ALPHA'S STRENGTH

Fallen Alpha Series #1

REBECCA ROYCE

Alpha's Strength (Fallen Alpha Series #1)

Copyright @ 2018 by Rebecca Royce

First Published 2014 by Fated Desires Publishing then 2016 Liquid Silver Publishing

Ebook ISBN: 978-1-947672-68-0

Paperback ISBN: 978-1-947672-69-7

Cover art by Glowing Moon Cover Art

Formatting: Ripley Proserpina

Published by Rebecca Royce

www.rebeccaroyce.com

❀ Created with Vellum

Foreword

Dear Reader,

Thank you so much for picking up Alpha's Strength. This is the first full length novel in the Fallen Alpha series. But, the story officially begins with a novella called Alpha Rising. It is also available on KU here: https://amzn.to/2qRW5cp While it is not necessary to read Alpha Rising to read Alpha's Strength, I know that many readers like to start officially at the beginning. If so please go grab Alpha Rising. We'll wait right here for you...

Rebecca Royce

Chapter 1

October had to be Cyrus' favorite time of year in New York City. Not too hot, not too cold, but with a slight crispiness in the air that beckoned his wolf to come out and play. Too bad he had to travel upstate to get in a decent run. He rubbed at the back of his neck and loosened his tie. His suit was expensive, but that didn't make it any less constricting. Or maybe everything simply pissed him off. The tension in the boardroom had become ten degrees too serious, and he refused to take any more bullshit. Not when the woods called to him.

"All right, gentleman, I've listened to you all day. Hell, I've been listening to this shit for the past year and a half since the subject of going public first came to light. I wasn't in favor then, and I'm not now. Why?" He slammed his hands down on the mahogany table in front of him so hard the coffee pot in the center of the too-expensive-to-be-practical piece of furniture jumped up in the air before bumping down.

The room fell silent as the other nine people in the room stared at the motion. Were they truly worried about the polished wood, or had he finally gotten their attention? He sniffed the air. He scented the correct amount of fear. Not too much, not too little. Like the weather outside, the pack's rapt attention —finally—made his wolf very, very happy.

"Well?" Cyrus stretched his arms over his head trying to ease some of the tension that had become his constant companion. "Aren't you going to ask me why?" He would gladly die to keep any of the wolves in the room safe. In a heartbeat. But right then, he'd like to wring every one of their necks. All at once.

"I don't think we dare ask right now." His sister, Lake called out from her seat towards the end of the table. Small and blonde as their mother, she dared speak when the others wouldn't. As his family, he allotted her more leniency not afforded to the rest of the pack. As pack Healer, she fell directly below him in terms of hierarchy. Healers didn't have to obey the normal rules of protocol with the Alpha—not in his pack.

For his part, he chose to ignore Lake's remark. If the pack feared him a bit, so be it. He'd never hurt any of them, and a little fear would keep them in line during tumultuous times. If they weren't careful, everything would be lost. With the death of Lucian, war loomed ever closer.

"I'm not going to take this company *public* because, in case you failed to notice, we are a company run by were-wolves. What we do *here* isn't for *public* consumption. This is *my* company. I built this place for you—it shields us, and provides for our expensive tastes. Tell me, have I not made all of you exceedingly rich?"

"You have, my Alpha." Justin, one of his most loyal Betas, spoke from the back of the room. As a wolf, Justin fought fiercely and, in his human form, ran the legal department with predatory skill. "But I imagine we've all thought about the potential here. We live in the human world and, when a communication security company is doing as well as ours, eventually, it is taken public."

"And then what happens to all of you?"

The attendants in the room stared without responding. This time, he understood their silence wasn't because he'd raised his voice, but rather because they didn't know the answer. What should they do in this situation? What was the right answer? How did werewolves stay hidden in the human world, but still live well?

He stood. He'd had enough for one day. "Everyone back to work."

Chairs were pushed away from the table, squeaking and groaning. His pack members quietly rushed from the room. None save Lake made eye contact with him. He clenched his fists. Why on Earth had he ever wanted to be Alpha? Some days, he'd prefer to be able to walk away, to lower his eyes, find something inside of himself that could be submissive and go home to a waiting family.

Instead, he always stood alone at the top of the power triangle, and he always went home to an empty penthouse.

Poor little rich wolf…

Cyrus shook his head. Hell, he couldn't blame any of them for wanting more money. Who didn't? Maybe if they all lived in the woods, they'd embrace their inner canines and not worry about any of this crap. But living in Manhattan meant co-existing with the humans.

He would keep them all safe, keep New York his own, and take over as Alpha Prime—no matter how much he hated the idea—if he had to in order to make the first two occur. Who the hell would ever choose to be Alpha Prime?

"Cyrus." Lake's voice caught his attention.

"Sister."

"I wanted to remind you—"

He let out a loud breath, interrupting her. "I haven't forgotten."

"—that Alexei Babikov is arriving tomorrow."

"Have I been acting senile? Like I'm losing track of major events I set up myself?"

When she spoke her tone sounded more chiding than he liked. "It's my job to tell you. Your bad attitude and surly temper are probably why you can't keep an assistant. If your own pack doesn't want to work for you, you need to make adjustments somewhere."

He picked up his brown leather Coach briefcase and tossed the satchel across the room.

Papers went flying. "Do you want to be Alpha, Lake? Fucking *challenge* me."

His sister had the audacity to roll her eyes. "Obviously I don't want to be Alpha. Keep the job. You do it so well when you're not acting like this. What's come over you lately?"

"Nothing." A lie. Lately, he wanted to crawl out of his skin, and the edginess had nothing to do with the full moon being two weeks away. As Alpha, he shifted whenever he wanted to. He didn't have to wait for the call of the moon to bring on his change.

"Right. Nothing." She walked over and placed her hand on his shoulder. "Well, misternothing-is-wrong-with-me-tough-Alpha-boy, you have nothing on the schedule for the rest of the day. As your Healer, not your assistant, I'm ordering you to get out of here before you explode and take the whole building out with you."

Healer or not, he didn't have to listen to her if he didn't want to, except, he really did need to take a walk. Nothing irked him more than Lake being right. She'd be smug about it for the next week.

"I'll go to lunch." He sighed.

"You do that." Her smile said he hadn't fooled her. "I promise the company will still be standing when you get back and still be privately owned."

He walked toward the door and stopped to stare at her. "You know you can't work at the hospital. I get why, for you, this job is not what you want, but what you want isn't possible. Not right now."

Sadness poured out through her scent, unobstructed for a second, before she reined the aroma back in, and nodded.

Good wolf. He'd trained her well. All of his people learned they had to be on guard with their weaknesses. No undo shows of emotions to give the enemy an edge, including scented feelings. Not with the werewolf world on the brink of war.

Maybe his orders screwed up their emotional well being, but he had no time to worry about psychological damage while the wolf world collapsed around them. With no Alpha Prime to manage them all, the smart, individual Alphas of the wolf packs prepared for war. And everyone gunned for New York City. His turf.

Over my dead body.

Cyrus stormed from the room and she followed close on his heels. Outside of the conference room were the desks of some of the assistants, including his sister's, which was situated right outside the door to his private office.

Apparently, she wasn't done with the subject. "I know I can't be in the hospital. I get all the reasons—full moon problems and the potential for discovery. But what is the point of living among the humans, if we can't interact with them, Cyrus? Why don't we go back to log cabins and hiding in remote, out-of-the-way towns? Why live in Manhattan at all if I'm not allowed to really *live* here?"

He raised an eyebrow, knowing his answer would

sound mean. Cyrus had no choice. How could he pacify her when he didn't know the right response himself? Lake and all the others needed surety from him, not indecision.

"You're ready to give up your weekly manicure, your chai lattes, and your corner dry cleaner to go wash clothes in the woods? Feel free, sister. I don't think you'd survive a week."

Turning his back on her, he left her standing next to her desk. These were not questions they could answer today. Cyrus pulled out his phone while he approached the elevator. He had three texts from other Alphas. Travis, from Philadelphia, wanted to discuss visitation rights considering their new blood oath not to attack. Some of Travis' people wanted to see distant relatives in Cyrus' pack.

Ultimately, treaties drove him crazy. Too many potential disasters came to light with the more deals he made. Blood-oathing Travis had been a necessary evil, even if Cyrus would have preferred to keep his borders permanently closed. The days of passing notes between Alphas at a diner in New Jersey had long passed. The treaty obligated him to be in constant communication with the Alpha of Philadelphia. The endless rounds of texts saying nothing, but still crowded with meaning, he didn't have time to decipher had replaced the simplicity of telling Travis to fuck off.

When the elevator doors opened, he growled and stepped inside. Two other texts came in from Alexei, the Alpha from Boston, demanding certain shows of respect while the Alpha visited Manhattan. He forwarded those notes to Lake. *Let her deal with them.* She'd decide if they'd reserve him a hotel room facing away from the sunset or whatever the bastard demanded to be difficult. Otherwise, she could call off the whole thing.

Cyrus really didn't give a shit anymore.

Six months ago, he'd wanted a treaty with Boston to help keep New York City secure. Now, with the constant back and forth with Travis in Philadelphia, Cyrus wasn't sure he should go any further down a worrisome road.

Cyrus stepped out of the elevator and crossed the lobby to the street. The noises of New York City greeted him. He'd heard tourists call it too loud, too busy, too tall of a city, but he found the sudden onslaught of sensory information calming. He couldn't overthink things when he was in the world that was Manhattan.

Or at least that's how he usually felt. At that moment, he wanted to crawl out his skin. What the hell was the matter with him? A growl left his throat, startling him. That was the second time in ten minutes he'd growled without meaning to. When was the last time he'd done that? Twenty-five years before? He'd probably been about eight years old, right after his first change.

Adult male werewolves didn't do anything unintention-ally—especially not ones who grew up to be Alphas. Control belonged to him.

He sniffed the air. A scent called to him, increasing his restlessness. In this case, the scent bugging him tasted like vanilla. But how to determine whose aroma he needed to find?

Cyrus looked left and right. This was New York City. Finding the scent of vanilla was like asking him to locate a needle in a haystack. Maybe whoever it was would go away and leave him with one less irritation in his cluster fuck of a week.

He stormed into the Starbucks across the street. Coffee, he needed some right then and there. If he could sharpen his senses and make it through the rest of the day, then he would let himself travel north that night for a private run —just he and the moon.

The smell of vanilla was stronger inside the coffee shop and not because of some syrup they used in the coffee. No, it grew in strength, far powerful than normal. Inside, his senses went high alert and his muscles bunched with tension. There was a threat. There had to be. What else could possibly elicit such a response from him?

He scanned the room until his gaze located the problem. Lilliana, the mate of the Alpha from Philadelphia, was sitting outside his office building in a Starbucks. *What the fuck? What the hell is she doing here?* He took a deep breath. Why did she smell different? Hybrid wolf, yes that had stayed the same, but why had she coated herself in vanilla? This close, he liked the smell. It made him dizzy, as if he needed to sit down for a while.

Cyrus steadied himself on the back of an empty chair and stared at Lilliana. She was petite with blonde hair that fell to her shoulders and curves in all the right places. He'd always been attracted to her, but she'd smelled too much like Travis, and something—indefinable—had been missing. She'd never really done it for him before. His eyes widened as he realized what he should have cued into immediately. She didn't smell like Travis anymore.

Something's wrong.

He walked over to her and threw himself down in the chair across from her. "What's going on, Lilliana? You know you shouldn't be here without permission. Very clear rules. I don't send my people to wander around Philadelphia. Explain yourself and why you smell different." Lilliana sat back in her chair. She stared at him for a few seconds, her brown eyes punching his gut as though she had struck him. He'd barely blinked when she looked down at the table.

"I'm sorry. I think you've made a mistake. My name isn't Lilliana." Her voice was softer than usual. She bit down on her lower lip. "Unless this is some kind of joke, sir."

Shock rendered him speechless. *Holy shit.* The girl in front of him was absolutely not Lilliana. She sounded different, she smelled different, and Lilliana would never in a million years be as submissive as the half-breed she-wolf sitting in front of him.

Lilliana knew nothing about her blood family— humans had adopted her. Since she'd been a latent shifter —unable to turn into a wolf—she hadn't even known she was a werewolf until Lake had healed her. Was it possible this woman in front of him was Lilliana's twin sister? They had nearly the same face.

The only slight difference, at least that he could see, was the woman in front of him had freckles across her nose, whereas Lilliana had none. On this unnamed she-wolf, the freckles were adorable.

Mate.

The thought slammed into him. Was such a thing possible? He'd never believed in a true mating. Most of the folklore about their origins was a bunch of crap. People mated for political maneuvers and strength. Sure, every young werewolf believed they'd grow up to find the other half of their soul, but, like him, most eventually grew out of believing in fairytales.

Life was all about choice, except, in this case, his wolf side seemed to have other ideas. Meantime, the she-wolf across from him wouldn't look at him. He'd liked that in the boardroom. Now, not so much.

What was the last thing she'd said to him before his mind had tilted sideways? Oh, right.

She'd asked if this was some kind of joke.

"No." He cleared his throat since his voice had actually cracked. He rubbed his forehead. Could that be any more humiliating? Alphas didn't lose it, not even when they met their mates. Or at least he didn't think they did. Other than Travis, he'd never known any wolf to actually find a true mating.

"Then I think you've made a mistake." She looked around the floor.

"Could you look at me? Please?" Wow, he really wanted her warm brown eyes to meet his.

She raised her eyes to his. He had one moment to drown in the caramel-colored windows of her soul before she turned red and looked down again.

Okay. He knew how to instill confidence in submissive wolves. No one in his pack cowered from him. He might growl a lot, but he never bit. Unless they did something very, very bad.

"Could you tell me your name?" He tried to keep his voice calm. All he wanted to do was to haul her over his shoulder and drag her back to his penthouse where he would keep her forever. If she was a full-bred wolf or had been raised in a pack, she wouldn't object. She might even bite him or run to make him chase her. But she was a half-breed and, if she was like

Lilliana, actually latent. She might think she was human. Hauling wouldn't work with her.

He needed to figure out how to behave.

"I don't think that's a good idea." She took a sip of her coffee. "You're some psycho who sat down here and said a lot of weird stuff. I don't tell my name to strangers, let alone deranged ones."

He laughed, a long, hard sound that surprised him with its intensity. All right, so she had claws. His nameless she-wolf wouldn't look at him, but she'd tear at him. The new discovery made him obscenely happy.

Now she raised her eyes. For a full thirty seconds, she stared straight at him. "That was funny?"

"No, but I found it amusing just the same." He dug into his pocket and pulled out his card. With a flick of his fingers, he slid it across the table to her. "I'm sorry I seem deranged. This is a case of mistaken identity. I have a friend who looks an awful lot like you. I thought you were she, but you are fantastically not. That's my card. I'm not insane. Google me."

She picked up his information and studied it for a second. "Are you somebody I should know? I don't watch the news or read the papers. I'm new to the area."

"I don't know that I'm somebody you *should* know. But you are going to know me.

Count on that."

"Look, I think you should go. It's not right, you sitting here." Now that was a statement. "Why isn't it right?"

"Because it's not."

He tried to keep his tone soft. "Look at me when you say that, and maybe I'll believe you."

She gripped the table in front of her. Her knuckles turned white, and she raised her eyes again. But he couldn't meet her gaze. Not this time. Not now that he'd noticed her left hand. It had been in her lap the whole time.

The she-wolf who was his mate—even if he didn't yet know her name—wore a diamond on the ring finger of her left hand. He couldn't seem to pull his attention from the spot. It was a tiny piece of jewelry. Square cut atop a silver base, it caught and reflected the sunlight on the table. Wolves didn't give rings to their mates. It was a human tradition that they saw no need for. But, by all that mattered to him, he wanted to rip that thing off her finger, throw it out the window, and go buy her the biggest, most expensive piece of jewelry he could find to replace the one she wore. Something that screamed she belonged to him, not to whoever had infringed on his territory.

Cyrus sat back in his seat. Protecting borders from outside invaders was actually something he did really well. He hadn't gotten to be Alpha of Manhattan by not knowing how to wage war. In this case, he'd have to take something that had already been claimed by someone else. This didn't bother Cyrus in the least. She was his mate, and she'd been placed right outside of his office building in the nick of time. There was still time to set this right. She wasn't married yet.

The fiancé could be dealt with. He'd yet to find a human male that couldn't be, and no wolf was going to challenge his claim in Manhattan. Cyrus took a deep breath. There was a faint hint of another non-wolf male on her, but not enough to indicate true, long-term inti- macy. *Even better.*

"Why do you want me to look at you?" She dropped her eyes again.

"Because your brown eyes are gorgeous." By asking that question she'd shown him she had no idea she was a wolf. Was latency a genetic trait? Did it run in families? He was going to have to ask Lake. Twin sisters and neither could shift. He'd never heard of such a thing.

"Thank you. I guess. You really shouldn't be speaking to me like this. It's not appropriate."

"Right. Do me a favor, beautiful. Tell me what I smell like to you." "What?" Her voice sounded breathy.

"Take a deep sniff and tell me. What do I smell like to you?"

She obeyed him. Of course she did. Even though she

clearly thought herself human, she had no choice but to obey him. The dormant werewolf inside of her knew better. As his mate, she'd learn to tell him to shove it when appropriate. But not yet.

"You smell like…"

He raised an eyebrow when her voice trailed off. "Go on." "Like power."

"Betsy," a voice hollered from the doorway. "What do you think you're doing?"

His mate jumped to her feet. "Nathan. Nothing." Her pupils dilated, and she looked left. Simultaneously, her scent took on the pungent aroma of fear. It irritated his nose, and he suppressed a growl. His mate should never smell like that.

Betsy, the name he'd now finally learned, shoved his card in her pocket and jumped forward on the tips of her feet. "I'm sorry, Nathan. This man sat down. I don't know what he wanted." She grabbed at *Nathan's* arm. "This is such a strange city."

"Well, it won't do to have you talking to other men. You know I don't like that." "Yes." She nodded frantically. "I do understand. I'm so sorry. Please forgive me."

Nathan, who was tall for a human but not a werewolf, shot Cyrus a look from the door. His dark-brown gaze started out hostile, but the quick intake of the other man's breath told Cyrus that Nathan quickly picked up on which one of them was actually dominant. Most of the time, Cyrus didn't bother with humans like this one. They were a waste of his time. But these were extenuating circumstances.

Nathan grabbed Betsy's arm. She flinched, and Cyrus stood up. It took every ounce of strength he possessed not to dart across the Starbucks and pound the other man to the floor. How dare he manhandle Betsy?

His mate was hauled onto the sidewalk and down the street. Cyrus took a deep breath. Nathan was a dead man if he left a mark on her. For now, he'd follow them from a distance. Find out where they went and plan his next move. His latent mate had to be handled with care, but he'd throw that all away if he saw anything else he didn't like from Nathan. Forget keeping their existence a secret. Cyrus would shift into a wolf and eat the man alive.

He smiled. The idea sounded better and better.

Chapter 2

Betsy Webber scurried along the sidewalk next to Nathan. If she kept her feet moving as fast as his maybe she would return home without bruises. His fingers dug deeper into her skin, and she sighed. She knew she should have made Cyrus leave—except she hadn't been able to do it.

What was wrong with her? The second he'd approached her she'd become a tongue-tied, spineless wimp who hadn't been able to look at him, never mind make him get up and go. Why? Sure he was handsome, but New York teemed with good-looking men. But Cyrus had been different. Sure, he was tall with blond hair, blue eyes, and a long scar down the side of his face that made him look…tough even though he wore tailored clothes that didn't give the impression of violence, but rather tempered restraint.

"So is this what you do now? Flirt with random men in coffee shops? Have you returned to your slut ways?"

She cringed at his coarse language and bit her tongue. Defending herself would not do her parents any good. She'd agreed to marry Nathan to save them, and that was exactly what she would do. Even if she wanted to claw his eyes out. And it wasn't as though he was wrong. Unfortunately, she had, in the past, been unable to control herself when it came to the opposite sex.

"No, sir. I promise I've not done that." *I haven't.* No one understood how long she'd fought to overcome that *quirk* of her nature. She wouldn't be punished for it now—she'd done enough of that herself.

"Good." Nathan yanked her out of the car, and half-dragged her through the front door of their rented house. "Because I'm not going to put up with any of your *nonsense*. You're going to be my wife. Don't forget that. Unless you want the worst-case scenario to happen." She shuddered. Betsy didn't want that.

At least he only called her *quirk* nonsense—other times he used more foul language. It didn't matter that she had her own theories about why she did what she did—sex addiction. She'd read that phrase somewhere and couldn't help but wonder if it applied to her. Every once in a while, she just had to...*do it.* The compulsion to fuck overwhelmed her. Even though she knew that meant she was going to hell with a capital H.

But that didn't matter now. She didn't want Nathan sexually—at least not for the moment. And even though he'd blackmailed her into this arrangement, she might be able to find redemption by his side. Her father said Nathan was so holy.

Now, if she could just remember that—instead of killing him in his sleep—everything would work out fine. She really did need redemption. From moment one, she'd been living a sinfilled life. Surely her commitment would help her fix things.

She sighed and made her way into the kitchen. Usually, Nathan's mood improved if she fed him. Her love of cooking and ability to create a fantastic-tasting meal was the one thing about her childhood that had turned out well for her as an adult. Her mother could cook, and she'd passed on the love of it to her daughter.

Betsy smiled at the thought. The hours spent together in the kitchen working side by side were her most treasured memories. Of course, she'd had no idea what her parents had been doing in the basement while she'd been upstairs stirring soups. If she had, she would have run for the hills.

"How does brisket sound?" Her mother had always called it pot-roast. She hadn't even known it had another name until she moved to Manhattan. The things a country girl could learn.

"Perfect." He spoke from the living room, and she knew he had sat down to start working on his emails. She let go of the breath she held. He'd be distracted for a while and maybe one of those correspondences would finally be the agreement to free her folks from their imprisonment in his family's compound.

Her mind swayed to the man from the coffee shop. She still had his card in her pocket. *Cyrus.* It was an unusual name that certainly fit the man himself. Did that sort of thing happen in New York all the time?

He'd been handsome; she'd give him that. Even if he was stranger than an owl perched atop a church in the middle of daytime during summer. He had almost made her fall off the nosex wagon. She'd noticed him the second he'd come through the door. And when he'd walked over, she'd stopped breathing for a moment.

What had he called me? Lilliana? Weird. She shook her head and started chopping onions. Had she preset the oven? She had this luxurious kitchen, but her mind was always somewhere else, it seemed.

Cyrus had smelled good. She closed her eyes and

stopped chopping for a second to let herself revel in the memory. She'd told him his scent was one of power. That had been an odd thing to say. Only it had been the first word to come to mind when he'd asked her such a strange question. Why had he done that?

"Betsy." Nathan's harsh use of her name jolted her, and she lost her grip on the knife. Her eyes flew open at the same time she cut her finger. With a gasp, she jumped backward and stuck her finger in the mouth.

"What are you doing?" he yelled at her. He always yelled. Even something as benign as her cutting her own finger aggravated him.

Nathan yanked her finger out of her mouth and pulled her to the sink. The cut had already stopped bleeding. She never stayed hurt very long. Cuts, bruises, and even broken bones all disappeared with very little effort. One time when she'd hit her head, she'd been dizzy for a few hours, but other than that, nothing ever seemed to linger.

A doctor had once called her an anomaly. Or maybe her father had made up that story. Not that she recalled seeing doctors during her childhood. Now, at least, she understood why. He turned on the sink. "Put your hand under the water."

She could have told him she wasn't burned. She'd been bleeding, but she'd long since learned there was absolutely no point in disagreeing with Nathan on anything. She stuck her finger under the cold water and tried not to wince when Nathan moved close to her ear and whispered in it.

"I think your attention is not where it is supposed to be today."

She swallowed. "You're right."

"I think you were bothered by that stranger in the coffee shop. I think he made you feel things, inappropriate things that you shouldn't be thinking about. I think that's why you cut yourself."

His voice was no more than a hiss, but she shuddered from the sick, creepy, crawling feeling that travelled up her spine—everything inside of her rebelled against Nathan touching her. She wanted to pull free. Standing by the sink with Nathan pressed against her and her hand stuck under the water was the hardest it had ever been to endure his presence. What had changed? It had to be her encounter in Starbucks. What else could have suddenly made Nathan so repugnant?

"It won't happen again." She fisted her hand under the water. It would be so easy to claw out his eyes. Betsy bit down on her lip. Where did those thoughts even come from?

"That's right, it won't. Do I need to remind you what my daddy will do to your daddy if I don't tell him each and every day that you are obeying my ever wish?" Nathan ran his hand down the side of her face. "Do I need to remind you what they did? How they were selling babies? Taking them from their mamas and selling them to God knows who? Do you even know how disgusting that is?"

She did, actually. Her body shook like it always did when they had this discussion. She could still see the scene she'd encountered in the basement. The way the baby her mother had held had cried. Her mother's stuttering response to where the child had come from…the guilt in the other woman's eyes, and the ugly sound of Nathan's father's footsteps as he tore into the house. Why had she thought her parents needed a soundproof basement to make moonshine? All the lies, all the years.

"Do you want them dead? Or in jail? They're only being kept alive because of you."

She opened her eyes and relaxed her jaw. "No. Please don't harm them."

Even though some days—when she felt disloyal—she did want them in jail. Her parents deserved to be put away. But how could she allow herself to feel that way? They'd raised her, and she hadn't been easy with all the stuff she'd pulled. And when her sexual needs had started...

Her parents had to find money some way to pay off the police from the time she'd broken into the mill, her father had explained. The whole thing was really her fault. Maybe if she had moved out when she'd turned eighteen? But then how could her mother have managed the house without her? And, besides, she had loved her parents. For their faults, they'd kept a roof over head and food in her stomach. Even when the incidents had happened, they hadn't seemed particularly upset.

"I have been patient waiting for the toxins of those other men to leave your system. Soon, after we say 'I do,' you'll belong to me. And then vengeance is mine if you even think of another man."

"I..."

The front door flew open. She heard the sound of it crashing into the table next to the door. Someone would really have to bang it hard to hit like that.

"What the...?" Nathan let go of her and stepped back, his eyes getting huge. "There's a wolf in the house." He screamed like a woman, and she whirled around, the sharp, loud noise drowning all other sound until it stopped abruptly when Nathan charged out the back door toward the street.

Betsy knew she should be running after him, but she stood frozen to the floor. The wolf in front of her held her entire attention. He was beautiful, bigger than any wolf she'd ever seen in the wild. He had gray fur with black spots. His eyes were blue, which really stood out from the rest of his body. The creature focused on her, and she couldn't help but stare right back.

Where had she seen eyes like that before? The knowledge hid in the corner of her mind, like an itch she wanted to scratch, before it quickly faded away.

She swallowed past her dry throat. Where had this tremendous creature come from, and why had he busted through their door?

He growled at the back door, crouching low as though he intended to chase after Nathan. "I think he's gone."

This must be how it feels to lose your mind. Why wasn't she running for her life? Why was she talking to him? Why did she assume he could understand a word she said? A giant wolf stood in her kitchen—smack in the middle of Brooklyn.

He huffed. Or at least she thought it was a male. How could she know for sure? Maybe it was a female wolf. The wolf narrowed his eyes at her, and she put her hand up to her throat. Was this some kind of punishment? Were her sins going to be handled by some old-fashioned, primal vengeance? Had the universe decided to let her be torn to pieces by a canine with huge teeth?

Her mind refused to accept what she saw. *My what big teeth you have…*

One second she stared at the wolf, and the next second he began to change. The face reshaped, elongating until it didn't look the same. The body followed suit. In seconds, it had shed its fur and, in its place, was a human being.

She'd been calm—maybe shocked—when she'd seen the wolf, but now all the fear she'd not felt seconds earlier rushed inside of her like a dam releasing its water. This was *wrong*—this didn't happen—wolves didn't suddenly become humans. That only happened in fairytales and horror movies.

Except this *was* happening. She darted backward, hitting the table behind her. She banged her hip and knocked over a decorative lamp. Not that she cared. It was Nathan's lamp. She hated the thing. Oh sheesh. Why was she thinking about the lamp when a wolf magically changed into something else right in front of her?

"Relax, princess." The wolf-man spoke from behind her, but she didn't dare turn around to look. Nathan had the right idea. *Back door. Running.* Yeah, all of it sounded fantastic.

"Betsy." The man spoke again even as she rushed toward the door. "I can smell your fear.

I get it, but you have no reason to be frightened of me."

She skidded to a stop—she recognized his voice. An image of the wolf's eyes flitted to her mind. Along with the voice, it all suddenly made sense to her. She wasn't crazed. She had seen those blue eyes—on the would-be-perfect-except-for-the-long-scar-on-the-side-of-his-face Cyrus Fennell.

After pivoting, Betsy faced him. "*You.*" Her world shifted off its axis. Dizzy, she gripped the wall next to her.

"Yes. Me." He was dressed exactly the same as he had been in the coffee shop. How was that possible? How was any of this possible?

"Is this some kind of joke? Or have I fallen asleep?" She rubbed at her head, desperate for any conclusion except the one in front of her. Maybe Nathan had set the whole thing up to test her or something. If she wasn't dreaming, then Nathan's involvement seemed as likely as any.

"No." He shook his head, his voice lower than she remembered. "I realize this was handled very badly. I guess I lost my mind when I heard how he was talking to you and then I smelled your blood. I saw red."

There had to be sense somewhere in what he said, in this whole evening. Somewhere in the chaos there was always order.

"What do you want with me?" The world didn't revolve around her, but first he'd approached her at the coffee shop and now—here he was in her house. She was the only common denominator.

"You said I smelled like *power*. How do you know what that smells like?"

"You followed me here because I said something flippant? Because I gave you a crazy answer instead of saying that you smelled like cinnamon or vanilla or coffee beans or something? I'm sorry. I'll sniff again and see if I can do better." She looked at the clock. It was almost six. She had to find Nathan and make sure he called his father for his daily check-in. That meant she had to get this man or wolf or whatever as good and gone as a turkey around Thanksgiving time.

But she couldn't chop off his head. He'd shift into a wolf and stop her before she could— *where the hell had that thought come from?*

"See, here's the thing." He held his hands out in front of him as though he wanted to pacify her. She stared at his long fingers, transfixed by his every motion. What was it about this man that was so interesting? Well, other than the whole wolf thing.

"The thing?" She scanned the room until she found what she needed. The knife she'd used to chop the onion. It was still on the counter. If she couldn't hurt him, she could at least make him aware she meant business.

23

"You're right. I do smell like power."

Ego much? "Great. I'm so happy I was right."

She moved to the left, keeping her gaze off the knife. Let him believe she was turning off the water at the sink. Anything, but what she intended to do. It helped that she still couldn't seem to look him in the eye. When this was over, if it ever was, and her parents were free of Nathan's family, she'd find a therapist. Someone who could explain to her why she did the things she did. And then how she could stop doing them.

"But that's the thing." Cyrus turned and walked away from her. She appreciated the sight of his backside when he moved toward the counter. What she didn't like was that he picked up the knife she'd wanted and placed it on the opposite side of the room where she wouldn't be getting to it. How had he known that's what she'd intended? He twisted to look at her and she almost gasped from the sheer masculinity pouring off him. Only her sense of self-preservation kept her from reacting.

"Go on." She had to find something else. Or maybe she should make a run for it. That would be the sensible choice, right?

"The fact that you know I smell like power is because you can really smell me. You're like me, princess. Do you understand what I'm saying? You're also a wolf."

Betsy stopped moving and forced herself to raise her eyes to meet his, even though it hurt to do so Why did it feel like someone had placed a weight on them and made them heavier when she tried to stare at him head on? "I'm not a werewolf or whatever you are. I think I would know if I had the ability to go furry. I get one visitor every month, regularly, and it has nothing to do with the full moon or walking on four legs."

Cyrus turned beet red. One second he looked all hot

and scary, and the next, he flushed and looked anywhere but at her. Men were all the same. Mention the period, and they had no idea what to do with themselves.

Betsy took her chance. She launched herself across the room and dove toward the counter where he'd placed the knife.

Cyrus rushed toward her, but she got there first. She held the knife in her shaking hand. Having never actually threatened anyone with a weapon before, she had no idea how hard it was to do, even if the person who needed the threat was actually part-wolf, had stalked her home— and busted in her door because he smelled her blood and wanted to protect her.

Or maybe that wasn't what he'd meant. Maybe he wanted to eat her because of her scent? Cyrus still hadn't said what he wanted with her, other than to talk about what he smelled like.

"Listen, I want you to go. Okay?" Her voice didn't shake and she had a moment of pride about it. Small victories were all she was going to get.

Cyrus crossed his arms. "Do you mean to stab me with that, princess?" He didn't look particularly threatened. If anything, he seemed bored. What the hell? She wielded a knife here.

"I don't want to have to stab you. I don't want that at all. I've never stabbed anyone. I'm not a violent person." Why was she explaining so much? "I want you to go. Leave me alone.

Take your crazy, you're-a-wolf talking self and get out of my house."

"This isn't *your* house. This is that coward's house. And I can't believe you're living here or wearing his ring because you want to."

"Why would you say that? You don't even know me."

25

"I know your name is Betsy." He paused, and, if anything, his gaze became even more smoldering. When he left, she was going to need a shower and vibrator to take care of all the heat coursing though her body. "And I know that you're *mine*."

She opened and closed her mouth. Her ears rang. She lifted the knife up higher. "Get out."

"I think you know it too. Deep down, your body and soul have always understood something was missing."

"Stop talking right now." She thrust the knife closer to him. "Just because I don't want to use this doesn't mean I won't."

"Oh, I know you would. Your wolf-side knows how to defend itself. Even if it's suppressed so deeply you can't find it. The latency has held it off. It did the same thing to your twin sister. But now, I'm told, she's quite the tough wolf lady."

Sister? The world seemed to shift beneath her feet. Betsy dropped the knife. Without thought, she grabbed onto his shirt. The werewolf discussion could wait. It was the last part of his response that concerned her. "What did you say?"

Cyrus ran his hand up and down her arms. She felt numb, his previous statement making it impossible for her to feel anything since all of her concentration had gone to staying upright.

"Which part?"

"The twin sister. How could you know I had one? How could you possibly?" She tried to shake him, but he didn't move. Why had the universe made men so big and bulky and left her so small? It wasn't fair. "She died when I was a toddler."

Her mother had finally admitted it a few years ago. Betsy had always known about her, had remembered her even though it should have been impossible to do so. Maybe twins didn't forget, maybe their souls always knew that they had shared a womb with another human. It had been an ache she'd never been able to shake.

"She didn't." Cyrus stroked a finger down her nose. "She's quite alive, and I'm going to get her for you. Get her here. Even though it's going to make my life hellish to make it happen. I'll do that for you because you're mine. My mate. My own."

"I…" She didn't have words. Oh, why had she dropped her knife?

Cyrus stepped back. "I'm going to go. This is too much for you. You need time. To process."

Betsy nodded. Good, that was what she wanted. Wasn't it? She'd wanted him to leave, except now she didn't. He was going to get her sister… "I…"

"Hear this. I'm going to stand outside this door for the next ten minutes. After that, there will never be a time when it's not being watched. That human will not come through the door again. If he does, he will be torn to shreds. Small ones."

His words snapped her back into the present. "No." She grabbed his arm. "Please, Cyrus, whatever is going on here, I still don't understand. But you can't keep Nathan from me. Not ever."

"I can, and I will." He growled his response, a glint in his eye telling her he was resolute in his answer.

"No." She shook her head. The tears, she always pretended she didn't have, fell down her cheeks. "You can't do that. If you do, all is lost."

In two seconds, he had her in his embrace. It shouldn't feel good to be held by a stranger. Not one who confused her, threatened her, and scared her so badly. It shouldn't. But it did.

"It can't be all that bad, princess. Tell me. How is all lost?"

"My parents are bad people. They've done horrible things. But they're all that I have.

And if you keep Nathan from me, they're dead. Please don't do that. Please. Please. Please." Begging had never gotten her anywhere in life. But she wasn't above it. Not when it mattered.

"I think you'd better start from the beginning."

She pulled back to look at him. "Talking about it won't help."

"I'm always going to protect you. You're mine. I can fix this. After I understand the problem."

Oh God. Could he? She didn't know about being his. It all sounded crazy. But maybe he could fix this. Was that even possible? She opened her mouth, and the words flew out.

Chapter 3

Cyrus wasn't certain he would survive it if Betsy kept crying. He'd never felt as completely out of control as he did in that moment. He did his best to fake control, but the truth was the little woman before him could bring him to his knees if she wanted. He had to find a way to make things right for her—*even if it means slaughtering villages and burning barns*. He blinked. Where had that thought come from? He hadn't heard—or thought—that phrase since his grandmother was alive.

Weird.

"My parents have done some bad things. Very, very bad."

He took a deep breath. "We are not our parents. Whatever others say, I don't believe we inherit their mistakes. What did they do?"

"Stole and sold babies." She choked on her words and buried her head in her hands as sobs wracked her.

He blinked. Well, he hadn't seen that one coming. Cyrus was used to solving the problems of others. His pack came to him for everything. Every problem they had, he tried to fix—from repairing hurt feelings between mated couples and managing unruly teenagers, to solving work heartaches—like his sister's need to work elsewhere, to define her life in some way other than pack. But stealing children? No, that was a new one.

Cyrus placed a hand on her shoulder. He really wanted to yank her against him and drag her back home. He'd gotten to hold her for a minute, but that was all he'd had. *For now*. She thought she was human, or at least she didn't yet believe that she was a werewolf, which was close enough to thinking herself a non-wolf. He had to treat her that way.

"Did you participate in any of it?"

"What?" She wiped at her eyes. "No, of course not."

"Then you're not responsible for it." *Simple. End of story.*

"You don't understand. Nathan's father discovered what they were doing at the same exact time I did. And now he's holding them prisoner at his compound. If I don't marry Nathan and make him happy every day, then he is either going to kill them or send them to jail."

"Wait." He shook his head. "What?"

"Nathan's father is going to either kill them or send them to jail if I don't make his son happy."

Bullshit. "Princess, are you sure? I mean that sounds nonsensical to me."

"Listen, I can't explain it. One second I was having the horrible truth of what my parents really did for a living explained to me. The next? Nathan's father, Franz, arrived and dragged them off. I've been living like this ever since."

Cyrus needed her to understand. "I'm not discounting that is happening to you. I'm sure it is. But something else is going on." His nose twitched, always a sign of a lie in the air. In this case, he didn't smell deceit on Betsy.

"Listen, whatever the details, my parents are at risk. I

need Nathan to make his call or…" His mate started to hyperventilate. He placed a hand on her shoulder, and she calmed, her shoulders sagging a bit. Cyrus knew how to take care of pack, how to make those for whom he was responsible feel safe, secure, and protected. Some of that was inherent. He may have been born with Alpha tendencies and abilities, but it had been Lucian, the former Alpha-prime, who had fostered it in him.

Now, with his mate upset and everything so unsure, he felt like a novice again.

"I understand your predicament." Not really, but he wasn't going to press her right that second. "Can you bear to be patient with me for a few minutes longer?"

With any other pack member—and even if she never shifted, that was what she was to him and more—he'd order them to stay still. But he really didn't want to tell her what to do. No, he wanted her to desire to do what he said.

By all that was holy, this was really fucked up.

"Sure." Poor thing sounded as bewildered as he. "I mean I should be throwing you out." He shook his head. "No one removes me from places where I want to be. However, I would go if that is what you wished." He paused, not wanting to leave. "This room. I'd depart this room, but you could be sure I'd remain on the front stoop until I was satisfied with things here."

"You're a very odd duck." Betsy scratched her nose. "You know that, don't you?"

"Wolf. Not a duck." He pulled out his cell phone and sent a text to the top members of his pack. He needed trackers and guards. They'd all be there pronto, or he'd know why before he smashed heads together.

Finished, he looked at Betsy. She hadn't moved, not

even an inch, and instead stood very still, worrying her bottom lip. He grinned at the sight. How had this happened? How had she existed in the world and he'd been completely unaware of it until now?

Moments like these didn't simply pop up out of nowhere. Events occurred because he planned for them, set them in motion. How could he simply walk into a coffee shop and meet his latent mate, who happened to look exactly like Travis' mate? Although Betsy was ten times prettier than Lilliana. No comparison really.

Betsy had freckles Lilliana didn't possess, and they made her so…sigh-worthy. "You're staring at me."

He blinked. Holy shit. What the hell had taken over his mind? "Sorry about that. Look, here's the deal. I've called the pack."

"Pack?" Her voice raised a notch.

"Yes." *Where had the anxiety in her voice come from?* "You know what a pack is, don't you?"

"I do, and that's what's made me concerned. How many of you wolf-shifting folks are there around Manhattan?"

"In Manhattan alone? Or do you want to count the five boroughs?" This was information he usually kept to himself. Numbers meant power, and no one needed to know the inner workings of his pack save him. Maybe his willingness to share with her should startle him. Only it didn't.

He knew she didn't trust him—he could smell it—but apparently the mistrust didn't go both ways. Cyrus would tell her whatever she wanted to know.

"No." She held out her hands in front of her as though warding off an attack. "Forget it, I don't want to know."

"Okay. Well, as I summoned the pack. Some are on their way here. Several will track Nathan." Cyrus could do that himself, easily. Humans didn't disguise their scents, didn't stay downwind, and didn't do anything to keep themselves from being found. But, if he left Betsy alone, she'd likely run, and he couldn't have that.

Although…the idea had merit. He'd go get Nathan. Then he'd track Betsy. *Chase her.* Maybe she would really run. His cock jumped, and he adjusted his pants. How could he have gotten so hard only imagining her running from him?

"What will happen when they find Nathan?"

Cyrus growled, loud enough that it echoed off the walls of her kitchen. She took a step back, and he forced his temper back down where it belonged. *What the hell is wrong with me?*

"Do you care about Nathan? Don't want him hurt? Care about his welfare?" If she said yes, he was going to have to take a walk to cool down. Even if it meant the chasing scenario had to take place again.

"What?" Anger—not fear—sparked in her eyes and she scowled at him. "Haven't you been paying attention? He's responsible for making my life miserable. No, I don't care about him, other than for his ability to call home and keep my parents safe."

Cyrus nodded. His temper cooled, and his hands stopped shaking. If her parents had really done what she said, then there would have to be consequences. He'd never condone child abductions or law breaking. If there was ever a person who counted on the rule of law, it was he. But he wouldn't allow his mate to be blackmailed. "Don't worry. That's not going to happen."

"How are you going to make sure of that?"

A knock on the door interrupted—two of his wolves were there. Betsy took a few steps back, her eyes widening at their presence. She was skittish. He needed to remember that when bringing her around new people.

"It's okay. This is Mitchell and Jenson. They're part of my pack. Senior members actually. I sent for them, remember?" He turned to his wolves, who stood stiffly and waited for him to address them. "You guys got here fast."

"We were already in Brooklyn." Mitchell spoke first. "There's a very good pizza place. We go almost every Thursday."

"I'm going to have to try the pizza."

Jenson nodded, but failed to mask his surprise. "My Alpha, you eat pizza?"

Cyrus didn't have time for this. "Not usually." He glanced at his mate, who still stared wide-eyed at his tall wolves. Jensen had at least three inches on Cyrus. Not that it mattered. He could best the other man anytime he wanted, and Jensen personified loyalty. "I usually prefer meat, chicken. That kind of thing."

"Does it matter what you eat? I mean when you're in your human form, can you eat anything or do you always have to eat like a wolf?" Betsy's attention returned to him. *That's better.*

"She knows?" Mitchell interrupted before Cyrus could respond to her question. "How did that happen?"

Cyrus raised an eyebrow. "She doesn't look familiar to either of you?"

"She resembles Travis' mate a great deal, but her smell is different." Jensen shrugged.

"Your sense of smell is better than mine. I thought she was Lilliana initially." Cyrus walked to her and placed his hand on her cheek. "But now I know better. She's my mate, gentlemen. And, to answer your question, Betsy, we can eat whatever we want when we're not in our werewolf forms. Our metabolisms are faster."

"I see." He really didn't think she did. Betsy's respiration was high; her pupils were dilated. She might even be going into shock. "I haven't really agreed to be your mate. Don't you think that's kind of, I don't know, presumptuous? Oh, hell in a hand basket, none of this makes any sense. I feel like an egg that just got cracked and stuck in a blender. Yep. That's how I feel." She said the cutest things. "You don't have to agree to be my mate. You are she. We'll work this out. Don't worry."

Mitchell and Jensen both walked inside. They nodded to him, and after a nod from each of them, he stepped back. Mitchell grabbed Betsy. She gasped before his pack mate pulled her into a hug. She stood stiff for a second and then finally hugged the other man back. It should bother him that other males were touching her, would make him nuts if they weren't pack. But they were all going to want to hug her. That was their way of welcoming her into the family.

Mitchell let go and Jensen pulled her into an embrace. She hugged him quicker this time, and Jensen stepped back.

"Well. Okay." Betsy rubbed her forehead. "This is really such a strange day." "Is she latent like Lilliana was?" "Yes."

Betsy stomped her foot, her fiery spirit reasserting itself. "Okay. *Enough.* All of you get out. I'm not latent or a werewolf or pack or whatever. I'm me. Normal *human* me. And you're all leaving."

Cyrus shook his head. Human women really did think they had a choice in these things. His own female pack mates would have known he understood the best thing to be done and not argue about their own safety.

"Actually, princess, there's going to be lot more of *our*

pack arriving shortly. However, Jensen and Mitchell do need to go." "Sir?" Jensen raised his eyebrows.

"Use that incredible nose of yours and sniff around the apartment. Pick up the scent of the human who lives here. His name is Nathan. He is a threat to my mate, but we need, for now, to keep him alive. Get him. Bring him to the office." He stroked the back of Betsy's hair. It was so soft, and he loved how it flowed through his hand. Someday soon he hoped to see it strewn over his pillow while she panted with pleasure.

"Through the back entrance?"

Cyrus nodded. "The service elevator."

The office building didn't really have one. The secret entrance through the basement of the building was called that in order to hide what really happened down there. Wolves in the big city had to be creative to hide themselves from prying human eyes.

"Got it." Mitchell nodded.

"Gentlemen, through any means necessary. I need his mouth to work. Not his arms."

Betsy gasped and covered her mouth. He waited for his pack mates to leave before he turned to her. "This is a violent world."

"Any chance you've made a terrible mistake and don't belong anywhere near me? Any chance you're going to change your mind?" Did she hope he had made a mistake? Or that he hadn't? It mattered little. She belonged to him. And he to her.

He pulled her close, sniffing at her hair. How could she have so many individual scents all at the same time? Cinnamon, vanilla, lilies…

"Do you really want me to? Ask yourself deep inside where that small, still voice resides. You know the one I'm talking about, the place where you can really hear yourself think. Do you really want me to leave?" He ran his hand up her back. "Or do you actually want me to stay? To be closer?"

She shivered beneath his hands. "That's not fair to ask me."

"Why not, princess?" His cock hardened. If he wasn't careful, he was going to lose all finesse and take her on the floor while the members of his pack arriving waited outside on the front stoop.

"I make poor decisions when it comes to men, and I always feel bad about it after. I'm not doing that anymore, no matter how desperately I want it. To say I'm not attracted to you would be a lie. I don't care about it though. Not being a slut means not being a slut."

He let out the long breath he'd held. "Don't ever call yourself that again No one is allowed to insult you. Not even you. Am I clear?"

She pulled back. "I think that if something is bad enough to use a bad word, then using it is appropriate at certain times. Sometimes I can't keep my legs closed. It's humiliating to me, to my family. I'm always sick to my stomach about it after. Maybe I have some kind of illness, but

I think slut is the right word."

"No." If she'd been raised as a wolf, as she should have been, she would have understood this better.

"Look, I get it. Here in New York City it may be acceptable for women to have as many lovers as they want. I get it. I even admire the way people are here, but where I was raised, and based on what we believe, what I do is not okay." And if she truly believed it, why did he hear doubt in her voice? Not a direct lie—that he would have scented, but her wolf side knew better even if her human half didn't understand.

"Oh?" He walked away from her—needing the distance to get his temper under control. How dare she think so little of herself? Touching her was only making his desire to claim her worse. Putting a little distance between them seemed the best course of action.

"So what happens now?" Betsy cleared her throat, a definite tic. She was as uncomfortable as he.

"I'm sorry. I can't let this go yet. You're *not* a slut. There is nothing wrong with you.

Female wolves go into heat in a different way than their female human counterparts. It has to be handled, and it's the male werewolf's pleasure to make them feel more comfortable." Although, since he'd become Alpha, he'd had to withdraw from the duty. Without a true mating, sometimes wolves mated for other reasons, even knowing they weren't the other halves of each other's souls. He didn't want to ever give anyone the wrong impression.

She gaped at him. "You guys go around screwing each other? Ooh, a female needs servicing, I'll go bend her over and get it on? Like it means nothing?"

He laughed, and she put her hands on her hips. Apparently, she hadn't meant her statement to be so amusing. Cyrus tried to drop his smile. After a second, he gave up trying.

"Listen, I think you are getting the wrong impression. We're not animals looking to rut. If a woman goes into heat, she picks a male to share the time with. Condoms protect against unwanted pregnancies. Mostly, it's a time shared by pack mates who care about each other. But you needn't worry, princess. Once a true mating happens, its one man and one woman forever and ever. What do you say? Do you want me to ease your needs? How did you put it? Bend you over and go for it?"

"You're an asshole. Did you know that?" Contrary to the fire in her eyes, she dropped her gaze.

"So, she gets submissive again after she delivers the blow to my ego." He grabbed his chest like she'd wounded him and moved toward her again. "I can be a jerk. Maybe more than I should be. You can help me with that if you want to. Make me a better wolf."

Someone knocked on the door. He sniffed the air. Another four of his wolves had arrived. Securing Betsy's safety came before anything else. He'd find a way to reach her heart one way or another. He had to. Anything else was inconceivable.

"Come in."

The four wolves that waited on the stoop entered, including his sister, Lake. She took one look at Betsy and drew in a breath. "She's not Lilliana."

"Congratulations. My entire pack is showing themselves to be more adept than I am at identifying the obvious." He returned to Betsy and took her hand. "Everyone, this Betsy. Betsy, this is everyone. She is my mate." He ignored the murmurs around him. There was no time for everyone to have an emotional response to this. "They'll all introduce themselves later. For now, we have things to do. Lake, I need you to call Travis. Don't tell him why; just get him here with Lilliana. The rest of you, search this place. I want info on the human who lived here with Betsy.

His name is Nathan. His family is threatening hers."

The males took off, moving through the house. He wasn't surprised. His pack was good at determining when he meant business. This was one of those times. Lake, however, didn't budge.

His sister stared at him, tears in her eyes. "This is your mate?"

Oh hell. He hadn't considered his baby sister's reaction. It had been the two of them against the world for so long before he'd won control of the Manhattan pack. Maybe Betsy was right. Maybe he was an ass. He should have handled breaking the news to Lake differently. A text message or something. *Shit*

"Yes. But she doesn't agree with it yet. Still trying to deny what's between us. Betsy, this is my sister, Lake Fennell. Lake, this is Betsy. Lake is the Healer in our pack. That's a special position. You'll get all the details of pack rolls and politics later."

Betsy extended her hand. "Look, I don't know if I'm his mate. If I hadn't seen him shift from a wolf into a human I wouldn't believe any of this. But, if you can all help me with Nathan and my family, then I'll be forever grateful. I'm Betsy Webber."

Lake took her hand in her own. "I've always wanted a sister. If Cyrus says you're his mate, that's what you'll be. Eventually." She winked at her brother and then closed her eyes.

"Lake. No." Seconds too late, he realized what his sister would do. In Lilliana's presence, Lake hadn't been able to control her need to heal. It was embedded in the DNA of the females in his family. They had no choice. He should never have let them touch. Lake would feel what was wrong with Betsy and need to make it better, whether the other woman was ready or wanted the change.

Cyrus rushed forward and grabbed their linked hands as Betsy collapsed with a scream. He managed to detach them and catch his mate before she fainted. He held her slight weight in his arms and stared at his sister's wide eyes.

"Is it too late?" Dread settled into his stomach. Betsy shouldn't be thrown into her wolf life any more than Lilliana should have been earlier that year. Everything it its time, and this was *not* that time.

"I'm sorry." Tears streamed down Lake's face. "It's done. She's going to change. Her wolf side is going to finally be free. As it always should have been."

Buzzing filled his head. This was happening, whether he liked it or not. "Damn it." "I'm sorry, Cyrus."

Betsy jerked against him. He petted her head. "Shove the sorrys, Lake. Help me get her out of here. This is nowhere for a first shift. We're going to my office."

Chapter 4

Her eyes had somehow been glued shut. Betsy wasn't sure how, but she couldn't open them. And someone had placed her in a fur coat and turned on the heater. Otherwise she couldn't explain why she felt the way she did.

Betsy groaned, and it sounded more like a whimper.

"She's waking up." A female voice. She'd heard it before. Who was it? *Lake*. That was right. Betsy sniffed the air, wanting to smell Cyrus' sister, which seemed weird. But since she couldn't seem to open her eyes, she gave into the instinct. Lake's aroma spoke of wind in the trees and sunsets.

Betsy forced her eyes open. How in the heck had she come up with that phrasing? How would she know what those things smelled like?

She looked left and right. Everything in the room looked a bit off. The colors were duller.

A loud bang sounded somewhere in the distance, and she winced at the sound. Where was she?

What was going on? Her heart rate kicked up. Something was wrong...she didn't know what.

Where was she? From the piping on the ceiling, it looked like some kind of unfinished basement. "Cyrus. She's fully conscious."

The man who had blown into her life and thrown it onto a tilt-a-whirl walked over to her. She stared up at him. He was so beautiful. She blinked. Women shouldn't think that about men. They weren't *beautiful*...they were handsome. Yet, somehow he was. So lovely, in fact, that she couldn't look at him for all of his tremendous perfection. She dropped her eyes.

"Now, now, princess. I thought we'd made some progress in that direction. You were doing a great job looking at me earlier." He patted her head, and she whimpered. It felt so good to be touched by him, so soothing. He was goodness. He had all their best interests at heart. He would... She whimpered. Her thoughts were so strained, so muddled. What the hell was going on?

Cyrus sucked in his breath. "Damn it. Lake, you're on notice for this. Learn control or don't leave your apartment."

In front of her, Lake looked down. "She needed fixing. That's what I do. It's like breathing."

He shook his head and furrowed his blond eyebrows. "I don't accept that. You're like a child. Do better." Cyrus turned her attention back to Betsy, and she took a deep breath.

Everything would be okay as long as he was there. She would do whatever he wanted, whenever he wanted. She belonged to him; they all did. He held their...

Wow. Betsy blinked rapidly. Where had those thoughts come from? They weren't hers. They had to belong to someone else, someone she didn't know, except they were obviously her own. Who else could be inside of her head making her think those things?

"Okay." Cyrus shook his head. "She's panting. I don't want her going into shock."

"What are you going to do?" Lake placed a hand on Betsy, and Betsy growled. She did not want the other woman touching her. No one should be placing hands on her right then. Betsy backed up, stumbling a bit. Why weren't her feet working, and holy cow she had growled. She needed to say something, anything, but her mouth wouldn't work. Sweat broke out on her neck.

"I'm going to shift and take care of her. What do you think I'm going to do?"

Lake retreated further. "Didn't you tell me that you shifted once today? You're going to shift twice in one day on a non-full-moon night? That's insanity. You're going to make yourself sick."

He laughed, and Betsy shuddered. There was no mirth in the sound. She could smell something on him she couldn't identity. It tasted tangy on her tongue. What was that?

And why couldn't she make her mouth work? Something was happening to her. She wasn't dense. She could tell something was off, but she couldn't put her finger on what.

"I'm not going to make myself sick. I'm Alpha." He shook his head. "And I suppose, if I do, you will fix me. That's what you do, what you can't seem to help yourself from doing."

Lake looked away, tears in her eyes, and crossed to the window. Betsy didn't know what the history between the brother and sister was, but she knew he'd hurt her feelings. She could smell it, taste it, a bitter pungent scent that burned her nose.

Distress didn't smell good. The scent resembled rotten eggs or something similar. She gagged.

"Have you realized that you're a wolf, princess?"

She jolted at his words. No, that wasn't possible. She whimpered and backed against the wall. *This. Can. Not. Be. Happening.* It had to be a mistake. Sure, Cyrus was a wolf-man. She'd seen him change. But not her. Not unless Lake had done something to her.

"No. Apparently, I broke that news to you, and it has placed you in utter terror. If I was worried about shock seconds ago, I'm terrified now. Don't worry, Betsy. All will be well."

Cyrus' body shifted. In the same way he had become a human from a wolf earlier, he shifted in the opposite direction now. Fur popped out on his skin and his nose, which had been adorable and human, elongated into a snout. She sucked in her breath and jumped when she realized the funny feeling on the back of her rear end was a moving tail.

She turned her neck to look at it. Oh God, she had a tail. Betsy wanted to cry, and it came out like a howl. She tried to stop, and it happened again. Heaven help her, she was a canine. She howled. She growled. She wagged her tail.

There had been things she wanted to do, plans she'd hoped to achieve after she settled the

Nathan problem and saved her parents. There had been food to eat. Now she wouldn't be able to even eat any chocolate. She sniffed—unless that rule applied only to domesticated dogs and not werewolves.

Cyrus had fully shifted into his wolf form. He stared at

her for a second, and she wished she could read minds, could know what he wanted from her. Currently, everything she craved most in the world left her in conflict. On one hand—or paw—she didn't want to look him in the eyes. The floor, the wall, anywhere but his eyes seemed a great place for her gaze. On the other, she wanted his total attention, wanted to rub up against him, to take him somewhere where no one would ever find them—where it would be the two of them alone.

She took a deep breath; she had to relax. They didn't even know each other.

Cyrus growled, and she forced her gaze to his. It felt akin to yanking a boulder skyward using only her neck. Yet, somehow she managed. Maybe it was the way he growled at her. Betsy would probably do anything to make that sound stop. Or maybe it was because he smelled like cinnamon and power. She loved that spice and she particularly liked how it surrounded Cyrus.

He crowded her until their fur touched. He was dark with gray specks and much bigger than her. Their fur wasn't dissimilar in color, and she wondered if all—*gulp*—werewolves were similarly marked.

His heat radiated into her body, consuming all of her attention. She closed her eyes. How could Cyrus feel so right when everything around her was so completely wrong?

Her body vibrated, and she opened her eyes, and then wished she hadn't. Betsy moaned. Oh God, how could such animalistic noises be coming from her? How could she be a wolf? She didn't even like wolves. They ate live-stock and made walking through the darkness in the woods a terrifying experience.

Pain radiated through her body. Her muscles ached, and she screamed out, but she couldn't even hear herself yell. What was happening to her? She was dying. That had to be it. She wasn't meant to be a wolf, and now she would die because someone had messed with her genes or whatever it was they had done to her.

The sound of her own pain changed as she realized she lay on the floor in her *human* body. It hurt to use her voice; her throat was scratchy. She raised her head, which pounded like she'd been drinking for days.

Cyrus knelt in front of her. "I forced the change back on you. It seemed the only way."

Lake squatted next to him. "How did you do that? I've never seen that before. You didn't do that with Lilliana."

"Lilliana belonged to Travis. It's an Alpha thing." Cyrus stroked Betsy's head, and she took a deep breath. His touch brought relief, which should have concerned her, except the ease of her aches made it impossible for her to think about anything, but the sudden absence of pain. "You're going to be okay, princess. The first couple times are awful. Then it's nothing at all." That was good news, she supposed, if she didn't want to ever have to go through that again. "Somebody had better explain to me what is going on, or, so help me, I don't care how much trouble it causes you, I'm going to the police. Where am I?"

Cyrus extended his hand, and she took it, allowing him to help her stand. If pride was the last to go before the fall, then she must have already tumbled headfirst into some kind of endless pit. The only plus she could see was that, apparently, clothes remained intact during these situations. She wasn't naked. That would be much, much worse.

Small silver linings...

"You're in my company headquarters. And two things, princess..." Cyrus spoke as he ran a hand down the side of her face. She shivered, and warmth invaded her core. Uh-oh. She knew that feeling. Any second she'd be begging him to take her from behind. The image made her wetter, and since her nose detected all sorts of new scents, she strongly suspected he knew what was going on inside her womb.

How could she make sense of any of this? Maybe it had always been an illusion; she'd never had privacy. Were-wolves had turned out to be very real, which meant they had always been able to smell things best left to the imagination. But she preferred the naïve ignorance she'd possessed before.

She swallowed. Thankfully, he didn't remark on her desire. They could both pretend the other one didn't know. "Two things?"

"Right." He nodded. "The first is I don't like threats, particularly ones I know you can't follow through on. They insult both of us. You going to the police is not a possibility."

Her temper flared. It might be hard to look him in the eye, but she forced herself to keep his gaze. "I can go to the police if I want to."

Lake snorted, and Betsy ignored her. She had nothing to say to Cyrus' sister. At least not right now. Her attention locked on Cyrus and his cinnamon smell.

"You can't." He stated.

She shook her head. "Unless you're going to keep me prisoner, I can." Her own statement startled her. "Are you planning to force me to remain here?"

Cyrus shook his head. She waited to see if he would say something, and, when he didn't, she had to speak again.

"Then I can go to the cops if I want to." She'd much rather they gave her some answers, but it seemed important he understand her—wolf or not—*she* would be the one to make choices regarding her actions. She was tired of everyone else ordering, blackmailing, or otherwise forcing her to bend to their will.

"I suppose technically you could, but you won't. Want to know why? Here is Wolf 101.

You will never want to do anything that could bring me harm—both because I am Alpha—*your Alpha* and your *mate*. The first would be enough to stall you, unless you felt compelled to challenge me, and the second would absolutely prevent you from betrayal and the challenge itself."

She couldn't deal with that at all. One thing at a time. He did smell fantastic, and she'd thought him handsome when she'd only been human. But mating? That had implications she would need to dwell on later when not in his presence. Or after a few stiff drinks like her father did.

"How do I even know if what you are telling me is true? You could have made this whole thing up. I don't know anything about werewolves. Not one thing. You could say all werewolves sleep in blue sheets, and I'd have to go home and do that because I know nothing. And this whole bit about me being a wolf before? I'm not buying it. I was a human until she,"—Betsy pointed at Lake— "did this to me."

"No." Lake gasped. "I could never make you a werewolf if you weren't one. You had a blockage, something keeping you from being what you should be. I removed it, and you shifted."

"Betsy." Cyrus pulled her against him. "Do you remember how you told me that sometimes you had urges, things you couldn't control?"

"You would bring that up." She struggled against him. If he kept her like that for too long, she wouldn't be able to stifle her need for him. Just like he'd told her. Female werewolves had to be taken care of when they were in heat. Like dogs.

"Only to tell you that there has *always* been a reason, and now you have to believe. There is no reason to berate yourself."

She had no response to that. He wasn't wrong. If this had always been inside of her, then at least it explained some things, like her need for sex and her propensity to crave raw, red meat. A door slammed open, and a shriek filled the room as Jensen and Mitchell dragged Nathan through the door. He was bleeding from the head, and his left eye had swollen shut. They carried him, but it looked like one of his ankles was twisted in an unnatural way. She winced. That had to hurt.

Cyrus poked her nose. "When the feeling of satisfaction hits you, embrace the sensation. You're a werewolf. We attack and beat our enemies."

What? She didn't get a chance to answer, because Cyrus released her and walked toward the new arrivals. As Cyrus moved away, Nathan noticed her.

"You." He hissed. "You're responsible for this, aren't you? You're the reason these creatures grabbed me off the street and invaded my home. After everything I did for you. See if I save your parents now, you slut."

Cyrus growled and with a swiping gesture too fast to be perceived, he clawed Nathan's face. An agonized howl left Nathan's mouth, and five red claw marks appeared on his face.

Lake laughed, a high-pitched snicker. "Don't insult the Alpha's mate, you stupid human." The Healer's words made Betsy gasp. Was that what Cyrus meant by embracing the destruction? Lake seemed joyful. But Betsy couldn't join her in her revelry. Maybe, if so much weren't at stake, she'd love the way the red marks on Nathan's face reflected Cyrus' rage. But Nathan had a point. He'd never call now. Her parents were doomed. A pulse of temper thundered in her forehead before she gritted her teeth. She hadn't really let herself get mad at them. There hadn't been time, but now, since it was all going to be over, she wanted to throw something at them. They must have known what they were doing was wrong on all possible levels. They hadn't been the ones to give up their lives to save her. They hadn't even tried to protect her and had been publicly ashamed when her sexual issues had come out.

And they had to know something about this wolf business. They couldn't have raised her and not known? Could they? Not to mention her sister. If her twin lived, as Cyrus said she did, then they'd outright lied to her. She growled and covered her mouth.

Cyrus turned around and looked at her. She couldn't read his expression, but it didn't matter what he thought. She had suddenly become the most disloyal daughter on the planet. *After everything they'd done, everything they'd put up with...*

...and all the lies they told me... The disloyal side of her soul didn't budge on that issue. But shouldn't they have known that her needs were normal? If one of them was a werewolf, shouldn't they have helped her to understand?

Heavens, she was conflicted. Her stomach hurt. She really wanted to go lie down, but that wasn't an option. Whatever she felt, she wouldn't hang her mom and dad out to dry. Maybe

Nathan could be reasoned with.

"Put him in the cage," Cyrus ordered, and his men— Jensen and Mitchell crossed the room with Nathan.

So much for reasoning.

"Cyrus." She crossed to him. "I know you said you'd

handle this, but I need him to make that call. Please. This isn't going to get him to do anything."

"Ssshh." He held out his hand. "Come."

Betsy took his outstretched fingers, embracing them with her own. She shouldn't be so willing to, but she needed his touch and not even in a sexual way. Cyrus could make this all okay. She shook her head. Was this some kind of Alpha thing, her constant need for him to make things right?

"Nathan." Cyrus walked with her over to the cage. "You owe Betsy an apology."

"I would never apologize to her. She should be kissing the ground I walk on. Instead, she's taken up with all of you. My father warned me that this could happen. This is the devil's work. You're all unnatural aberrations that need to be hunted down and killed."

"Oh. We've got a true believer here." Cyrus laughed. Mitchell and Jensen joined him. Betsy didn't really see what was so amusing, but the male werewolves seemed to really enjoy his statement. "I haven't had one of you in a cage for years. Tell me, how long ago did you guys join up?"

"What are you talking about?" If she was going to stand outside the cage and listen to this stuff, she needed to at least understand.

"There have always been humans who try to hunt us. Most dismiss our existence completely, but the ones who believe typically want us dead. It's long been my pleasure to show them the error of their ways."

"You're saying your father knew about werewolves?" No one from her hometown went around talking about myths. They were too busy drinking and managing the livestock industry. Maybe doing both at the same time. Her parents didn't even let her watch horror movies with were-wolves or vampires—she'd snuck those.

"Everyone knew, you bitch."

Cyrus growled again, but Nathan didn't seem to notice. He kept talking. "My daddy killed more werewolves before I was born than he can count. He only stopped because my mom didn't want him getting killed after I was born. But he could have been the greatest ever. In Montana, where we're all from, he's like a god."

What the hell is he talking about? Because what Nathan described—that didn't fit her image of his parents either. So, had everyone known the secret—except her?

"That so?" When Cyrus spoke, Betsy shuddered. She'd never heard him use that particular tone before. Calling it menacing didn't do it justice. She turned to look at him, rubbing the goose bumps on her arms with her free hand. Hearing him that angry made her want to hyperventilate.

She struggled for composure. Why did it matter that Nathan's family knew about werewolves? She was a were-wolf. Had they known that? And why didn't she know about her parents? Were they all latents? There were so many questions and no answers coming.

Cyrus dropped her hand and surged forward. In a blur of motion, he gripped Nathan by the neck and pulled him up against the bars. The other man gagged.

"Here's how this works. I'm going to hand you a phone, and you're going to use it to make your daily phone call. You aren't going to use any code words to tip anyone off that all is not well. If you do that, I'll know. I'll smell it. My *kind* can do that. Make your call or die when my pack hunts you down during the next full moon. You'll be the rabbit. We'll be the wolves. There's always a choice. This one is yours."

Cyrus dropped him, and Nathan rolled around the floor of the cage and gasped for air. "What's it going to be? Call or die?" "I'll call." He had to strain to talk.

"Good." Cyrus turned to Jensen. "Get him some water. I wouldn't want his daddy to suspect anything is wrong. Not even a sore throat."

"Well, this is unexpected."

Betsy jumped at the new voice and whirled around. A man she hadn't met yet stood in the doorway. He was tall, maybe even an inch beyond Cyrus, which was impressive. He had long brown hair that hit shoulders. He was dressed impeccably in a black-on-black suit that reminded her of gangster movies she'd watched alone at night.

But it was his eyes that struck her. They were pure white. She'd never seen anything like them before. Her mouth hung open, and although she knew she must look like a landed fish, she couldn't seem to shut her lips. In the same way she'd known Cyrus smelled like power, she knew the scent of power.

"You're early." Cyrus didn't take his eyes off the cage to address the newcomer.

"I come when I please."

"Not to my city you don't, Alexei. You come when you're invited and not a second before. Get out."

No one in the room moved or made a sound except Nathan, who wept on the ground of the cage. Yet, Betsy knew Cyrus' words amounted to a very big problem. She smiled, finally closing her mouth. Prickles of awareness broke out on her neck. Heavens, Cyrus had issued a challenge. There could be bloodshed with whoever this Alexei turned out to be. And the idea titillated her.

Heaven help her—what had happened to her?

Chapter 5

Cyrus hadn't become Alpha of New York by being a pushover. He wasn't scared or impressed with Alexei's shtick, and he had no intention of letting the Alpha of Boston waltz into his city—let alone his headquarters—willy-nilly without some kind of response. As he was certain Alexei would expect nothing less, he had to wonder what the fuck the other man really hoped to accomplish with this.

Behind Alexei, two wolves entered and, growled loudly. One of them showed his teeth. Cyrus took a deep breath to confirm what he'd already scented. Alexei had brought only those two wolves with him. The other Alpha might not mean war, but his wolves didn't want him threatened. That was fine. Cyrus had his own protectors.

Jensen lunged forward as Cyrus anticipated he would. "You would come here and threaten our Alpha?"

Alexei laughed, tilting his face towards the ceiling when he did. " Call off your attack dogs, and I'll turn off mine. We can discuss my early arrival civilly over a drink. You can tell me why you have a human in a cage and I can explain the situation of baby kidnappings in Boston that has brought me to your door."

His words cooled whatever smart remark Cyrus would have made about attack dogs. "Human babies or werewolf?"

Both were completely unacceptable, but Cyrus had faced a situation the year earlier in which his pregnant females were getting attacked. He'd thought Travis Michaels to blame until that misunderstanding had been cleared up. Now he had to keep the impregnated pack members hidden. Cyrus had assumed the perpetrator of the crimes had wanted the deaths of the women, but maybe it wasn't that. Maybe the target had been their children...

He glanced down at his mate. Her parents had been selling children.

Could this be that large? Could it cross the continent? An ache for Lucian's leadership swept through him like a hard wind, threatening to knock him over. Not that anyone need know—certainly not the pale-eyed warrior across the room.

"I don't think any other topic would have allowed you entrance. Shall we talk upstairs?" Alexei nodded and turned around. But Cyrus wasn't quite done yet. "Your two pack mates can stay down here. They can help Jensen use some of his aggression to get Nathan to do what I say. Jensen, I need him to call home. You'll tell me if anything is wrong scent-wise. Get him his water."

Jensen's pupils were huge. His trusted friend and pack member would have preferred a fight to his task, but since that wasn't happening, at least not yet, Jensen nodded. Cyrus patted him on the back when he passed.

Mitchell spoke. "Alpha, I don't feel comfortable with

you going with him alone. Take one of us with you or call others."

Alexei turned around. "Going soft, Cyrus? There was a time when no one would have doubted your ability to take me in a fight. Do your pack members doubt your skills?"

"Perhaps they don't want me dead. Is your pack accustomed to letting you enter possible deadly encounters without any assistance from them? Are they hoping someone will take off your head or set you on fire?"

Alexei's pack members growled. Cyrus winked at them, which made them growl louder. "Down, boys. Your leader is in no danger from me unless he opens his mouth to say something threatening. I don't think he travelled here to do that, not if he needs my assistance with baby snatchings. Betsy, Lake, you're with me."

This stopped Alexei. The other Alpha raised a brown eyebrow. "You wish to bring the females?"

"Yes." He didn't need to explain more. The man could have the women in the room, or he could save his issues for another day. Cyrus had no intention of leaving his mate or his sister alone in the room with Nathan. The male was stuffed in a cage, but he might say something upsetting. Cyrus would not allow that to happen. They'd all had enough for one day.

Lake groaned loudly. "Hello." She nodded to Alexei and led him away toward the elevators. Alexei followed in her wake. His sister would see to settling the other Alpha in Cyrus' office.

Betsy cleared his throat, and he turned to look at him. "I need to go?"

"Yes." Why did he keep having to explain himself? Had this suddenly become some kind of democracy and he'd not been informed? If he said come, his pack came. Of course he'd never had a mate before. His parents had not been true mates. Yet they had loved each other as couples who'd spent their lives together did. Their shared history had deepened their communication. Maybe he needed to work on that…

"Why do I have to go? Don't you think I would be better off down here with Nathan? Just to make sure he doesn't try to pull anything."

Cyrus shook his head. She still thought like a human. Eventually, she would come to see how pack worked. "Jensen and Mitchell can handle him. I'd rather you not be here for him to taunt."

Betsy dropped her eyes, and he inwardly sighed. Some day she wouldn't feel so unsure around him. He had to believe that. Everything had just happened, and adjustments took time. The only problem was that he'd never been very good at being patient.

"If you are not with me I am going to worry about you. This is an important conversation. I need to be able to concentrate." It pained him to admit such a weakness, but there it was.

She raised her eyes slightly, still not quite meeting his gaze. "What's going to happen to me down here in the basement? Nathan is in a cage. Your pack mates are here. If I get my feelings hurt, it won't be the first time in my life. I'll live through it."

She was used to being brave, and she didn't trust him completely yet. That much he could understand. If she'd been raised as she should have been, with pack, she would know to trust the instincts inside of her that had to be telling her she was pack and belonged to him. A sudden thought almost brought him to his knees. What if she didn't feel that way about him? What if she felt that way toward someone else? Felt more connected to another Alpha and a different pack.

What if Alexei connected her more to the pack in Boston than Cyrus had managed so far? Oh hell. Could that have happened?

"Are you okay?" She reached out and gripped his arm. "Your smell changed."

He cleared his throat; he could imagine it had. None of his pack members would mention it. But she was his mate, and she didn't know better.

"How so?" He needed to get upstairs with Alexei, but this was more important. Instead of a lifetime to hone her senses, he needed her to do it in a few minutes. If that meant she needed blunt, unrelenting honesty no matter how uncomfortable? Then he'd do it. Unreasonable, yes— but life wasn't fair.

"There was a surge from you, a change in the way you smelled, for a split second." She wrinkled her nose. "You usually carry the scent of cinnamon, you were suddenly filled with vanilla too. And mint."

"You think I smell like cinnamon?" *Huh.* He'd never heard that before. To him, aromas were connected to seasons and places. *The woods. Fall. The city.* Betsy had a very specific sense of smell.

"Is that a bad thing?"

"No." He shook his head. "My scent changed because I got nervous. I've trained my wolf pack to do their best to disguise that, but I didn't follow my own instructions."

"You got scared that I might stay down here and get hurt?"

"I got nervous that you aren't connecting to me." He shook his head. This conversation had to cease before he ended up curled under a table in a fetal position. "Stay down here if that is what you prefer. I would like you upstairs with me where I know you're safe, where I don't have to worry that the basement might spontaneous combust and you'd be somehow killed in the process. But, if you don't want to be there with me, then don't come. I can't force you to want to be with me. Not even as an Alpha wolf."

He turned on his heel and headed toward the elevator. Maybe he should order her to go with him. That's what he'd do with any other pack member. Only he didn't want that from her. He wanted her to choose him, to want to be with him, and to stand at his side.

Shit. Wasn't true mating supposed to be easier than this? What if he'd gotten this whole thing wrong and she would never—could never be mated to him? What would happen to him then? Would he be stuck in this perpetual, unrequited need for her for the rest of his existence?

She ran to him and grabbed his hand. He looked down at their joined fingers for a second before he pressed the elevator button to go up to the offices. She'd chased him, and he hadn't seen that coming. What did it mean? And was her taking his hand an indication of feelings on her part? Why was this woman so confusing to him? He'd dealt with females his whole life and Betsy made him feel like a dolt.

"I had no idea you were so insecure." She raised her eyebrows.

"What?" He wasn't insecure. He'd taken over a wolf pack when he'd barely been twenty years old. He couldn't have done that if he was *insecure*. Humans had neuroses, not Alpha werewolves.

"That was a pretty good display of passive-aggressive back there. If it was that important for me to go with you, why didn't you say so?"

"I did." The elevator dinged when it opened, and they stepped inside. Hadn't he made that clear? He wanted her to come. He'd told her to, and then he'd relented out of respect to her wishes. How and why had this gotten so complicated?

"Not really. No, you said you didn't want to worry about me. And you didn't want Nathan to hurt my feelings. That's not the same as you *need* me with you."

He wanted to growl. This infuriating woman was going to make everything complicated. He could already tell, and he really wanted to kiss her for it. "You say that to me while you can't even look me in the eyes."

"I know. It's very bizarre. I'm trying to work on it, believe me. Sometimes I can't stand the idea of it, like I'm going to be overwhelmed by you if I dare to take a really good glance at your blue eyes." She shrugged. "It's got to be a wolf thing, right? I mean animals do this. They have pack relations or whatever. We had three dogs for a while when I was growing up, and they had an order. One of them was in charge. Although come to think of it, they always acted like I was really the one in charge. In this case, it's you. I'm working on my order. Or maybe I'm really the passive-aggressive one."

"Betsy." He sighed loudly. How could he want to snarl at her and bite down to mark her at the same time? By the end of the day, he might very well lose his mind. "You're my mate. I

can guarantee you're not passive. You've said some things to me humans wouldn't dare utter without even understanding why. You sometimes manage to regard me perfectly well. I'd say that your looking down is something else entirely."

Her heart rate increased dramatically, enough for him to hear it. His words struck a nerve.

"What do you think it is?"

"You want me," he answered bluntly. It only seemed fair she be as off-center as he. "And if you look at me, you're afraid both of us are going to know how much you do."

The elevator stopped at the top floor, and he exited, pulling his mate with him. She'd sucked in her breath with his proclamation, and it had confirmed that his suspicions were right on. Betsy was hardly prepared for that level of intimacy...yet. But, eventually, she'd have to admit to her desires, and then things would change. Then they'd finally make the connection he knew they could have.

Screw insecurity. Things finally made some sense. He smiled at the thought.

Mating matter settled, he only had to deal with Alpha politics and stolen babies. And figure out what to do about Betsy's family.

Just that...

He walked into his office, and from the scent of discomfort—a pungent smell, like decaying garbage outside a restaurant—he wasn't a moment too soon. Lake had never liked Alexei. Nothing had changed. Alexei, seemingly oblivious to her feelings—although Cyrus seriously doubted that since Alexei never missed a trick—sprawled on the leather couch across from Cyrus' desk.

Lake tapped the back of her head against the wall where she leaned. "What took you so long?"

"Betsy and I needed to have a conversation."

Alexei interrupted. "This must be a new thing between the two of you. Did it only just happen?"

"That's not your concern. This is Betsy. She's with me. That's all you need to know." The how, the who, and the fact that she'd been a latent who'd only just turned—yeah, none of Alexei's fucking business.

The Alpha from Boston nodded. "You were such a fun

guy when we were younger. Where did the stick that is perpetually up your ass come from?"

"Years of handling problems like you. Be careful. When you get home, your own people might be there waiting to take off your head. I'd hate for you to go through that. Again."

Alexei growled. "You know that was a rumor."

"Or you wanted us to think it was."

"Are you two finished? Do you think you could get to the matter at hand?" Lake cut off their argument, as he'd known she eventually would. It was always a question as to whether or not he was going to claw off the other were-wolf's face. That was why he wanted Lake with him. She tended to force him to keep a cooler head.

Sisters could occasionally be useful.

"We were attacked last week," Alexei must have agreed because he sobered. "Seemingly out of the blue. It was brutal. We lost a lot of females. I've been trying to keep this under wraps. The scene produced no results in terms of scent. Not were ones anyway. Lots of humans but none known to us. This is happening more and more."

Cyrus nodded. This was always a problem. The human police carried fingerprints, not scent ones. "Did you try their authorities? Maybe there is some kind of forensic evidence."

Lake raised an eyebrow. "Been watching *CSI* again?"

"Don't undermine him. He's making a good point." Betsy stepped forward, and his heart stuttered. Had she stood up for him? For a second, he forgot to breathe. When had that ever happened? His father had thought he had to toughen him up practically from birth, his mother never contradicted the man, and he'd always been an Alpha in training. *Put up or shut up and don't whine when you don't get your way.*

63

"I'm sorry, my Alpha." Lake glanced down. He would comfort her, except he wasn't going to undo Betsy's lovely gesture by making it appear less than it was. Lake should probably be sorry.

He'd let her handle that emotion for a while.

Alexei tapped his nose. "We did try to use the human police. There aren't any fingerprints in the system."

Of course not. That would be too simple.

"But it told us that we are dealing with humans. I had heard that you faced similar problems, and I came a day early to see how you had handled it. However, I'm now wondering, as I sit here, if we aren't dealing with something more nefarious than I originally thought. Do you think it's possible that there is a conspiracy happening?"

"What kind of conspiracy could there be? Humans setting out to steal werewolf babies? That would be..."

He trailed off and turned to look at Betsy. Her eyes were huge as she stared back at him. Alexei wanted to know if it was possible for humans to be stealing werewolf babies, and the answer was yes; it was *very possible*. Only he couldn't tell the other man that because the only people he knew who were stealing babies were his mate's parents. His little mate had stood up for him in a room with another Alpha. She'd defended him from his sister, a woman with considerable dominance of her own.

And to reveal that crucial piece of information about her parents to a vengeance-seeking Alexei would be a betrayal. He would die first.

Fantastic. He was about to ask the man to enter into a treaty with him, and he was going to start the negotiations by lying to him. Or, at the very least, and it wasn't much better, by omitting a very big piece of information.

Alexei turned left and right, watching all of them. "There are some amazingly hard to decipher emotions happening in this room right now. Would someone like to tell me what's going on?'

Cyrus shook his head. "I've been considering the implications of your suggestion, and clearly my mate is doing the same. It's a big, broad idea, and one we'll have to dwell on another time."

The most important thing for him to do at that moment was to get Alexei sent to his hotel and keep him distracted while Cyrus worked things out with Betsy. Then, once he knew what he could do for her parents, he would figure out how to undo this moment with Alexei. The other Alpha would never understand. Alexei had lost females and babies. He'd want revenge. Only he wasn't going to be getting any off Betsy's parents. Not if Cyrus could help it.

"I don't believe you. Something else—"

Cyrus shrugged. "It's really not my problem if you can't decipher smells anymore. I can loan you my Healer if you're in need of one. Otherwise, perhaps you can chalk it up to old age." "I am exactly two years older than you. Do you expect to lose your senses anytime soon?"

"I'm not you." Cyrus shrugged again. Irritating the other Alpha would also distract him. Petty—but effective. "I don't know when members of your family start to head toward the grave."

Alexei stood up and then rolled his eyes. "I know that you're baiting me. It's easy to do, and I'm working on controlling my temper. I wouldn't want to scar up your other cheek in anger."

At the reminder, Cyrus rubbed the long mark that marred his left cheek from next to his ear all the way to the middle of his chin. He hadn't thought about it in years. He'd had it such a long time. The battle that had taken his parents had also left him with that mark. The scar hadn't bothered him in so long, he didn't notice it anymore.

Did Betsy hate it? Did it bother her to look at it?

Shit. Maybe she was right. Maybe he was *insecure* and pathetic to boot.

He turned his attention back to Alexei. Easier to handle the ego-driven werewolf than whatever was happening to him. "If you think you'd ever get close enough to me to scar me, you're sadly mistaken. I'd eat you alive before I dropped what was left of your body in the Hudson."

"You're funny. It's a good thing I find you amusing, or I'd have to kill you."

Cyrus walked forward like the wolf whose soul he had inside of him, with sheer and purposeful intent. "You came into my city a day early, uninvited. I get why you did it—I don't trust phones any more than you do. We have business to conduct together tomorrow. A treaty to agree to in blood, if you're willing." Another agreement that would burn in his belly, but anything to keep his pack safe during this tumultuous time—until another Alpha Prime could be found...

"But you're not ready to talk terms tonight. Is that it?" Alexei raised an eyebrow. The man liked to play game.

Cyrus wasn't in the mood. "Tomorrow. As agreed."

"I need to find my pregnant females. Dead or alive, they have to come home. To their mates and lovers. I came here to keep our appointment but I can't talk treaty until something is done about this. How do you do it? How do you manage to handle all of it at the same time in a human world?" Did Alexei really want an answer? Cyrus wasn't used to the other Alpha wanting to really *talk* about anything.

He sighed. "Call upon your strength. You wouldn't be

Alpha if you didn't have deep resources." Truth was, he understood Alexei completely. He wouldn't want to focus on anything other than the search too. His cell phone beeped, and he glanced at the device. Travis had arrived in the building and, unlike Alexei, had done him the courtesy of informing him of his arrival. Unfortunately, Travis and Alexei hated each other. "We'll talk treaty tomorrow because we must."

They couldn't be allowed in the same room, even if he couldn't prevent them scenting each other.

His nose itched. A quick look at his mate told him what he'd smelled. She was in distress. All the color had vanished from her cheeks.

This day wasn't getting any better. Philadelphia and Boston couldn't go to war in the penthouse of his New York pack's headquarters. Not when he had to go to Montana to rescue his mate's criminal parents. She'd never even told him where she was from but Jensen's investigation of the house had given him at least that much information. Everything was so complicated. Shouldn't mating be simple?

Cyrus had never missed Lucian so much in his life.

Chapter 6

If she could have turned into a puddle and been absorbed into the wood floor beneath her feet, Betsy would have gladly done so. She knew what Cyrus had to be thinking. Her parents. Stolen babies. And the fact that she was a werewolf and hadn't known. She'd have to be a giant moron not to know what he thought.

She wasn't educated like she wanted to be. Her home schooling had been a necessity. They'd lived too far from the main road to get her to school and back every day while still running the home properly. But she could read, and she could do arithmetic, more or less. One and one always added up to two.

In this case, the numbers all pointed in the direction of her folks. How much worse could any of this get? Only her parents were locked away, so unless they'd arranged a bunch of kidnappings months ago before they were found out, they hadn't done this.

Betsy had a bad moment when she thought Cyrus was about to share his theory with Alexei. Only he hadn't.

Instead, he seemed to be trying to get the other wolf out the door.

"Alexei. I need you to leave." Cyrus motioned toward the door.

The other Alpha laughed, a long, hard sound that rattled the pictures on the wall. She winced. He took up all the space in the room with his personality, at least to her. She was so glad that Cyrus wasn't like that

Only Alexei didn't go, and his pack mates had been willing to throw themselves into a fight to protect him. That kind loyalty impressed her.

Alexei snorted. "You need to work on your subtlety. Ask me nicely. Convince me to share a meal with you and then we'll see if I feel like leaving."

Cyrus shook his head. "Not having dinner with you. You need to go. Travis is here on another matter, and I won't have the two of you stinking up the place with your pissing contest. Get in the elevator. Get out. I'll see you tomorrow."

All joviality fled Alexei's features. His eyes turned feral, a wolf in human form. She shuddered and took a step backward. Betsy never wanted to find herself on the other side of that gaze. She turned to Cyrus, instinct pointing to him as the safe harbor in the room. What would he do if Alexei refused to leave?

"I don't know how you can have a positive relationship with that poser. He has no business being Alpha. He runs Philadelphia like it's a democracy."

Again, Cyrus only shook his head. "There are ranges between democracy and autocracy. You know what Lucian taught us. To each his own. If it works for Travis, I have no comment. I don't want war, not again."

She squirmed in her seat. Cyrus rubbed at his cheek, and she wondered if his scar had come from some sort of battle. Betsy sighed. It was hard enough navigating human politics. What kinds of things did wolves do to each other, and why did the idea of watching Cyrus in battle make her so hot and bothered?

She really needed to have her head examined.

"I'll leave, but only because I need you to give me what I want tomorrow. I need you to help me find them. Pissing you off tonight is only going to make you more obnoxious." Who was Alexei trying to convince? Cyrus or himself?

For his part, Cyrus raised an eyebrow. "You scratch my back, I'll scratch yours."

Alexei nodded and stalked from the room. A few seconds later, the elevator dinged. She sniffed the air to see if she could confirm his departure, but his scent remained too prevalent in the room to determine if Alexei was there or not. Maybe others could tell, but her skills weren't there yet. Processing what had happened would have to wait—she needed to survive all these changes and freak out about them later.

"Cyrus." She needed to say something about how he had kept her parents' illegal activities to himself. His protection of her family deserved recognition.

"Not yet, princess." Cyrus cut her off.

Lake looked left and right. "What is going on? Is someone going to fill me in? I only know the smallest amount."

"Not yet to you too, sister." Cyrus walked to his desk. His face gave her no indication of his mood; neither did his scent. The man who'd consumed her thoughts since they'd met retreated behind an unreadable mask.

She didn't like the feeling. It made her want to claw at

something—to howl. Instead, she cleared her throat. "When can we talk about it?"

"Later." He didn't look up when he addressed her, and the sound of the elevator dinging again caught her attention. She didn't like Cyrus ignoring her—how he avoided her as though she wasn't in the room. Whoever was getting off that elevator—Travis, he'd called him—had thrown him.

She sniffed the air. He was regrouping. How did she know that so clearly?

Because he was just…perfection to her. She bit her lip. How was she going to survive if they ever slept together? Hell, if he affected her this way and she'd never seen him naked… She swallowed hard. What would happen when she did? And why was she thinking *when*—shouldn't it be if?

A couple entered the room and Betsy transferred her attention to them. The man was tall with brown hair and dark eyes. His arms, where they were visible, showed ink. He had a stern visage, his eyebrows furrowed and his jaw line hard. His smell spoke of Alpha, the same way Cyrus's and Alexei's did. Power tasted like fire in her mouth. It demanded attention.

She shifted her gaze to his companion and sucked in her breath. The woman she regarded must have noticed her at the same time because she had a similar reaction, covering her mouth with her hand. They stared silently for a moment. Or maybe it was longer than that. Time ceased to have any particular meaning when she gazed at the impossible—her mirror image in living, breathing, and smelling-of-wolf form.

Tears pooled and then fell from her eyes. Betsy had known this person before, had dreamed about her, asked after her, and mourned her when her parents had told her, eventually, that her twin sister had passed from the earth. It had seemed excessive to weep as she had, considering she'd never really known her sister. Yet, she had. They'd shared a womb, and Betsy had felt her absence like a wound that festered and wouldn't heal no matter how many salves she put on it.

Her twin pointed at her. "I knew you were somewhere..." The other woman's voice hitched. "I've been waiting for you."

Tears slid from Betsy's eyes. "Me too." Her voice sounded hoarse.

The other woman walked toward her slowly. "How did this happen? How did Cyrus find you?"

The other male in the room growled. "Cyrus, I think you'd better explain yourself."

"Gladly. But later. Why don't we let our mates catch up?"

"Mates? As in you have one too?"

Betsy tuned out the rest of what they said. They could growl, hiss, or pee on each other for all she cared at that moment. Her world had become solely focused on the woman who shared her face. Well, almost shared it. On closer inspection, it appeared as though her twin sister had not been cursed with the abundance of freckles across her nose that Betsy had to live with. She hated the way they appeared. Yes, it was settled; her sister was gorgeous. Much prettier than Betsy, and it didn't bother her. She was so darn glad to see her.

Cyrus had promised he'd bring her twin to her. And he'd delivered.

"Well." The woman laughed, taking her hand. "Are you going to tell me? How did he find you?"

Betsy laughed. "In a coffee shop."

"Really?" The woman she'd been waiting to find raised

a blonde eyebrow. "I need to hear this story. I'm Lilliana, by the way."

She knew the name. Cyrus had said it several times, particularly in the first few minutes when he'd thought that was who she was. "I'm Betsy." She smiled. "It's so lovely to finally find you."

Lilliana's arms came around her, pulling her into a tight embrace.

Betsy sniffed. "Oh thank goodness you're a hugger too. I didn't want to weird you out by grabbing you if you didn't like it."

Her sister laughed. "If you didn't like hugging, I was going to force you to embrace me anyway. I knew you existed. I just did."

Betsy closed her eyes. This was a small miracle in the midst of a hellish day.

IT AMAZED Betsy how fast Cyrus could get things done. Someone, maybe Lilliana's mate, Travis, had suggested food, and the next thing she knew they were all seated in a conference room with people delivering a huge meal. Was it having money that made this happen or being the Alpha of Manhattan? Maybe both?

A woman entered the room, smiling at all of them. She smelled like roses, and she carried another plate of food. How many sandwiches did Cyrus think they needed?

"I'll set this down." The woman with brown hair grinned at her. "Do you need anything else? I can go get anything you need."

It took Betsy a moment to realize she spoke to her. "Oh no, we're fine."

"Wonderful. I'm Kyra, by the way."

"Hi, I'm Betsy."

"I know."

The other woman did something Betsy did not anticipate, crossing to her quickly to give her a hug. Betsy wasn't used to being embraced, particularly by people she didn't know. Jensen had done it earlier and it had freaked her out, and consequently stayed stiff as a board through the whole thing. Her discomfort didn't seem to bother the other woman, though.

Finally, Kyra let go and stepped back. "It's wonderful to have you, Betsy."

With that wonderfully weird exchange, Kyra left the room. Betsy turned to look at Travis and Lilliana, they both ate their food like nothing strange had happened. Why would they have thought it odd? She was the only fish out of water in the room, the only one struggling to find her way in her constantly shifting world.

Cyrus had stepped out. She had no idea what for. He hadn't told her. In fact, he hadn't regarded her very much since Alexei had left. What was that about? Her skin itched, and she wanted to claw at the table. Had she done something wrong?

It couldn't be Travis. He and Cyrus had been downright cordial in comparison to how he'd reacted to Alexei.

"Where were you living before today?"

Betsy turned her attention to Travis, who was eating a bag of potato chips as though he had no cares in the world. It had to be an act. He was an Alpha like Cyrus. Even if she didn't fully understand it, her nose knew the difference between pretending to be calm and actually being that way.

"Brooklyn. In a brownstone." She drummed her fingers on the table trying to do something with her nervous energy. Where had Cyrus gone? "Well, that must have cost a pretty penny."

Lilliana elbowed her mate. "It's not polite to talk about money. Don't mind him.

Werewolves never have a clue on niceties like that."

"Oh, I don't mind. I don't know what it cost. Nathan handled all of that. He told me where to go, and that's what I did." She picked up her water and took a sip. Had it suddenly gotten hot it the room?

"Nathan?" He crunched his chip. "Who's that?"

Lilliana growled. "Stop interrogating my sister."

"We've just met her. I'm trying to get a sense of her history, my love. I'm not interrogating her. I'm asking questions so she can tell me about herself." He crunched again and his gaze didn't waver from her. So much for thinking he lacked intensity.

"Nathan is the human"— she squirmed when she used the word. When had she started adopting the language of werewolves?—"who has been blackmailing me for some time. I suppose that is going to stop now that Cyrus has him locked up in the basement."

Travis jumped to his feet. She could smell the surge of adrenaline in the room. "Cyrus has a human in the basement? And he didn't think to share that news?"

"Oh, sit down, Travis." Cyrus reentered the room. He'd taken off his tie, and his collar hung open. He'd decided to get comfortable? Why? "We'll get to the details. You need to know them too. Oh good, it smells like they got the chicken I ordered correct. Last time there was too much garlic."

He grinned, and it took Betsy a moment to realize he'd

made a joke. Or attempted to. "Isn't garlic a vampire thing?"

Travis clapped his hands slowly before sinking back down in his seat. "Look who's trying to be amusing."

Cyrus' smile fled, and she missed it. If it wouldn't have been weird, she would have reached out and tried to smooth the lines away from his eyes.

"You have a human locked in the basement?" Travis continued speaking, this time with one eyebrow raised.

"Yes. Don't you? We should all have at least one human locked in our basement at all times, don't you think?"

"Why do you have this man locked up?" Travis played with a strand of Lilliana's hair. "I'm sure there had to be another way to get your mate's attention without kidnapping her boyfriend, lover, or husband."

"Oh, he's not any of those things." Betsy spooned some rice, anything to handle her nervous energy. Travis would be great at interrogating prisoners. She might confess her every sin to him, if he asked. What was it? His tone? His eye contact? Were all male wolves like this? "He was going to be my husband because he's holding my parents hostage. I had no choice."

"I think you'd better start from the beginning, Cyrus." All the humor fled Travis's voice and he leaned forward.

Cyrus sat down next to her. "I would have told you this already, but all you wanted to talk about was Alexei's scent permeating the room."

"I think I have the right to know why the Alpha I'm in a non-aggressive treaty with is entertaining my worst enemy."

"Someday you're going to have to get over what happened that summer." Cyrus waved his hand in the air.

"You're both powerful werewolves, and Lucian never held it against either of you."

There was a story in there somewhere. But, since Betsy could barely follow who was who at this point, she didn't want to ask. It would make things more confusing, and there was enough of that in her life at that moment.

Lilliana interrupted. "Back to the point. Locked human in the basement. Blackmail. How you came to be mated to my sister that, up until today, I thought I'd made up in my head."

"I can't believe you never mentioned you thought you had one." Travis eyed her sideways.

"Would you go around advertising someone who may or may not be your imaginary friend?" Lilliana rolled her eyes. "Cyrus, a little illumination please."

"I met Betsy in a Starbucks. As she told you, I thought she was you until I realized her scent was different and she had the gorgeous freckles over her nose."

Betsy's cheeks heated up. He thought her spots attractive? He didn't find them grotesque? She stared down at the table. How could that be?

"Why didn't you call me immediately?" Travis leaned forward. "Why did it take you hours? As it is, if I hadn't been in Jersey, it would have taken twice as long to get here."

"Because I had scented my mate for the first time and decided it was more important to ensure her safety and well-being than to inform you about something that I was still unclear about. Speaking of which…" He turned to Betsy. The force of his regard took her breath away. He hadn't looked at her in hours, and now she felt as though she couldn't take deep breath from the intensity of his stare.

"Yes?" Her mouth went dry.

"Give me the ring."

She had no idea what he was talking about. "The ring?"

"Left hand. Ring finger." He exhaled loudly. "Take it off."

"Is that an engagement ring?" Lilliana raised her voice in question.

"Nathan, the guy in the basement who has been blackmailing me, insisted I wear it. He wants me to be his wife. It's part of the deal."

Cyrus growled, and she narrowed her eyes at him. "Look, I don't love the thing either or what it happens to represent, but you can't order it off my hand. Mate or no mate or whatever, I'm not going to take it off because you command my obedience."

There. He hadn't wanted her docile. He'd insisted she look him in the eyes, had been the one to point out she probably wasn't passive. Well then, he could live with her temper and see how he liked that. She'd never been able to hold back hers, even with her parents who hadn't liked it. Maybe it had been some werewolf thing always stored inside of her. In any case, if he couldn't deal, he could go find himself another mate. Even if the idea of that made her stomach ache.

When he spoke again, this time it was barely above a whisper. "Maybe you could take it off then, Betsy, to spare me the energy it takes to restrain myself from ripping it off your finger. I'd love to be able to take it, sell it, and give the money to some human charitable organization as opposed to flinging it across the room or throwing it twenty stories down into traffic. In that case, though, I guess we'd get to find out if it's a real diamond or some cheap knock-off. Want to give that a go?"

Her heart rate had picked up during his little speech,

and she noted her sister and Travis had fallen silent as well. Would Cyrus actually rip it off her finger? She swallowed, not wanting to find out. Her panties soaked. Oh boy. She didn't want to deal with why that happened. . He wouldn't hurt her. She knew that beyond a shadow of a doubt. If he'd wanted to do that, he could have done so in the brownstone. She tugged at the ring, and it slipped off her finger easily. It had never fit perfectly, which had always seemed sort of apropos somehow.

"Here." She handed it to him, and he exhaled a breath loudly. "Thank you."

"Yep." She nodded, looking away. "Maybe you should finish up telling them what happened and how Nathan ended up in the basement. I have a headache. I want to go home." Cyrus stood up. "I'll have Mitchell take you."

She nodded and tried to ignore the sting of his easy acquiescence. He really must not want her to stay. She tried to be reasonable. It would be too much to expect him to take him herself. He was Alpha. There were things for him to do, plans for him to make in regards to her parents, especially now that it seemed to directly concern him. He'd not spoken to her in hours except to order her ring from her finger—Cyrus had made his feelings toward her very clear since they'd arrived in the building. He wanted her out of the way where he didn't have to worry about her.

Lilliana stood up. "I'll walk you out."

"Thanks." She smiled, still not looking at Cyrus. Her head really was pounding, or she would never leave her newfound sister. She hoped she didn't have to go too long without seeing her again.

They walked a distance into the hall, and Lilliana pushed the button for the elevator. Her sister held up her hand to her own mouth indicating she wanted her to be quiet. They entered the device and were halfway down before Lilliana spoke.

"You don't have to stay here with him if he's awful to you."

Betsy touched her head, wishing she could rub away the ache. "What?"

"We can take you back to Philadelphia. I mean, Travis has a treaty with Cyrus, and I'm sure it would be breaking some clause of it to do that, but there is no way I'm going to allow my sister to be abused—arrangement or no arrangement."

"Abused?" It took Betsy a full thirty seconds to realize what Lilliana meant. "Cyrus? Oh, he's not abusing me. If anything, he saved me from that."

"Betsy, he threatened to rip the ring off your finger."

"He wouldn't have done that." She believed that despite all the turmoil. "He wanted to. He'd thought about it. But he never would have touched me."

"How do you know?"

Betsy smiled. She'd been a wolf for only a couple of hours, but she'd picked something up her sister hadn't? "Because underneath his bluster, I smelled something else."

"What was that?"

"Fear." They stepped out of the elevator together. "Cyrus actually asked me to take it off so he didn't have to think about it anymore. There was a difference."

Lilliana nodded. "Well, I certainly know how it is to live with an Alpha male who occasionally has dominance issues. Travis can get possessive to the point of my eyes crossing." Her sister sighed. "Look, I guess I know we technically met only today, and we don't know each other, but you have family, okay? And somewhere to go if you don't want to stay here."

"Thanks." Betsy liked the warm feeling Lilliana's words created. She didn't fear Cyrus, and the thought of leaving him actually made her kind of nauseous. Not because she was his mate—that word still felt foreign—but because she belonged to him. He'd shifted for her, brought her back to her human self, cared for her, and now he was working to solve her problems. Even if he ignored her when she'd rather he paid attention, that didn't warrant abandoning his care.

But it had been a long time since she'd known she had somewhere to go if she needed help—that was a gift unto itself.

She exchanged numbers with her sister and headed toward Mitchell, who waited at the entrance for her. If she hadn't seen Cyrus endlessly texting, she'd think the other wolves could communicate with him telepathically. Nathan had given her a phone for the sole purpose of allowing him to reach her. Her sister's number was the first one she'd ever gotten to enter.

She walked out onto the street toward Mitchell. He stood by a blue Town Car and held a door open. Once she was inside, he climbed in after her. Betsy could have easily taken the subway, but if someone wanted to take her downtown another way, she wasn't going to complain. Besides, if Cyrus had ordered the car, that's how they'd be going. Mitchell would never contradict him and she'd never be able to convince the driver to turn around if Mitchell didn't agree

"Anything I can do for you, ma'am?" Mitchell leaned back, stretching his long legs when he did.

She laughed. "You can never call me ma'am again."

Her companion furrowed his eyebrows. "But you are the Alpha's mate. You deserve the term."

"Right." Were people really going to ma'am her from

now on? She sighed and stared out the window. Maybe it was her exhaustion from the day, the emotional upheaval, or the fact that she tended to be spacey when she was this worn out, but it took her five minutes before she realized the numbers were going in the wrong direction.

"Mitchell, I live in the other direction. Brooklyn is downtown from here."

"Brooklyn?" Mitchell shook his head. "I'm bringing you home, ma'am. To Cyrus' uptown apartment. By the park."

"You're what?" *Oh hell*. She'd really not seen this coming.

Chapter 7

"You know she's basically still human. You're going to have to do better than that." Travis shook his head and walked to the window. "It's not that I don't sympathize with the problem. I dated Lilliana for weeks, holding back the instinct to flip her over my shoulder, bite her, claim her, and make her mine."

"The ring was like a thorn in my side all day. I couldn't look at it anymore." Cyrus rubbed his head. Part of him couldn't believe he was even having this conversation with the wolf that less than a year earlier he'd been on the brink of war with. "And the moron in the basement shouldn't get to show any possession over her. Not in this lifetime or any other."

What he really wanted to do was tear the asshole's throat to shreds. Short of that, removing the ring had been the best possible solution. "Do you think I scared her?"

Travis shrugged. "I think you pissed off my mate, who dug her fingers into my knee."

If he'd done damage to his relationship already, this whole thing might be fruitless. Why had he been given a true mate? He didn't have the slightest idea what to do with one. She consumed his whole existence. How could he function if it stayed like this?

"Listen, here's the deal. Betsy's parents did something bad. I'm not going into the details, but if what I suspect happened, happened, then it would at least explain where Lilliana came from and how she didn't know of her wolf heritage. Until Lake messed with her, Betsy was the same damn way."

Travis turned around, shaking his head. "Going to do something about your sister and her inability to leave the latents alone?"

"Man, if I had any idea what do about Lake, I'd have done it a long time ago." His sister had slunk out some time after Travis arrived. What she did with her nights was her own business, but lately she'd been moping because she couldn't work in human hospitals because it risked discovery. This wasn't a new thing for her, and why it had suddenly flared up, he had no idea. Another thing he couldn't focus on.

"You think Betsy's parents have done something that may affect my mate, and you aren't going to tell me what it is?"

Cyrus shrugged and pretended indifference. Truth was he'd be pissed as hell if he were in Travis' position. But he wasn't going to share until he was damn well ready, which was why he always tried to know what was going on, at all times.

"Cyrus…"

He rubbed his nose. "This isn't up for discussion. I assume you have your mate properly protected. She's not at risk. Nothing I'm going to do in Montana can touch her anymore. Feel lucky I let you know Betsy existed so quickly at all."

He'd done that for Betsy, not Travis or Lilliana. Seeing her sister, a changed latent wolf who now functioned as a fully transformed werewolf, mated to an Alpha, had to help Betsy in some way adjust herself. Not to mention having family went a long way to making things easier. Or harder, depending on the day.

"You weren't always like this."

Cyrus swung around. He needed to collect his stuff and get out of there. His mate waited for him in his apartment. If he'd frightened her, he needed to undo that. He hadn't scented fear, but maybe he'd missed it because of all his turmoil.

"All Alexei wanted to do was reminisce too. Something in the water making everyone want to talk about our summers with Lucian? I was a fifteen-year-old kid. Who cares how I behaved back then? This is who I am now."

"The three of us share very little history except those few summers. I think it would be natural for us to want to talk about whatever we do have in common." Travis paused. "Which now I suppose includes our being mated to sisters."

"Feels a little coincidental, doesn't it?"

Travis shook his head. "Are you seeing some sort of divine plan all of a sudden? You don't even believe in any of the old stories. No truth to the myth, isn't that what you say when asked? You told my mate it was all bullshit."

"It is. Bunch of wolves praying to be human to save a raped girl. It's a sick story if you break it down to its parts." Why was he always sucked into these conversations?

"You have a problem."

That was it. Cyrus snarled. "I don't have a problem. If I chose not to believe in the bedtime story you prefer to subscribe your life to, then it's my business, not my *problem*."

He stalked into Travis' space. If the man wanted a fight, he could have one. A rip-roaring fight. Forget their treaty. He'd take him, take Philadelphia. Then Travis could see what kind of problem *he* had.

"Down boy." Travis shook his head. "Shit, I forgot how tense I was before I got things straight with Lilliana. You're lucky I'm in such a forgiving mood."

"Stop patronizing me." In another second, he was going to shove him. Right to the ground. He'd hit with a giant thump…

"You have a problem *with Montana*."

Travis' words penetrated the anger haze that threatened to take over his existence. He took a deep breath. "Montana."

"Right. With Montana." Travis patted him on the shoulder. "There's no Alpha there."

Travis' words floated around in Cyrus' mind for a second before they made sense. "Shit."

"Yep. Shit." Travis laughed. "You know what? I'm happy not to know what Betsy's parents are involved in. I wouldn't want anything to do with going to Montana right now. You have fun with that, buddy."

"Are you telling me that there isn't one Alpha in the whole state? Whom did Lucian deal with?"

"None of the lone wolves in Montana ever dealt with Lucian, as far as I know. And since the Alpha Prime's death, there hasn't been any communication."

The elevator dinged, and Lilliana stormed into the room. She walked straight to Cyrus, bypassing Travis altogether. Cyrus had a moment to realize how strange that was before she jammed her pointer finger straight into his shoulder.

It didn't hurt, but the intention behind it startled him. Lilliana always seemed so docile. "If you hurt her, I'll rip out your eyes. Or I won't. I'll have Travis do it. But the meaning is the same. Get nicer. I found my sister, and she seems lost, fragile, and confused. Don't be such a bully. There must be a kind man inside of you somewhere."

"Yeah." He nodded, forcing himself to take a deep breath. Lilliana's newly discovered relationship with Betsy didn't grant her the right to order him around "You'd think that, wouldn't you?"

———

MITCHELL NODDED to Cyrus when he approached the door. He hadn't asked his pack member to stay and watch his mate, only to deliver her inside his apartment, but it didn't bother him in the least that Mitchell had.

He stopped to regard the wolf for a moment. Did his pack member like him? Did it matter if he did? Mitchell would step in front of traffic for him, go to war for him, and stand outside his door to keep his brand-new mate safe.

Cyrus knew a lot about Mitchell's life. He knew the man's family history. He'd been there when his parents had been shot dead by hunters before Cyrus had taken over as Alpha and made their full-moon shifts safer. He'd presided over the ceremony where Mitchell's sister had taken a true mate and then moved to the other man's pack in Canada. But he had no idea if Mitchell had a girlfriend, no idea if the man had dreams or aspirations he hadn't fulfilled.

Did he need to know these things about his pack mates? Alphas were leaders, warriors, protectors, not nursemaids, mothers, or best friends.

He'd bet Travis knew all about his pack members. They probably called him when they stubbed their toes. Alexei, by contrast, would probably drown himself in the ocean before he sat around listening to pack members' problems.

Cyrus shook his head. He had a mate to woo. Why was he pondering life problems he'd never considered before?

"How are things?"

Mitchell stepped away from the door. "It's quiet inside, my Alpha. I showed her around and then left her to her own devices. I didn't want to invade her space."

"Thanks." He nodded. "But, uh, I meant with you. How are things with you?"

"Sir?" Mitchell shook his head. "I don't understand."

"Oh damn it." He threw his arms in the air. "I'm asking how you are. How is everything with you?"

Mitchell stared at him for a second before answering. "I'm fine. How are you?"

"Good." Well, this was awkward. Maybe this was why he didn't do this kind of thing. He'd clearly made Mitchell uncomfortable with this nonsense. "Thanks for the help. I do appreciate it."

"You don't have to thank me, Cyrus. You know it is my duty and pleasure. You're my

Alpha."

That was the first time he'd heard Mitchell use his name. Asking how he was had produced a result. He kind of liked it.

"Good night."

Mitchell stepped toward the elevator. "'Night."

Cyrus walked into his apartment. He took a deep breath. Already Betsy's scent had permeated the room. He loved the way it drifted into his skin, attaching to his pores, entering his blood stream until he could practically exist on her scent alone.

He dropped his briefcase on the floor next to the door. Tension pulled on the muscles at the back of his neck, but

Betsy's presence in his place helped a lot. She might not like it here. Someday, when she was officially his, if she wanted to move he'd let her pick any place in the city she wanted. Anything to make her happy.

Of course if he told her that, he'd fuck it up and she'd probably refuse to live with him altogether.

He wandered through the place, knowing she was in the guest room with the door closed. Her scent was strongest there. She could have gone anywhere she desired, and the guest room with the door closed certainly spoke volumes. *Go away. Don't bother me.*

Cyrus walked into his room and let out the growl he needed to release. His mate was in his apartment. Beautiful and untouchable—at least to him. He could break down the door if he wanted to. With very little effort, he could yank the door off its hinges, throw it to the side, and be in there.

Could he make her want him as he did her? Could he show her with his body what he'd never be able to say with his words? That the years of doubting, even that such a thing as a true mate existed, had turned his soul into a hardened shell. It had been a long time since he'd even paid attention to it.

But he wanted her to. She'd stood up for him against Lake—and against Alexei. Would she do it again? He sat down on the edge of his bed and rubbed his shoulder where Lilliana had jabbed at him. It didn't hurt of course, but the guilt he'd felt at Lilliana's words had burned him like a branding iron.

Thinking of her brought on another memory he'd not dwelled on for a while. When Travis had first mated her, he'd given her a necklace, a totem of a female wolf. It was meant to be Lily, the first female werewolf, the woman who, legend said, all Alpha werewolves descended from.

She'd been tough, been a survivor through horrendous circumstances.

The whole story always brought a sour taste to his mouth, but the necklace had been passed from female werewolves to their offspring for generations. At some point, it had gone from his great grandmother to an aunt and then eventually to Travis' mother. He and Travis were very distant cousins.

It had bugged him immensely. With one choice, one aunt takes the necklace, and somehow his sister ultimately gets screwed out of a legacy she should have had. The necklace, however, rightfully belonged to Lake. Lake had never wanted for anything. He'd seen to that once his parents had been gone. Strangely enough, Lilliana had turned the necklace over to him. She'd said he needed it. Whatever that meant.

He'd tried to give it to Lake, and she'd refused it, some-thing about not liking old things. It had been sitting in his sock drawer ever since.

Without another thought, he retrieved it. Betsy needed to have it. It should belong to her now. And, if nothing else, giving it to her would give him an excuse to talk to her tonight, and that was what he really needed. To speak to Betsy one more time before he lay down for the night and stared at his ceiling, which was all he did lately.

Totem in hand, he knocked on the guest room door.

"Come in," Betsy called, and he turned the door handle.

He walked into his spare bedroom wondering when he had last gone in. The room was consistently cleaned, thanks to the staff he employed, but he never had any reason to enter himself. No one came to his apartment. *Ever.*

Betsy sat in a chair next to the window, knees pulled up, and seeming very, very small.

Her bed appeared untouched, completely unwrinkled as though the housekeeper had made it. The glow from small lamp next to the bed cast the room in shadows.

"Are you okay?"

She sniffed and wiped at her eyes. Hell, had she been crying?

"I guess so. I mean, why shouldn't I be fine? I'm a werewolf, which before today I didn't even know existed outside of horror movies. My parents are locked away. I'm so angry with them I can't even express it. And I'm basically at your mercy, which actually feels okay, probably because of the wolf thing, and that alone scares me to death." She sniffed again. "So, yeah, I'm fine."

"Betsy." He breathed out her name as he walked slowly toward her. If he could have taken all of her fears and stored them away inside of himself where she never had to face them again, he would in a heartbeat. When he got to the chair, he dropped to his knees in front of her.

"I am at your mercy, not the other way around."

"Please." She shook her head. "Look, I don't blame you for this. You went to get coffee, and ended up with a mate who didn't know she was a werewolf, had no idea how to be a mate and inherited all the problems that came with her. I'm sorry for my tears."

"You were exactly what I was looking for." When she snorted, he continued talking. "Do you know that it's possible to be surrounded by people and yet totally alone?"

Cyrus didn't do this easily. Talking about his feelings had never been part of his training.

"I don't actually. I'm almost always alone." She

shrugged. "I guess I understand why now. I was really a werewolf among humans. And I guess my parents aren't really my biological parents either."

"I'm responsible for a pack full of souls, and I don't think any of them know me at all. I needed you so completely, and I was too dumb to even know it. Your scent drew me to the

Starbucks. I scented you on the street and followed it inside."

She raised her eyebrows in shock. "You did?"

"Absolutely. And then I thought you were Lilliana, which drove me crazy, because no way was I going to cross a street to follow her. She's nice, but she's not mine."

"Thank you for bringing her here tonight."

He touched her knee, needing any kind of connection. "You're welcome." *Anything, Betsy. Anything at all.*

"I'm not sure what you expect. I mean you know I'm attracted to you. You'd have to be dumb to not know that, and I know you can even smell it. But I'm not ready. My head, it's all over the place."

"I have no expectations." All he wanted was to spend a few minutes in her presence. "Not sexual ones anyway. Actually, I have a gift for you."

"You do?" She sat a little forward in her chair. That had to be a good thing. She wasn't leaning away from him.

"I do." He held up the necklace. "This is a very old necklace. A totem. It's travelled through a lot of different people to get to me. Your sister wore it for a while. But it's always belonged in our family."

If she noticed the use of "our family", she didn't respond. Ordering himself to relax, he took a deep breath. Calling her family before they'd even slept together would probably be presumptuous among humans.

"It's beautiful." She took it from him, running her finger down the length of it. "Is it a werewolf?"

"The first one. Her name was Lily. Or so the legend goes."

She stared up at him, meeting his gaze straight on. There were no tears in her eyes, which was a huge relief.

"Legend?" She wanted to hear more, and it seemed as though he was going to have to tell her. The creation story, the one he had rolled his eyes at since the death of his parents, had taught him not to believe in fairytales. Still, she looked at him so expectantly; he thought perhaps for that evening he could tell it like it had been told to him.

"There are many versions of this story. I think every werewolf knows it slightly differently. What changes is that there are variations in the number of people and the exact details." She sat back a little. Shit, he'd already lost her. Maybe qualifying it had somehow dimmed the mystic element of it. He needed to do better. "But I'll tell it to you the way it was told to me. How does that sound?"

She nodded. "I feel like a small child, but, yes, I'd really like to hear it the way you know it. Where did werewolves come from?"

He almost answered "alterations in DNA over time", but instead, he stood up. "Can we sit on the bed while I tell it? I can't stay on my knees like this indefinitely."

"Oh." She jumped from the chair, moving toward the bed. Truth was he could stay like that all day, but he wanted to be closer to her, and kneeling in front of her chair did not get the job done.

Betsy sat on the bed and patted the spot next to her. He tried not to look too pathetic as he eagerly accepted her invitation and joined her. They were still too far apart, but anything short of deeply pressed inside of her was going to feel too separate at that point. He'd have to deal with it for the moment.

"There was a woman named Lily, and she was human. Lily was beautiful. More beautiful than the other women in the town, but not wealthy or well connected, and the other women were jealous of her because of her beauty and didn't include her in their circles."

Betsy rolled her eyes. "Some things never change I guess. I never went to high school, but they're always talking about this stuff on the news."

"You're right. Some nastiness is universal." He tried to remember where he was in the story. It was hard when he was so close to Betsy that all he wanted to do was reach out and hold her. "Um. Right, okay. The men all desired her, but none understood her. She was creative, strong, and brilliant. Not necessarily qualities they wanted in a docile wife."

"This feels ominous to me." Betsy scooted back on the bed until she leaned against the headboard. He followed her back, positioning himself on his side to look at her. There were dark circles under her eyes, but the tension around her mouth had lessened. She was relaxing, and it was a beautiful thing to witness.

"It should. Lily went out into the woods to get water from the stream, and a group of villagers watched her go. Some of the men decided to follow. They didn't have good intentions, and while her back was turned, they jumped her."

Betsy gasped. "No."

He wished he could tell her differently. "They raped her, and when she resisted, they beat her and left her to die, alone in the woods, with only the moon for company."

A tear slipped down her face, and he brushed it away. "Or so she thought. Lily was actually not alone. There was a pack of wolves nearby. Three male wolves came across her as the men were leaving. They attacked and killed her assailants."

"Good." There was a growl to her voice that made him grin internally. The wolf wasn't far from the surface with Betsy. She hadn't yet learned to conceal it. Eventually she would have to, but, for now, he loved seeing it develop. There was nothing wrong with craving a little violence when appropriate.

"And then they turned back to her. She touched something in them, something that wasn't purely animal. The need to have her, to help her, and to possess her overwhelmed them.

The Alpha wolf prayed to the god of the moon to hear them, to save her, to let them be with her." "The moon listened?" Her voice was barely a whisper.

"He did." Cyrus smiled. Somehow, in the midst of telling the story, he'd discovered he could see it again as he had when he'd been able to believe. The cold night. The light from the moon. Lily's beautiful face marred —she would always appear as Betsy to him now in his imagination—and the wolves that wanted her more than anything. Cyrus could understand them now. He'd beg any power in the universe to give him Betsy.

"And he changed the wolves to men, well, animals and men, and he changed Lily too. They were the first werewolves. The other two wolves would eventually find worthy women to love, and, through all of them, we became as we are now."

"And Lily was the Alpha's?"

He stroked a side of her face with his fingers. "That's right, princess. Lily belonged to only her Alpha. Forever."

Chapter 8

Betsy fingered the beautiful necklace Cyrus had given her, the one of Lily, the first female werewolf. It felt old, and beyond that, it felt...powerful, which was ridiculous because she wasn't two years old and she knew that objects only held the power assigned to them by people. She gently tapped the blue eyes of the representation of Lily. Someone had assigned this totem power, and even though it hadn't been she who had done it, she could still feel it resonate from within.

Cyrus hadn't said anything for a minute, and she found him regarding her with an unreadable expression. She preferred the open intimacy he'd shared when he told her the story earlier. The sound of his voice, coupled with the way his gaze had bored into her as though the story belonged to only the two of them in the universe, had given her the shivers.

Sheer force of will alone kept her from begging him to rip off his clothes and take her hard right then and there. But she had to live with herself in the morning. Besides, he smelled...tired. His cinnamon scent had dulled since that afternoon.

"Are you okay?"

He nodded. "Thanks for asking."

"You're welcome." Cyrus always seemed so genuinely grateful for small niceties. All she'd done was ask if he was fine. Her mother had always cared about her, in the only ways her mother could show affection. Someone had at least cared, most of the time. "Thank you for the necklace. Would you help me put it on?"

"Ah...sure." He sat up. "How do I do that?"

She raised her hair off her neck. "Just attach it for me."

"Okay." His scent altered slightly, becoming sweeter.

Had she made him nervous? When he'd come home and not instantly made a beeline for her, she hadn't known exactly what to do about it. She'd watched the minutes tick by on the clock. It had taken more than seven minutes for him to come to her. An eternity. What was the purpose of hiding in her room if he wasn't going to seek?

Cyrus finished fumbling with the necklace, and she dropped her hair back down before turning to look at him. "Can I ask you something?"

"Anything."

She stretched sideways until they were face to face. Stifling a yawn, she forced herself to stay awake. She had questions, and he was being quiet and accommodating. It was too good an opportunity to let slip away. Who knew if she'd ever see him this free from tasks again?

"Why is this starting to feel okay? I liked when you said that the wolves killed her attackers, and earlier tonight, I... wanted something that seems really silly now."

He took her hand in his and stared at their joined fingers as though they were the most interesting things in the world.

"The violence attracted you because it was a justified kill. Don't misunderstand me. It is not okay as a werewolf to kill indiscriminately. One of my jobs as Alpha of New York is to hunt down and destroy those types of werewolves if they enter my territory. Not only is that kind of murder immoral, it is also one of the ways we get discovered, and we can't allow that to happen. I can't know for sure, but I'd hasten to guess that Nathan, your captor who is caged for the foreseeable future, or someone connected to him, came into contact with an out-of-control wolf in the past. Discovery can almost always be traced to something like that." "So the fact that it made my mouth water doesn't mean I'm sociopathic?"

He grinned, meeting her gaze. The heat in his eyes left her mouth dry. "No. You're not sociopathic, Betsy. Can I ask you something?"

"Sure." Anything to get her eyes off his mouth. Maybe talking was a bad idea. A very, very bad idea.

"Is Betsy short for Elizabeth?"

She shook her head. "You'd think so, but I'm just Betsy. I've never been, that I know of, Elizabeth."

"Betsy suits you. It's...sweet and sexy at the same time."

She blinked rapidly. He thought she was sexy? "Thank you."

"You're welcome." He lifted their joined hands and kissed her knuckles and she forgot to breathe. "What was the second thing you mentioned, the thing you wanted but were so vague about?"

He would remember she had mentioned a second thing. Why had she? Why couldn't she keep her mouth closed when she needed to?

"I don't want to tell you." There, she's said it. He could be a gentleman and leave it alone.

"Why not?" *Shit.*

"Because it's embarrassing."

He tugged her against him until her head rested on his chest. She could hear his heart beating beneath her ear. The urge to snuggle deeper overwhelmed her, and she gave into the urge. When had she last been held? As a baby?

"I'm sure it's not embarrassing. It's probably a wolf thing."

He was warm, like heat from the sun on her cold skin. "Do you promise not to laugh or think less of me for it?"

"I promise not to think less of you. I can't promise not to laugh if it's funny."

Fair enough. At least he seemed to never lie. "When I was hiding in here, I was kind of hoping that you'd come home and chase me."

He didn't say anything, and she wondered if he hadn't heard her or if she had actually stunned him into silence. His scent changed. The dull aroma of cinnamon roared back to full blast. Cyrus no longer smelled tired.

Well…all right… Her words had certainly garnered some attention. Even if he had yet to answer.

Cyrus sat up and moved away from her. Oh hell. She hadn't considered that he'd be so turned off by her odd thought that he wouldn't even want to touch her. She felt bereft of his warmth. Why hadn't she made something up? *Oh, Cyrus, I don't know. I was thinking that I really wanted to eat raw meat. Is that a wolf thing?*

No, she'd gone and opened her stupid mouth.

"Betsy."

She raised her head to look at him. "Yes?"

"Run."

"What?" His command didn't immediately register with her. Had he told her to run?

Cyrus raised an eyebrow. "Run."

He wanted her to run? Her blood pumped faster—he

meant what he said. That must mean he was going to chase.

Happiness burst inside of her, and she took off running. The apartment wasn't that big, even if it was huge for Manhattan—three bedrooms, one being used as a home office, and three bathrooms, kitchen, eating area, and an outdoor balcony that ran the length of the place. She didn't want to go out there. It was cold. That would be a last-resort hiding place.

She dashed into his bathroom, looking for anything with a scent. There was some Lysol under his sink, and she sprayed it around the room. Anything to throw him off from finding her right away. She rushed through the hall spraying the Lysol everywhere before running into the kitchen.

"Stupid," she muttered to herself. There were not that many places to hide in the kitchen. But it at least would give her cover while he searched elsewhere.

She kneeled on the floor, watching him when he stepped out of the guest room. Cyrus sniffed the air, looking every bit the predator. Would he fall for her trap? Would he go the way of the Lysol?

"Clever maneuver for so little time, princess." His gaze turned to the kitchen, zooming in immediately to where she poked around the corner. "But I hunt for a living. I thought you wanted to run."

He rushed toward her, and she yelped, dashing down the hall as he rounded the back end of the kitchen. All she could think about was getting back to the guest room, back to where he had held her on the bed and…

Two strong arms heaved her upward. She yelled when he slammed them both down on the soft bed, his body above hers. Betsy's heart beat frantically, but Cyrus still seemed to be in control.

His face was above hers, and heavens, she craved him. She'd never known the meaning of that word before, but she did now. She *craved* Cyrus like she needed to breathe in air.

"Two things."

He wanted to talk? "Yes?"

"I'm going to teach you how to run and hide from a werewolf so that, if you ever need to, you can." He licked his lips, and she watched the movement of his tongue, fascinated. "And this desire to run, to be chased, is very wolf. Not weird. Not funny. It's part of the mating dance. If you had been born to a pack, if you had known what you were, when we encountered each other for the first time, and recognized that we were mates, this is what we would have done. You would have run—and run—until I caught you."

"And then what?" She lived for his next words. Please don't let them be *I would have left you alone and not touched you for weeks.*

"I would have hauled you up against me." He'd done that. That's how they'd landed on this bed.

"And?"

"I would make you mine. Mark you. Put my scent up against you. Ravish your body until any thoughts of ever being with another fled from your mind. I would fuck you until neither of us could stand again." He panted, and his pupils were huge. She was glad to see she wasn't the only one affected by his words. "But you don't want that. You've already told me no, and I need to respect that. I'm not an animal. Not entirely anyway. I can dictate what instincts I give in to. If you want that, if you want it now, you need to tell me that. Say yes."

He wanted her to speak? To form words? It took her half a minute before she could.

"Yes."

"You're sure?"

"How many times are you going to make me say it?" She pounded on his chest, but he didn't move. "Yes. Yes. Yes."

"No regrets tomorrow. I won't allow it."

Ever the Alpha. She leaned up and bit down on his bottom lip. Of course, if anyone could dictate how someone else would feel, it would be her Alpha. And she had no doubt that, after what they were about to do, that is what he would be. *Her Alpha.*

His mouth crushed hers. There was nothing gentle about Cyrus in that moment. He commanded her mouth to acquiesce to his, and she did. She softened beneath him, wanting to be complete in the way she could be only if he claimed her.

She clawed at his chest, wanting him naked, wanting no barriers between them. He stopped her movements. "Not so fast. We'll get there. I promise."

His words did stop her frenzy and she took a deep breath. Cyrus was right. There was time. She could savor this. When he kissed her again, it was gentle, and she sighed against his mouth.

The heat she'd experienced earlier when she lay against him rushed back. Her body felt languid. He lifted his head, planting kisses all over her face and down onto her neck. "You taste just like I knew you would."

She hoped that was a good thing and decided it must be because he didn't stop kissing her. Instead, his hands fumbled with her buttons, a sign that perhaps Cyrus wasn't as composed as he pretended. Task completed, he removed her shirt and stared down at her.

"What?" Her cheeks heated up. She wasn't super

skinny—she could probably afford to lose a few pounds. Did he not like what he saw?

"You are the single most beautiful woman I've ever beheld."

"Stop it." She shook her head. Not that she wanted to even consider any of the other women he might have *beheld,* but she didn't need pretty words to fill her mind with non-truths. It wasn't that she thought herself unattractive, but Cyrus was rich and handsome. There was no way some drop-dead-gorgeous werewolf or human hadn't been where she was.

"You don't believe me?" He seemed surprised. "I think we're going to have to do something about that."

"No, that's really not necessary."

"Oh. I think it is." Cyrus hauled her up against him, and she gasped. Where was he going to drag her off to now?

"Are we going somewhere?"

"The bedroom." He rounded the corner back into his bedroom. She could still smell the Lysol she'd sprayed earlier and now wished she hadn't. Cyrus dropped her on the bed and walked to window. He must have had the same thought as she because he cracked it, letting fresh air into the room.

"Weren't we in a perfectly good bedroom?"

He shook his head. "No. This is our room. That's for guests. You're not a guest. Guest implies impermanence. You live here now."

While she waited on the bed, he yanked open his closet door. On the other side of it was a full-length mirror. "Cyrus, what are you planning?"

He didn't speak and, instead, walked over and picked her up again. She never would have thought she'd liked being handled this way, but she loved it. Anytime Cyrus wanted to pick her up and bring her somewhere, she'd gladly go.

"Look at yourself."

She shook her head and tried to squirm in his arms. He set her down on her feet, holding her still in front of the mirror. "I'd rather look at you."

"We'll get to that. But I told you that you were the most beautiful woman I'd ever seen, and you didn't believe me. You thought I lied to you. I can't have that. I think you need to learn to believe me."

"Are you going to spank me?" The idea had merit. If he wanted her to bend over and be punished, she'd not say no.

"Maybe another night." Cyrus leaned over, his face right above her shoulder blade. "Tonight, I'm going to bite you." "What?"

She'd no more asked than Cyrus' teeth sank into her shoulder, right next to her neck. Betsy gasped, but not from pain. Liquid heat pooled inside of her and slid downward toward her thighs. Her knees buckled, and he caught her. "That's the first. I'm going to bite you again. When we've reached completion, I'm going to bite down on you so hard it will mark you forever. When it starts to heal, I'll bite it again. This will happen for the rest of our lives."

Betsy nodded, her brain in a haze of pleasure. Yes, bite her again. He should bite her over and over. All the time.

"Now look at yourself." She did as he asked and stared at the woman in the mirror. Betsy hardly recognized herself. Who was the woman with the heated eyes, the messed-up hair, and the flushed cheeks? It couldn't really be her. Pressed up against Cyrus, she didn't look too rounded where she'd thought she should be more slender. No, she came across as sultry and small.

"Do you see these breasts?" Cyrus ran his fingers around her nipple.

She nodded. Not that she usually gave them that much of a look, but she could certainly see them now. "Yes."

"They're beautiful. More than a handful cupped in my grip." He smoothed his fingers over them, and she shuddered. "So smooth and tender to my touch. Your nipples are pink. I want my mouth on them, but first, I have to hear you tell me how beautiful they are."

His cock pressed up against her ass as he held her. This was turning him on. Betsy smiled and could see in the mirror that she suddenly appeared as a woman who knew how much her man wanted her. He controlled an entire pack, and he belonged to her.

Maybe it was a werewolf thing…maybe it was her discovery that actually belonging to a powerful man was a hot thing…but Betsy believed him. If she said that her breasts were beautiful, then they must be.

"They're beautiful. Won't you touch them, Cyrus? Please?"

He growled and picked her up again, bringing her over to his bed. The comforter was soft beneath her back, and she pushed down farther into it.

"You like the silk, princess? I'll drape you in it. When I let you get dressed."

They undressed each other. Betsy had never felt such strong intensity as that radiating off of Cyrus. His focus was entirely placed on her, and, once he had her naked, he grinned in a way that could only be called wolfish. She narrowed her eyes. "What?"

"I'm going to do as you asked now."

"What was that?"

"To please touch your breasts. I'm going to do that. A lot." He bit down on her nipple, and she writhed on the bed beneath him. He smiled at her, his eyes crinkling. "Sensitive?" "Apparently." She panted.

"I can see that." He knelt over her and stroked his thumb down her stomach while his other hand cupped her breast. "I can also see that you have the most delicious curves.

Everywhere they're supposed to be, and they all belong to me."

She ran her hand down his chest. He was built like some kind of mythical god. How many women talked to him every day while he wore his designer suits and had no idea of the body underneath? Betsy hadn't imagined he looked like this. Her mouth watered, and for the first time, she let herself look all the way down at the complete package.

Something on her face must have given away her thoughts.

"Like what you see?"

"Yes." There really wasn't any other response. Cyrus was huge, bigger than any man she'd ever encountered. She'd had sex with only humans. Were all werewolves built like him? Werewolf women must be happy all of the frickin' time.

She reached down and stroked him from his balls to the top of his cock. He groaned, and she grinned. "Roll over, big guy, and I'll show you how much I like what I see deep in my mouth."

"What?" He shook his head.

Had she not been clear? "I want to give you a blow job."

"You do?"

She wasn't exactly sure what was going on here. "Is that a problem? I mean, I don't have to if that's a problem for werewolves." Had she committed some kind of sexual *faux pas*?

"No. I would love that." He cleared his voice. "Another time. Okay? Tonight is about you."

"It can be about both of us."

"The night is young." He kissed her hard. She wasn't going to forget this part of the evening, but she wasn't going to complain either. She'd get his cock in her mouth. He pulled back to grin at her before he scooted down toward the end of the bed.

"I need to taste you." His voice sounded gravelly. "Right now."

Before she could blink, he had his mouth on her pussy. She closed her eyes. His tongue was doing wicked things, and before long, he'd found her clit. He pushed on it, and she cried out. At this rate, she wasn't going to last very long.

"Cyrus." She cried out his name. "I'm going to come very fast like this." "I know. And then again and again."

She laughed. Who was she to argue with that?

Chapter 9

The woman drove him crazy, and if he didn't find some kind of steadiness soon, he was going to lose it before he properly pleasured his mate. He hadn't been this overexcited since…well…he couldn't remember when.

She tasted like heaven, and her little noises of breathless delight spurred him to give her more. That's all he wanted, to take care of her, to make her so happy she'd never think about leaving and stay with him forever like Lily had stayed with her Alpha.

His brain stuttered at his thought, and he pushed it away. This moment had nothing to do with the legend, and it had no place in his thoughts.

"Cyrus, please."

He raised his head to look at her. She was a vision, sprawled on his bed with her hair fanned out in every direction with total abandon. Betsy belonged to him, and he wasn't ever letting her go, even if he had to keep her like this all the time to convince her.

"Please what, princess?"

"I want you inside me." She grabbed onto the sheets

when he circled her clit with his thumb. Such a responsive lover. He could play with her for hours.

"I kind of am already. A part of my body is inside of you right now." He swirled his hand over her clit again, and she gasped. Yes, he was going to make his mate come. Right then.

"Not the part I want in there."

"Oh really?" He loved playing with her. "You're not enjoying what we're doing? I guess I could stop. Go make a sandwich."

"Don't you dare," she fumed, her eyes turning wolf. Wow. He was impressed. Most werewolves couldn't do that, even threatened. His mate, now that she wasn't latent, had no trouble accessing her animal side. It showed power. He wasn't surprised. Betsy was a survivor, and her life spoke to a core of steel he respected.

"All right. That's good because I really do like doing what I'm doing right now."

His cock was so tight and hard he thought it might explode. Cyrus had never been this turned on before without doing something about it. But even the discomfort of wanting her didn't make him want to hurry. This was too much fun.

She was slick, smooth, and hot inside, and he pressed his fingers deeper, stroking her inner walls while he messaged her swollen bundle of nerves one more time. He used a circular motion, finding that her body responded the most when he did. She bit her lip, her head tilting backward.

Betsy was close. Every nerve ending in his body told him she would come any second. He'd never been so attuned to a lover before. Not that Betsy was just any lover. No, she was *the one*. He could get lost in her body for the rest of his life if he wanted to.

"Come on, princess. Let go, for me. Make me a very happy werewolf tonight."

"Cyrus…" She called out his name as her sweet juices coated his fingers. He stroked her to completion, reveling in how long and hard she came around his hand. His cock twitched, begging for attention.

He wasn't ready. Not quite yet. He wanted her settled down so he could bring her back to the edge again.

She opened her eyes to look at him. "Wow."

"I'll take wow. That's a good word." He licked up her body until he got to her mouth. "I can think of some other particularly good words you could use."

Her mouth was soft, and she smiled when he kissed her. He breathed in her scent. This was a great moment.

"Thank you." She kissed him over and over. "I don't usually come that way."

"It's all new now. We're brand-new to each other. Deal?"

"All right." She kissed the edge of his nose, which was so cute he couldn't help the grin it placed on his face. "Brand-new with Cyrus. I'll take it."

"That's good because I need to come inside of you now, princess." He needed it more than he'd ever needed anything else in the universe.

He maneuvered himself until he was positioned by her pussy. His mouth watered. Maybe he could go down on her again.

"What is that look?"

Her voice brought him back to the moment. "I'm thinking of licking you again."

"Listen, wolf-boy, I loved that, and I would never, ever say no to you doing whatever you wanted down there. But you promised me your hot cock in my pussy. And I know you always keep your promises because that is what you told me."

Damn. Talk about using his own words against him. *Fair enough.*

"I'm not going to complain. I'm going to do what my mate wants." He sniffed at her, loving the sweet scent of her. After this, the scent would be all over his skin. He would get to smell like Betsy.

"Couple of things."

She ran her hands through his hair. "Go on."

"I can't get you pregnant unless you're in heat." He took a deep breath, not because he wanted to confirm what he already knew but because he liked to have as much of her inside of him as possible. "And you are not."

"So you're saying that I want you because I want you and not because it's my biological incentive to fuck every man I see since I'm a werewolf?"

He laughed, a long hard song. Sex could be fun in the midst of the desire. Who knew? "No, you're free from the mating compulsion right now. And when you feel the need to fuck, charming phrase for it by the way, you'll be doing that only with me."

"Okay." She pinched his shoulder. "What else? You said a couple of things."

"We'll never have to worry about sexually transmitted diseases. Can't get them or give them." How was he supposed to think rationally when her legs were spread and she was hot, ready for him?

"That's great. I wasn't really worrying about that, even though I guess I should have been."

He bit the top of her knee. "And I want to make sure that you understand the biting. I'm not going to be able to control myself. I'm going to have to bite you. Do you think you're okay with that?"

"More than." She paused for a second. "Was that it, or do you want to employ any other delay tactics?"

"Oh, I'm not delaying, princess, not in the least." He lifted his cock and pushed inside of her. She gasped, and he tried to slow down when he felt her body stretching to accommodate him. The last thing he wanted in the universe would be to hurt her in any possible way.

"I'm sorry." He bit down on his bottom lip to force control on himself. "I shouldn't have plowed in there like that." Damn it, he was such an asshole…

"Don't you dare apologize. I love it. I want more. What are you waiting for?"

"Ha." The girl might be trying to kill him. "All right."

Truth was it would have been hard to stop him from moving. He fit inside of her like a glove, like he had been made to be there, which he supposed he had. Betsy moved her hips, and he surged forward, even deeper into her core.

He closed his eyes, sweat forming on his forehead. This was what coming home felt like. Cyrus jerked his cock out of her, rubbing against her clit as he did. She dug her fingers into his back. "More."

He opened his eyes to find her heated gaze on him. "As my mate commands."

Repeating the movement, he was once again rewarded with Betsy's pleasure sounds. Gasps, moans, and the repeated litany of his name from her lips created a sexual soundtrack he knew would play over and over in his mind. Or at least he hoped it would. Nothing had ever sounded so beautiful.

His balls tightened, and he clenched his teeth. *Not yet. Damn it.* Betsy's pussy squeezed him tight, milking him with every movement and making it harder to maintain his cool.

Pushing in and out of her, he found a rhythm that she

liked. Looking down at her, he couldn't get over how lucky he was to have her there, to have been given this gift.

With one hand, he gripped the headboard, shaking it with every thrust. He held on by a very thin shred of control.

"Cyrus." Wow, he really loved how she said his name. "Please don't hang back, darling. You don't have to be in control all the time."

She wrapped her legs tighter around him, and he was lost. Any control he had over his movements ceased to exist. There was only Betsy in the universe. Time disappeared, and as he moved in and out of her, he was vaguely aware of the fangs in his mouth descended. When he'd bitten her earlier, it had been with his regular teeth. This time he would mark her, make her his permanently.

He jerked forward, going deeper inside of her, knowing that he wouldn't be able to hang on much longer. Cyrus fought a losing battle. But—*oh by everything in the universe*—he wanted her to come first. She cried out his name, her muscles pulsating around him, and her juices wetting him with her warmth. Betsy was heat—molten lava—and he was drawn into her flames gladly. Maybe he could exist inside of her forever.

With that thought, he lost it. His balls tightened to the point of pain, and he came over and over again inside of her. His opened his eyes and found what he searched for—the spot on her shoulder that would show she belonged to him. Yes, he knew what he needed to complete this, to take her in the way of his kind.

Cyrus shook his head and howled his human side battling him in the marking. He did not want to hurt her, and that was what he was going to do if he let go of his control. She had delicate, porcelain skin. His wolf teeth couldn't tear into her, not like this.

"Damn it." Betsy clenched her thighs around him. "Bite me. Don't make me beg you for what we both need."

How did she know the battle that raged inside of him? Her words had given him permission, so he bit down on her. She jerked beneath him, and he felt like the worst soul on earth. But then her muscles spasmed around his cock again. It took him a minute to realize she'd come again. He swallowed and tried to make sense of what had happened. His mind fogged over, and it was hard to think.

Betsy writhed beneath him, and he stroked the top of her head. He still couldn't let go of where he'd bitten her. She'd liked it. That much he could grasp, but why he couldn't release her didn't make any sense. He growled and finally released her.

The marking was customary. All male werewolves did it to their mates, but no one had ever told him what that would be like. The line between man and wolf had thinned, even more so than when he made the change on full moons, but Cyrus was an Alpha. He never lost control of himself, even to the animal. What the hell had happened?

Betsy panted, kissing his chest in between words. "That was… Wow. That was just wow."

He'd come hard enough that he should be passed out in exhausted bliss, but all he could think about was how close he had come to tearing the skin from her body, the way he had been brought to the edge. That couldn't happen again. Was he some kind of monster?

Cyrus kissed the top of her head, and drew her to him so he could look at the damage to her shoulder. He leaned down and licked it. Some of the healing properties of his wolf saliva were always present, even when he wore his human form. Maybe it would help.

She pinched him, and he turned his attention to her smiling face. "What the hell? You promise me marking, biting, and then you almost don't deliver?"

"Betsy. Um…" His own voice sounded foreign to him, as though he was listening to it from a distance. "Are you okay?"

"I'm better than okay. Was that what your hesitancy was about? Were you worried I wasn't okay? We had that whole conversation right before about what would happen. I gave you permission."

He shook his head and drew her up against his chest before he rolled them until he was on the bottom. "The reality of it was different. I was so close to unacceptable—"

"No," she interrupted him, "you don't get to take the single best sexual experience of my life and alter it by making yourself to be some kind of scary wolf. You're not. You were never going to hurt me. Sheesh, I may ask you to bite me daily to come like that."

"Really?" He wasn't entirely convinced she wasn't trying to spare his feelings. . "It didn't freak you out that my teeth changed and I bit you really hard?"

"No." She waved her hand in the air. "Like I said earlier, there are certain things that should be bothering me, certain responses I'm having that should make me scared, but they're not. Remember which one of us wanted to be chased?"

He grinned, stroking the silky strands of her hair through his fingertips. "Trust me, we both wanted that."

"I should be certifiable right now and instead," she yawned, "I'm sleepy."

"It's the wolf inside of you. You were always a were-wolf. Those instincts were always there. They were repressed. Maybe it's all falling into line because it's somewhat of a relief for you to finally be who you should be."

"Maybe." She kissed him, and he petted her back. "Can I ask you something?"

"Sure. But wouldn't you rather sleep?" Her scent had dulled. Her body craved sleep, and he would see to her needs if she wouldn't see to them herself. How long had it been since Betsy had a good night's sleep? He suffered from insomnia, but he'd be damned if she wouldn't be rested in his care.

"I will. I may even drop off mid-question."

He laughed, picturing the image like something out of a cartoon. "What do you want to know?"

"How old were you when you became in charge? When you took over as Alpha?"

"Oh." He wondered what had sparked that thought in her mind. "I didn't take over. I battled for it when I was twenty. When I won, I took control."

"Hmmm." Her voice was getting softer. She really might pass out at any time. "What happened to the last Alpha?"

"That's not really for a late-night conversation. It won't give you good dreams."

She growled low in her throat, and he stared down at her. How had he ever imagined she was passive? "I'm not going to run away in fear. What happened to him?"

"I killed him." He'd torn his throat out and had his blood dripping from his muzzle. Just stating that he'd killed him sounded much nicer.

"So you challenged him for Alpha, you won, and you

killed him?" She drummed her fingers on his chest. Nothing about her scent had changed. Betsy really did seem to want to discuss this, right before sleep, after great sex, and it didn't bother her at all. His little latent princess was becoming a full-fledged she-wolf.

"Exactly." There was a lot more detail to all of that, but it seemed enough for the night.

"What made you decide to do that?"

He shifted his position a bit, her words biting into long buried memories he didn't allow to surface into the light of his consciousness very often. "Shepherd was a bad Alpha.

Werewolves kept dying under his leadership. He didn't take care of us."

"I'm sure he was." In the darkness of his bedroom, with her face buried in his chest, it felt okay to answer her. He wasn't so certain he'd want to discuss this over breakfast. Some things were better left put away. "But I meant, what prompted you to suddenly challenge him? Did you feel overwhelmed with the need one day, or did it happen over time? You could have died in that battle with him. You couldn't have made that decision lightly. You wouldn't even bite me without holding back."

"Oh, well, actually it wasn't me who thought it was time. Lucian came to me and let me know he thought I was ready and that Shepherd had hurt enough people."

She yawned again. "Who was Lucian? I know you might have told me. I got a lot of information today."

"Lucian was our Alpha Prime. He was in charge of all the Alphas. We all held fidelity to him. He was a great man. When I was a teenager, he used to run wolf training, which is I guess the equivalent of camp, at his home in Virginia. He had acres of land. We used to go there to become better wolves. The summers started off with about fifty wolves, but by the time he stopped doing that, there were fifteen of us total. They were special times."

"And your parents sent you?" Her voice had perked up a little bit. Where was she going with this?

"It was an honor to be asked, to be noticed by him. Even Shepherd liked the idea. He wanted strong fighters since we were always at war."

"And Lucian told you to go challenge the Alpha of Manhattan when you were twenty years old?"

"He did." Cyrus scooted her over a little bit to look at her. "Where are all these questions coming from?"

She stroked the side of his face. "I'm trying to understand you. I feel so connected to you, but we don't know each other that well. Becoming Alpha was more than taking over a job, right?

It became your identity in the same way that, I guess, my identity will have to shift as your mate.

Mitchell keeps calling me ma'am, and he's older than me."

He laughed, loving the way she touched him. "I can make that stop."

"I think it would make him really uncomfortable if he couldn't do it."

She was probably right, but he wouldn't have worried about that. Mitchell would adjust to whatever Cyrus' mate needed. He had no doubt the whole pack would.

"It did change things. I think sometimes I was born to do it." There, he'd said it aloud, and he never had before because it sounded presumptuous and stuck up, as though he had some kind of special destiny when, in truth, he knew that things happened randomly and he'd been lucky.

Lucky he'd not been killed when he took down Shepherd—and luckier every day since that the world hadn't fallen apart. Lucky that whoever had managed to take down Lucian hadn't come after him. Lucky that he'd walked into the Starbucks and found Betsy.

"Well, Lucian must have thought you were born to do it." She snuggled closer. "All right, enough. I'm closing my eyes. I can't think straight. I don't even know what I'm saying."

"Goodnight, princess." He stroked her hair and listened while her breathing got more even, and she fell into a deep sleep.

Well, Lucian must have thought you were born to do it. Her words resonated in his head while he stared at the ceiling. Had Lucian thought he was born to be Alpha Prime? How had he determined which ones of his students got invited back year after year to his home? They all had Alpha tendencies. Which ones did he keep and why did he let some of them go? What had been the determining factor? And why had he done it all?

He watched the ceiling fan spin. Betsy hadn't cured his inability to sleep, but that was okay. He'd probably doze off at some point for an hour or two, and he was more comfortable than he'd ever been before.

She mumbled something, and he grinned. It was nice that she could be so at ease with him.

The windows in his apartment had been designed to keep the noise of the street out, but with one of them cracked, he could make out some of the traffic noise from below. Easing himself out from under Betsy, he crept on silent feet to the cracked opening and closed it. New York was always awake, like him, it seemed. He could order Thai food if he wanted it and have it at his doorway in half an hour. Or have his dry cleaning delivered at three a.m.

He shook his head. What was the matter with him? Why couldn't he get his brain to shut off?

Cyrus closed his eyes and leaned against the cool pane of the window. What had Lucian said to him that day he'd told him it was time to be Alpha? He hadn't thought about it in so long. *"Shepherd is destroying New York. Your parents are dead. Do you want your sister to be?"* The Alpha Prime had always seemed ancient to him. He'd probably been about a century old when he delivered that question. They lived to be one hundred and fifty or so if they managed not to get killed. Cyrus had been so young himself, thinking his mentor so old when he wasn't.

Such a childish way to be…

Cyrus had pulled a drink from his beer bottle and set the alcohol down on the table. All of his enjoyment of the afternoon fled into the wind. "It's not customary to simply go and challenge an Alpha. Especially not one as powerful as Shepherd."

"Who made him powerful, boy? The pack that follows him. If you kill him, they'll follow you."

He couldn't imagine that. How would they follow him, the kid who destroyed their leader? Even his wolf instincts couldn't clear up that distinction for him. Would Shepherd's mate follow him? His children? Would they flee and plot against him? Who was to say he could even manage to do it? Sure, Cyrus was strong but so was Shepherd.

"It's time, Cyrus. Take your place or get out of the way and let someone else do it."

Betsy sighed in her sleep, and he opened his eyes to look at her. She had asked him how he'd decided to be an Alpha, to take over the position. Well, he hadn't wanted to get out of the way. It wasn't in his nature. And he'd been stronger. On that one day, he'd won, and it hadn't been his blood left on the ground.

Chapter 10

Betsy opened her eyes and knew two things instantly. First, it was still the middle of the night. There was no light anywhere in the room. The curtains were even closed. And she didn't think they had been when she'd conked out. She rolled over and checked the clock, confirming that it was three a.m.

The second thing she knew was that she was alone in the room. Cyrus was gone. Not even the bathroom held more than a shadow of his scent. She got up and walked to his closet. Having no idea where her clothes had been discarded, she was going to have to wear something of his since she wasn't going to go traipsing around the apartment in her birthday suit.

She tugged on a T-shirt that said Columbia on the front. It fell to her knees, and she supposed it would have to do. It smelled like Cyrus, and she grinned. It was hard to imagine him in a T-shirt. Naked? No problem. Wearing a designer suit? No problem. T-shirt? Maybe if he was lounging around, but did he even do that?

Betsy padded out into the living room. She stopped in

the archway and took in the scene in front of her. Cyrus was passed out at his desk, his head down on top of something he'd been reading. She approached slowly and stared down at what he'd been doing when he fell asleep. A bunch of spreadsheets and numbers looked up at her. She'd never been able to make sense of them before and didn't want to try at that moment. What concerned her was the man head down on top of them. He couldn't be comfortable like that.

She smoothed his hair off his forehead, and he jolted backward as though he'd been stabbed. He jumped to his feet before she could even say anything.

"Are you okay?" He turned left and right.

"I was going to ask you the same thing." She walked around the desk toward him. Did he always awaken like he had to fight something off? "I'm sorry I woke you like that. You didn't look comfortable head down on your papers."

Cyrus grinned a big smile. "Wouldn't look good to drool on the spreadsheets in front of my new mate."

"Amazing, you still use spreadsheets. Don't you high-powered people all do everything digitally? You actually printed paper?" She still had no idea exactly what his company did except serve as a front for werewolves and cage humans in the basement.

"Sometimes I have to have things printed out to really see them. I'm missing something in the marketing department. There's a problem with their budget."

She took his hand in hers. He was such a mixture of contradictions. The tough Alpha, the focused business man, the lover who didn't want to bite her for fear of hurting her, the playful guy who told her to run. *The twenty-year-old kid sent to kill an Alpha by a man who should have been powerful enough to figure out a way to handle that Alpha himself.* She pushed that thought away. What happened years before she was here couldn't be the focus of her time.

"Is it standard for the CEO to go over budgets?"

"It needed doing, so I figured I might as well get it done." He cleared his throat. "Why aren't you sleeping?"

"I could ask you the same thing." He'd dressed himself in a white undershirt and a pair of boxers. Cyrus was far too clothed for her taste. He should be naked. All the time. "Was I snoring?"

"What?" He shook his head. "No, of course not. I can't sleep. It's nothing to do with you. I have insomnia problems. I can't sleep, and then when it gets quiet enough at night, I kind of nod off for a few hours here or there."

Her mate needed to relax, and he needed caring for. Whatever her parents' issues were— and she clearly had a lot of them—her mother and father had taken care of each other. Cyrus required some tending, and she was glad she was here to do it.

"I can't imagine that even a werewolf should be running a company and a pack on a few hours of sleep, here and there."

"Not much I can do about that. We don't respond well to traditional medicine. Lake has gifts that can heal us, but it's not like I can go take a sleeping pill. It's likely to have the opposite effect, and I'll be jogging the streets of New York for two days straight." He shrugged. "Come on, let's get you back to sleep."

She took his hand. "I have a different idea."

He led her into the bedroom. "Oh?"

She walked to the side of the bed and turned on the reading light that sat there. "Sit on the edge of the bed."

Cyrus stopped moving and gaped at her. "What?"

"Come on, Alpha-boy, do what I say. Sit on the edge of the bed."

"Betsy, what do you have planned here?" He stretched his neck, and she could see the tension in every muscle. If what she wanted to do didn't work, she'd start reading on how to give massages. Maybe she would anyway.

She waited, deliberately not answering him until he sat down on the bed. He grinned and shook his head. "If you are planning on making me do deep breathing exercises, I can assure you, I've already given that a go."

"No." She dropped to her knees in front of him. "I don't want you breathing deeply while I do this. I'd rather you get really excited."

"What…"

His voice faded away when she kissed his leg. She started at his ankle and moved upward, planting a kiss every few inches on her way up. Cyrus had muscular legs, and there were lots of places to explore. His body vibrated slightly beneath her ministrations.

When she reached his thigh, she tugged on his boxer shorts, letting them drop to the floor. His cock, which had clearly come to attention when she'd started kissing him, was in perfect position for her to stroke it.

He hissed in a breath. "I can't wait to get inside of you again, princess. I wouldn't have suggested it. I thought you might be a little sore."

"I am." She wasn't, but she didn't want him arguing with her about what she wanted. It had been apparent to her during their lovemaking that he wasn't used to having oral sex

performed. "The only place your cock is going is in my mouth."

She purposely didn't look up at his face, but she felt his whole body tense from where she kissed the top of his thigh.

"Betsy." He lifted her chin to look at him. "Please don't feel like you have to do that."

"I don't have to do it. I want to do it. I like to. What's the matter? Only had bad ones? Someone bite you?"

"It's not that." He seemed so uncomfortable in the way he squirmed that she almost felt bad for him. But she actually liked to give oral sex, and if he had some kind of problem with it, better to find that out now. "Then what is it?"

"I never chose to have sex with humans. Too fragile. What if I hurt them?" He wiped at his brow. She really didn't want to make him more stressed out. The idea had been to relax him. She hoped she hadn't made some massive miscalculation.

"And? Werewolf women don't give blow jobs?"

"Not really, no." He drummed his fingers on his knee. "Our longtime relationships turn into either our version of marriage or, if we're lucky, a true mating. Casual sex is usually because she's in heat and needs to feel better."

"And that kind of encounter doesn't lend itself to blow jobs, just in making her feel better, which is why you were so fantastic at going down on me earlier."

Things were finally clicking together for her, and a picture of Cyrus, the Alpha caretaker who never even got to relax in bed, formed in her mind. No wonder the moon had picked her to be his mate.

"Did you really think I was fantastic at it?" His eyebrows rose slowly.

"Oh, I'd say the whole thing from start to finish was an A plus, plus. Don't get all ego-y about it though. I'm going to expect repeat performances." When he laughed, she took a deep breath. Apparently, he could be teased, which was a good thing. Lack of a sense of humor would be a problem over time. "Here's the thing though. You mated a girl who thought she was human most of her life. And human girls sometimes—if their men are really lucky— give them blowjobs. I happen to really like to so, unless you have a real objection to the act, I want to put my mouth on your cock as soon as possible."

He visibly swallowed, and she watched the muscles in his neck clench. "I don't have any objections at all."

"That's good." She cupped the head of his penis, and it stood up straighter. "Now you've got a very impressive piece of manhood here. I can't wait to taste it."

She licked the remainder of the way up his leg, squeezing his balls on the way up. He sucked in his breath. Betsy had always loved this part of sharing sex, and now that she knew she was supposed to be with the werewolf in front of her, it was even more fun. She could do this for him, and she could revel in being able to give him pleasure in a way no one had ever before. Moving to the top of his getting-larger-every-second cock, she wet the head with her tongue. Cyrus made a little moan, and she knew he had enjoyed it. She moved lower, exploring the ridged part of right up against his head of his cock. She licked it slowly, savoring the taste of Cyrus, the heat of him. Was there any part of him that didn't warm her body?

She proceeded slowly. This was his first time on this part of the rodeo. She wanted him to enjoy it and didn't want to rush the experience for him. Finally, when she felt his body jerk beneath her ministrations, she knew he was ready to be really pleasured.

Betsy opened her mouth and took him as deep inside of her throat as she could. Cyrus was huge. There was no way she was getting him all the way down, even with her considerable skill set in this department. She compensated as best she could, running her hands up and down the part of his shaft that she couldn't quite get in her mouth. He moaned, moving in and out of her mouth with thrusts.

She reveled in the act, loving that she controlled it, loving that she could do this for him. For Betsy, this moment was powerful. She gripped him tighter, squeezing his balls with her free hand.

He called out her name, his hips moving at a rapid pace. She raised her eyes to look at him. Cyrus was lost in rapture and to witness it qualified as a moment of beauty. He came in her mouth, saying words of passion over and over, and she swallowed it down, loving every pulse.

She had given him his first blowjob, and she'd bet the farm that he had loved it.

Betsy had no sooner wiped her mouth than she found herself pulled down on top of him.

"That was…"

She grinned. Good, if he couldn't come up with words then she'd accomplished what she set out to do. "Yes?"

Betsy checked out the clock. Half an hour had passed. Maybe he'd be ready to get some real rest in the bed and not on top of his desk.

"Amazing."

She would have responded, but he pulled her mouth down on his. God, she loved kissing him. He pulled back to look at her. "You're such an amazing gift to me."

Betsy rolled her eyes. Sentimentality didn't work for her. The television shows that she saw on where it got too gooey made her want to throw something. She had no idea how to handle it. "Sheesh, one blow job and you're writing poetry. I'm not a gift to anyone."

"Yes you are." His eyes were serious. "Do we need to go back to the mirror?"

"Oh." She smiled at the memory his words invoked. "How about we do when I'm not sore?"

"I don't need to penetrate you to show you what a gift you are to me."

"Cyrus..." She swung her leg over him to keep in place. Not that he couldn't get out if he so wanted. She hoped he didn't want to. "Let's go to sleep."

"I don't know if I'm going to be able to sleep again."

His scent said differently, but she didn't want to point that out lest he get riled up and defeat her purpose. "Would you try with me?"

"Sure." She'd known he wouldn't deny her request. Only, this time she wasn't falling asleep until he did.

They snuggled back into the bed, and she placed her head over his heart so she could hear it beating. Strong and steady.

"What time do you have to get to the office in the morning?"

"I'm usually out by six-thirty."

Well. That wasn't going to work. Not for today. Would the world end if he got there at nine?

"Why so early?" She kissed his arm.

"I always have so much to do."

"Here's the thing." Betsy had never really figured out how to manipulate people into doing what she wanted. Or at least any attempts she made hadn't worked. Maybe it wasn't fair to call it manipulation when she was really trying to take care of him or to get him to take care of himself.

"Yes?" She could now hear the fatigue in his voice.

"I'm not going to be able to get up that early. I'm so tired. Do you think we could go in a little later? That is, if you want me with you..." She let her voice drift off.

"Oh. You're with me tomorrow. That's a given. Okay, we'll go in later."

"Great." She snuggled closer. When she hadn't been

able to sleep as a child, her mother had petted her head until she'd dozed off. Given that she didn't have any other solutions, she gave into the urge and ran her fingers through his short blond hair.

They lay in the darkness, and she deliberately avoided eye contact with him so that he wouldn't think about anything but how warm they were together, the quiet, the dark, and the sound of the ceiling fan gently moving the air in the room.

She willed him to believe he could relax with her, to not feel as though he had to be doing something, to let whatever was troubling him leave for the night.

It was everything she could do to keep herself awake, given that all the things she wanted him to feel she'd experienced herself. But she was determined to see that he slept and wasn't going to give up until she'd done that.

Betsy felt rather than saw when he fell asleep. His breathing changed, and he relaxed. She let herself glance up at him then. He appeared different than he had passed out at the desk. With his eyes closed, and his mouth slightly open, Cyrus came across as younger. They'd not discussed his age, but she'd guess him to be in his mid-thirties. Maybe that was wrong. Maybe werewolves aged differently.

She bit down on her lip. How could she feel so connected to a man and not know how old he was? Betsy exhaled the breath she'd been holding. Somehow, she had to change her thinking. It was okay to feel the way she did about him—they were mates, and she wasn't human. She was mated to the Alpha of Manhattan. She'd gotten him to fall asleep when he'd claimed it impossible after giving him his very first blowjob.

She'd ask him his age in the morning. And what his company did. For now, she knew that he had a really big heart that no one had taken proper care of in however many years he happened to have been on the planet. That would change now that she was around.

Not daring to move for fear of waking him, she snuggled closer and gave into the lethargy threatening to overtake her. Sleep would work for both of them.

———

THE NEXT TIME she opened her eyes, light streamed in underneath the curtains into the room. Her muscles were sore from lack of movement, and she had to blink several times to clear the fog from her brain. The clock read eight in the morning, which meant she'd been asleep for five hours.

Betsy grinned. Not only had she been asleep, but the Alpha snoring lightly next to her still slept on. It had taken a little TLC to get Cyrus to conk out. Now she wanted to make him food before he woke up, checked the clock, and panicked.

He didn't stir when she got out of the bed. She'd made it to the bathroom and out when she heard his phone vibrating. Betsy bit down on her lip as she debated for a second whether she should leave it alone. People were very private about their cell phones. Still, she wanted him to sleep, not get awoken by somebody needing something the second he opened his eyes.

She grabbed the phone and walked out of the room. The screen read Lake, and she answered.

"Hello?"

There was a pause on the other end before Lake spoke. "Betsy? Is Cyrus okay?"

"He is." She cleared her throat. Having not spoken yet, she still sounded hoarse. "He's actually asleep."

"Really?" The tone of Lake's voice raised a fraction in surprise. "I've never ever known him to sleep late."

"Well, today he is, unless there's an emergency I need to wake him for?" She glanced back at the door toward the room where he slept. Betsy would hate to disturb him, but an emergency was an emergency.

"No." His sister laughed, and Betsy had no idea why. Something was funny? "I'm getting texts from Alexei's people wanting to know the time for the meeting today."

Betsy rolled her eyes. She hadn't liked the Alpha, and he had certainly not cared about timing the day before when he'd shown up announced and uninvited. "Lunch time. He'll be in for lunch."

"Thanks. Oh, hey, Betsy?" Lake stopped her before she could hang up.

"Yes?"

"I'm really sorry if I harmed you in any way by making you turn into a full-fledged werewolf. There's no excuse. I should be in better control than that."

"Oh." Betsy smiled. That was nice of her to say. "Thanks for the apology, but I think it was the best thing that could have happened to me."

"Good. And you're clearly the best thing that's ever happened to my brother if he is sleeping in. I mean he has never done that. Not even when we were kids."

"I don't think I had anything to do with that. The Alpha wanted to sleep in, so that's what he did."

She heard the words come out of her mouth as she said them. There had been no conscious decision to lie to Lake. The other woman was his sister. Surely she'd want him rested and healthy. But it had felt as though the way to protect Cyrus had been to not let anyone know he needed extra sleep. Betsy would never purposely expose anything that might be considered a weakness.

"Right. Of course." Lake continued, "Would you be interested in doing something with me and some of the other pack women some time? Like a movie or dancing?"

Betsy gasped. "Oh, I'd love that. So much." She'd never had friends. It hadn't been possible. She's had her parents. They'd gotten less and less attentive as she'd gotten older. But they'd been there.

"Great. Then we'll plan that. I'll see you at lunch."

"Sure." Betsy hit End on the phone and walked into the kitchen. She had no idea if Cyrus even had any food in the house. The one thing she could do was cook. It was what she had hoped to do once the business with Nathan was over. That would obviously not be happening now. A pang struck her heart. She was never going to school, never going to become a chef. Never see the world.

Tears threatened, and she blinked them away. She had this whole new world to explore; she'd become a werewolf, or, rather, she had discovered she had always been one. Nathan was being dealt with. Her parents would be okay, one way or another. Cyrus, who was hot as hell, and sweet to boot, belonged to her. What business did she have to be crying over culinary school, which probably would never have happened anyway?

She found the eggs in his fridge, along with some bacon and biscuits. Someone kept it stocked, but she'd guess it wasn't Cyrus. She smiled at the thought. There were trade-offs, and even if she hadn't been given a choice, she couldn't let herself dwell on the negatives. Other things were too good to complain about.

Betsy broke the eggs on the side of a bowl and got started in making breakfast and quit thinking about things that wouldn't do any good anyway.

Chapter 11

Cyrus opened his eyes and took a deep breath. His muscles were loose, and his head clear for the first time in longer than he cared to remember. He rubbed at his eyes and sniffed the air. His apartment smelled different. He scented…eggs. Someone was cooking breakfast.

A rush of memory pushed into his head, and he grinned. Betsy was here. He'd fallen asleep next to her after she had, well, given him immense pleasure the likes of which he had never known before. She'd tried, very badly, to trick him into falling asleep. He'd gone along because the woman had wanted to take care of him and it had felt so nice to he had no intention of arguing with her. Besides, he hadn't really thought he'd fall asleep.

He threw his legs over the bed and glanced at the clock when he stood up. Did that say nine o'clock? Shit. He wasn't just late; he was seriously late.

Cyrus bounded into the kitchen and took a deep breath. Wow. Her cooking whatever she prepared smelled like heaven. He'd never actually lived in a house with someone who could cook before. His mother had burned water when she tried. They'd all preferred meals she could reheat.

"What are you making?" He came up behind her and wrapped his arms around her. She fit perfectly to him, and he inhaled her vanilla scent into his lungs. A man could get used to this. "Eggs."

It was the sound of her voice that alerted him. He hadn't smelled distress over the scents of cooking and the vanilla, but it was there. Betsy was upset. Cyrus took a steadying breath. Yesterday had been a lot. It was ridiculous to think she wouldn't be overwhelmed. Of course, he'd woken up happier than he'd ever been. But that was neither here nor there. This was her first day greeting the dawn as a werewolf. Maybe it didn't look so pretty in the light of morning. He resisted the urge to chuck something across the room.

"What's wrong?" Whatever she needed, he'd figure it out. If she wanted space, she could have another apartment in the building. He owned the whole thing. He'd court her or date her or whatever. Surely some member of his pack could tell him how to do that.

"I'm being stupid." She wiped at her eyes. "I hope you like scrambled eggs. I didn't want to wake you to ask how you liked them. Oh, and I spoke to Lake. The meeting with Alexei has been moved to lunch. No need to rush in."

"You did?" She turned off the stovetop, and he turned her around until she faced him. One thing he would not do was stop touching her. That might kill him. She'd adjust, but she'd damn well do it in his arms even if it were three apartments down from his. "That was very kind of you to take care of that. I like my eggs however you want to cook them, and I don't expect you to cook and clean, by the way. That's not necessary. You don't have to."

"I actually like to cook."

His cock jumped at the reminder of exactly what those other things she *liked* to do were, one particular act had knocked him for such a loop he'd completely conked out afterwards. He forced his attention back where it belonged. "You're crying. This doesn't seem like joyful cooking to me."

"Look…it's not your fault. You didn't make me a latent werewolf. You didn't even change me into one—and Lake has apologized, and I've forgiven her, so we don't need to keep rehashing it—I'm sort of letting things go, that's all." She sniffed, and it stabbed him in the heart as if she had taken a knife and pushed it inside of him.

"Like what?" He stroked the back of her head.

"Well, I had these ridiculous dreams about what I would do when this was over with Nathan." She pulled away from him, and he let her go. He wanted her to talk, not to clam up, and if she needed space to do so, then that was fine. For now.

"Why were they ridiculous? Were you planning on doing something so outlandish it could never happen?" Because his pack had resources, he could probably make about anything she wanted an eventuality.

"No." She laughed, and he felt better. Betsy picked up a bit of egg on a fork and motioned toward his mouth with it. He opened and let her feed him the food. It was warm and melted on his tongue. He savored it for a second before swallowing it down. She'd put heaven in her scrambled eggs.

"Then what?" He wasn't going to let this go. It wasn't in his nature.

"It was ridiculous because I was never getting away from Nathan, so they were never going to happen. I think I wanted to hold onto the idea."

"Which was what?" If she were trying to be deliberately evasive, she would quickly find that, once he started to dig out a problem, he didn't stop until he'd fully uncovered it. His mate had been crying while she cooked scrambled eggs on their first morning together. This constituted a problem.

Not to mention he was feeling all kinds of rested and energized. No way would he let this go unfinished.

"I wanted to go to culinary school." She looked down at the pan of eggs before she scooped them out onto a waiting plate.

"Why can't you still do that? This is New York. We have such schools here. You can certainly go. I went to college. And got a master's in business actually."

Betsy raised a blonde eyebrow when she handed him his plate of eggs. He took it and went to sit at the counter. She sipped at a cup of coffee before placing one down in front of him. This whole thing seemed really domestic. If only she were happier, he'd be ready to declare it the best morning of his life.

"How old are you exactly? You took over the pack at twenty, and you look about thirty-five. Where did you find the time to go to college, business school, and then develop a very large company that does whatever it does in the last fifteen years?"

He grinned. Oh, there were things about their life that were going to blow his mate's mind. He hoped in a good way. She might be really weirded out by the whole thing. His smile fell.

"I'm older than I look. By a considerable number of years. Werewolves have longer life spans. We look younger, longer. Given good nutrition and no one killing us, we tend to come to the end of our lives at about 150 years, give or take some." He sipped his coffee.

Betsy's eyes seemed to dance around in their sockets.

She processed what he said quietly, but her body was absorbing every shock. He might need to get her a massage. Or give her one.

His mood brightened considerably at the idea. She'd taken care of him...

"Which would make you how old exactly?" Like him, she didn't let go of a carrot once it had been dangled in front of her.

He cleared his throat. "I will be forty-six on my next birthday, which I guess would make me about twice your age."

She set down her mug "Holy cow. You don't look a day over thirty-five."

"Thanks." He needed to lighten this up. "But most people would say thirty. Maybe the stress of the last twenty-four hours has aged me all of a sudden. Thirty-five? I should be insulted."

She threw her napkin at him, and he caught it. There was some humor back in her eyes.

"I had no idea I'd mated such an elderly gentleman..."

"Elderly?" He lunged for her and pulled her up against him. "I'll show you elderly." He kissed her, and she melted against him. This was how they should start every morning. After a moment, he withdrew, wishing he could stand there and kiss her forever. If only the outside world didn't wait for them.

"My company handles privacy issues for business in terms of telecommunication. We identify potential spy issues, breaches in security. Basically, we're a private company that helps public companies keep their business secrets safer."

She sighed. "You say the most romantic things. Kiss a girl, talk about breaches in secrecy."

He rubbed his finger down the slope of her nose,

memorizing the features of her face. "You said you didn't know what my company did. I thought you should. Now, tell me again why you thought you couldn't go to culinary school?"

"Well, besides the small detail of not having a high school diploma since I was educated at home? I don't think my parents ever took care of that officially."

Another check-minus for her family. He ground his teeth together. Were there manuals for dealing with horrendous in-laws? How did human males deal with this? How long did they wait before they threw them off cliffs?

"Other than that? Your educational background can be handled." Or forged if need be.

"Why should I bother? I'm never going to get to work in a restaurant, am I? I mean, all of your people work at your company."

Cyrus let go of her and took a few steps away. She had no idea how closely this resembled a conversation he'd had with Lake weeks earlier. His sister was desperate to work in a human hospital since she was now educated to the point of being a nurse practitioner.

"You are fortunate in that you will never know what it is to live here, in New York, under the rule of Shepherd. We used to have much higher numbers than we do now. The pack was under constant attack both by other werewolves and from snooping humans. It is a lot trickier than you might imagine to arrange a life as a werewolf out there in the human world. Can you disappear from a normal job every full moon? Can you explain to your bosses why you have to?

People start to ask questions."

"Listen, I get it, I'm not arguing with you. I just became a werewolf. I'm going to have to let some of my human dreams go." She shrugged. "You do the dishes. I'm going to go get ready to see what today has in store for me. Oh wait, I can't." She turned back to him. "I don't have any clothes."

"That's taken care of. I sent two of the females to the brownstone to collect your clothing. It's all put away in the second closet in my room. Also, you have a set of drawers in there too, next to mine."

She shook her head. "Do you always think of everything?"

With a spin of her heel, she turned and headed back toward the bathroom. If he thought of everything, he'd have remembered to tell her where her clothes were before then. Of course, forgetting had granted him the gift of seeing her in one his college T-shirts.

He cleared his plate and carried it to the sink. When was the last time he'd cleaned a dish? Never eating at home meant never having to clean up after himself. He scrubbed at the dishes before going after the pan. She'd never cooked the bacon so he put that and the biscuits away. His mother would be so proud that he still remembered how to do the things she'd made him do when he was a child. It had been so many years since he'd done 'chores.'

Always need to be able to take care of yourself... Her voice sounded in his mind, and he smiled at the memory. He almost never thought of his parents anymore. The memory of them simply didn't fit into his daily life. Nothing about his life now resembled anything about his time with them.

Well, maybe now it did.

He turned off the water and took a deep breath. Giving up her dreams. He hated the thought of that. As soon as the Nathan problem was settled, he wanted her as blissfully happy as she could be. And then when she wasn't, he'd kiss her back to happiness.

There really wasn't anything he could do about her dilemma short of purchasing a restaurant for her to work in. But then he'd have to buy Lake a hospital, and he suspected that his handing them careers was not what either lady had in mind. Although that wasn't much different than what he did at the company.

Cyrus shook his head. He wasn't going to solve the world's problems standing over a sink. He had to get dressed and get to the office. Alexei would be bound, by the end of the day, by a blood oath to not invade Cyrus' territory, or there would be hell to pay. Then they would move on to Montana.

Some things he could be sure of. Cyrus had always known how to get things done.

━━

NATHAN QUIVERED in the cage like a shaking leaf. Cyrus hadn't even spoken to the pathetic excuse for a man yet, and the human was about two seconds from pissing himself out of fear.

Cyrus glanced at Jensen, who leaned up against the back wall. The other werewolf only pretended to be at ease. He could smell the tangy taste of Jensen's vigilance across the room.

"Join me," he called out to Jensen, and his pack mate walked over immediately.

"Yes, my Alpha?" Jensen held eye contact for a second before he looked slightly down. It was the appropriate behavior to show respect, although Cyrus had no doubt that, given the provocation, Jensen could easily meet his gaze for extended periods of time.

"Anyone abuse him last night?"

"No." Jensen shook his head. "I was here the whole time. He got fed, watered, and was allowed to use the bathroom. He even got to take a shower this morning."

"Fed, watered, showered. That's good." He laughed, and Jensen's eyebrows furrowed downward.

"Sir, I didn't mean that to be funny."

"I know." He patted Jensen on the arm, and Jensen stared at the spot he'd touched as though he couldn't believe the contact.

"He thought your phrasing was funny." Betsy walked up next to him and handed him the coffee she'd purchased across the street.

"How so?" Jensen followed the conversation. .

"It's like you were talking about a dog, sort of." Betsy shrugged. "If you'd said you let him outside, it would have fit perfectly."

Cyrus smiled into his cup. Betsy understood his sense of humor perfectly. Bizarre, really. Very few people ever followed the direction of his thoughts.

"Sir, if I may say, the whole pack is thrilled by your true mating. We look forward to your moon ceremony." Jensen smiled broadly. Cyrus wasn't entirely certain he'd ever seen that particular expression on the other man's face before.

"Thank you."

"What's a moon ceremony?" Betsy sipped her drink.

"Kind of like a wedding. But better." He'd get into the specifics with her later. Someone would have to preside over it since he couldn't do it himself, and she'd have to be comfortable with the nudity.

"My mate is looking forward to the movies tonight," Jensen continued.

"Movies tonight?" Cyrus regarded at Betsy. "This is the first I'm hearing of it."

"Oh." Betsy shook her head. "Lake asked me if I'd like to get together with some of the women sometime to do something. Very vague. I had no idea she'd planned it for tonight. This is a lot sooner than I expected."

"Sounds like my sister." Cyrus grinned. Leave it to Lake to disrupt the evening he had planned. "You should go. I have Alexei to deal with and this fool here. You'll be safe with the pack, and after the movies, we'll meet up back home."

"Oh. Okay." She flipped her hair over her shoulder, and it was everything he could do to not to tug at her shirt to look at his mark there. He salivated to see it. Betsy turned to Jensen. "What are we seeing?"

"I'm afraid I don't know, ma'am. I didn't think to ask."

"You," Nathan called out from his cage noticing Betsy for the first time. "You're with them now. I should have known it. A leopard can never truly hide his spots. My father warned me you'd always be mostly animal, even if you hid it better than the other abominations. You're an animal. We should never have thought to save you."

Betsy jerked as though he'd struck her. "What did you say?"

Jensen growled, launching himself at the cage. Nathan screamed like a woman and darted to the back of the bars. "You will not insult the Alpha's mate."

"Oh, the Alpha?" Even as he shrieked, Nathan continued his insults. *Stupid boy.* "You're fucking the Alpha, you slut. Can't you ever keep your legs closed?"

"I never slept with you." Betsy sipped her coffee, and he could smell her fighting for calm. It burned his lungs. He hated to smell her so stressed out. "Then again, I'd never sleep with a rat like you."

Cyrus walked toward Jensen and nodded for him to get off the cage. This was one of the reasons he hadn't left her within talking range of Nathan the day before. The pathetic excuse for a life form couldn't be trusted to not hurt her in some way.

"How did you know she was a werewolf? How did you know when she didn't?"

Nathan laughed, a hysterical whiny sound, but it did little to disguise the disgust in his gaze as he focused on Betsy. "Oh, everyone knew. We kill your kind. We do it when you're babies."

Cyrus almost gave in to the urge to claw out the man's eyes. The human shouldn't be allowed to look at Cyrus' mate. Instead, Cyrus held onto his calm and took a sip of his coffee. It wasn't time to kill Nathan...yet.

"But you didn't change, and neither did your sister. So, even though we knew you had animal parents, my father—who is a great man—said it was our duty as true believers to give you the chance to be saved from the pit."

Betsy had gone very pale. "So you all knew I was a werewolf this whole time? And my sister too? What did you do with her? Send her off to another true believer?"

"I don't know anything about where your sister went. I just know what I know. My father saved you from the pit, and I was supposed to save you the rest of the way. Until you went and started sleeping with *him*."

"Cyrus." Betsy's voice was very low. "I think I'm going to be sick."

He put his arm around her. "Take some deep breaths. Jensen, go get my sister."

"Yes, my Alpha." Jensen shot Nathan a look that could have scorched the earth before he ran from the room.

"Betsy, listen to my voice. You aren't going to give this man the satisfaction of seeing you throw up." She raised her now red-rimmed eyes to look at him. He would make Nathan suffer tenfold for the pain Betsy endured. "And we don't know what is true. He is a stupid asshole."

He'd said the last part loud enough for Nathan to hear and was rewarded when the other man cried out. Good, Nathan should know how lowly Cyrus viewed him. The man was nothing more than a coward pretending to be a tough guy.

"We'll find out what is true and what isn't. Then, I promise you, Nathan and his like will know the pain of crossing us. I give you my word."

Betsy nodded, giving him a small smile that broke his heart for its bravery. Jensen rushed back in the door, followed by Lake. His sister must already know the situation because she walked right to Betsy and placed a hand on her arm.

"You feel sick? Like you might lose your cookies?"

Betsy laughed, a shaky sound. "Great phrase."

"Thanks. I use it with the pack pups. It always makes them laugh. I think you're doing better. I can feel some of the pain leaving you, and I think we can credit my brother for that."

She nodded. "But I can help the rest of the way."

Lake placed a hand on Betsy's arm, and Cyrus let go of his mate. Betsy needed the healing, not he, and he wouldn't suck any of Lake's magic touch from his mate by accident. He never thought about his own healing abilities. His pack's Healer happened to be his family, and he used her whenever someone needed help, but Alphas could heal with their touch. There was no kind of magic to it, just plain old comfort in being held by the person who was responsible for the person's care. It went along way to relieving fear and angst.

He didn't know that he'd done that for Betsy. Their relationship would never be entirely Alpha and pack member. She belonged to him differently. Maybe his holding her would be more effective because of that. They'd have to find out together.

Cyrus walked to cage, where Nathan trembled. "You have a venomous mouth for someone so terrified."

"You're just an animal."

That had clearly become the human's standard reply and ultimately what all true believers said when they found themselves in this kind of situation. Lucian had held a policy of not dealing with them at all. His last summer with the Alpha Prime, Cyrus had witnessed him beheading two of them. Cyrus could remember that day vividly, not because of some kind of horror associated with it— beheading was certainly a brutally effective way to send a message back to the other true believers—but because he hadn't felt anything at all about what he'd witnessed. Not one damn thing. They were humans who wanted to kill his kind; they needed to die, like removing a wasp's nest before the creatures inside could sting anybody. Death was the only answer.

"You're right." Cyrus nodded. "I am an animal, sort of. But I'd never do to a woman what you did."

Nathan spit from the cage, almost hitting Cyrus' two-thousand-dollar suit.

"Spitting is a dirty habit." Cyrus set down his coffee. "It spreads disease, and your fragile little bodies can take only so many encounters with illness before your hearts stop beating. If I were you, I'd be more careful, although I suppose it doesn't matter. You aren't going to live long enough to get sick again. When I'm done with you, I've decided to give you to my friend Alexei.

I hear he likes to play with his food before eating it. You'll beg for death before he's done."

Nathan cried out, big fat tears streaming down his face. The man wasn't a true believer— he was a bully.

"Jensen, see that he calls his father for his daily report. He'll be leaving with Alexei later and get the plane all set up for a trip, will you? A bunch of us are going to be visiting Montana tomorrow."

Chapter 12

Betsy sipped her strawberry daiquiri and regarded the other women who surrounded her. They were all members of her pack, and they were all talking at once. She smiled at one who had said her name was Liana before she took another sip. The whole evening was different than she had imagined it.

"This is our version of the movies." Lake laughed, taking a large swig from her pink-colored drink. Betsy had no idea what it was. In fact, she had no clue about what most of the women were consuming. She'd never been to a bar before. She'd ordered her own drink because she'd seen it in a movie once, and at least she had something to order other than the whiskey her father preferred. She hated the smell of that and detested the taste even more.

It was loud, and everyone in the place seemed to be having a good time. Her group had a table in the corner.

"We can't admit we go to bars." Lake shrugged. "Or the men send a representative to guard us. What point is it having a ladies' night out with them watching over us like we need babysitters? We're female werewolves. We can take care of ourselves."

"Here. Here." A redheaded woman on the other side of the table saluted with her beer. Betsy tried to recall the woman's name. Rachel? Raquel? There were fifteen women with her, and, if she was lucky, she'd remember the names of five of them by the end of the evening. It might be a year before she could remember the name of every wolf in the pack. She sighed, stirring her drink with the little plastic umbrella someone had stuck in it.

"So," Lake continued, holding her hands over her head as though she was stretching her arms into the sky, "we say we're going to the movies, and we all meet here. No harm, no foul. For some reason, bars seem more risky to the men."

Betsy tried to digest her words and found she couldn't ignore the twinge they gave to her insides. "I don't think I'm comfortable lying to Cyrus."

The whole table fell silent. The women seemed to be making eye contact all around her, as if they were silently communicating in a way she couldn't follow. Wouldn't anything ever be easy? Couldn't she just make friends? *No.* She bit down on her lip. *Not if it meant betraying Cyrus.* That felt wrong.

"They don't understand." One of the women, who had been quiet most of the night, whose name she could actually remember since she'd met her briefly in Cyrus' office building as Kyra, smiled at her kindly. "They're not in a true mating. You and I are the only ones here— actually, the only ones in the pack—to find a true mating. The others have mated with men who are not their true mates, which is fine and their decision, or they are still single. They don't understand what deceit feels like to us."

Kyra had brown, shoulder-length hair and kind blue

eyes. She was slightly on the chubby side, with ten pounds she might not need hugging her hips and breasts. Betsy liked her tremendously, and she'd never exchanged more than hello until that moment.

"Who are you true mated to? I've met only a handful of the werewolf pack members." Actually, she'd spent most of the day closeted away in a room with a man named Luther who was about ninety and who'd given her a history and mysticism lesson about werewolves. By the end of it, her head ached, and she wondered if she'd made a mistake thinking she could get her high school diploma since she obviously could not retain information the way she needed to.

She still couldn't figure out the difference between all the moon cycles and why they had anything to do with the chemistry inside of her body.

"I think you've met him several times actually. And talked to him. His name is Jensen." She brightened at that, letting go of the breath she held. Yes, she knew Jensen. He'd come to Brooklyn and thrown himself on the cage today. She could see them together. They fit in the way people seemed to do on television, as though they'd been cast to be together by some authority that knew these things. His dark hair would complement her lighter brown, and he'd gaze into her blue eyes adoringly every morning.

Like Cyrus had looked at her when she'd fed him the eggs. She sighed at the memory. What was she doing in a bar when he was not with her? She was making friends. Or blowing it so the whole pack ended up hating her

Liana, who sat next to her, spoke. "Let's not make it seem like those of us who fell in love with our partners are somehow slumming it, because we aren't *true mates*. We met someone, fell in love, committed, and have families—like the humans do. It's a commitment, and I won't have it dismissed because you smelled your mate and it happened to work. Our unions are just as sacred."

Kyra nodded and bit down on her bottom lip before she spoke. "I would never disparage your relationship or anyone else's, sister wolf. It's that while you might choose not to lie to spouse, and I commend you for that, it's physically painful for me to do it, and I don't blame Betsy for sensing that she doesn't wish to give that a try."

"Then how do you come here when we do this? How do you lie to Jensen?" Lake took another swig from her drink. How many had Cyrus' sister had?

"I don't lie. Jensen knows where I am and what I'm doing."

A hush fell at that response. Finally Lake spoke again, this time with temper in her tone.

"How do you know he won't tell the Alpha and Cyrus will put a stop to this whole thing?"

"I don't." Kyra shrugged, smiling at Betsy. "But if he does, it's not the end of the world."

"Not the end of the world? My brother has never seen a good time he didn't want to break up."

Okay, Lake was drunk. Betsy had seen it many times with her father. She hadn't liked the look of it then, and she didn't now. Only now, the toxic alcohol fumes coming off the pack Healer made Betsy want to sneeze too.

"That's not true. He wants you all to have great lives. His only concern is keeping you safe." Her defense of him was swift. If Lake believed that, then she really didn't know her brother at all. What had he done to make them all so completely misunderstand him? She drummed her fingers on the table. He needed to hire a PR person for his own pack mates.

"Don't get us wrong," the Raquel/Rachel person said. "We love the Alpha. Things were so bad before he took over. My parents call him the savior. They say the pack was all but decimated and he put it back together. We could never get on without him, but, no offense, he has a real stick up his ass sometimes."

"No offense? How am I not to take offense? He's my mate and your Alpha." She growled. "I can promise you he'd never speak about you so disrespectfully."

This had been a mistake. She couldn't have friends, not if it meant listening to them complain about their Alpha, who happened to be her true mate. She didn't need this kind of stress.

Liana put her hand on Betsy's. "Ruth is drunk. Don't mind her. I would never speak about Cyrus Fennell any way but with reverence. He is my Alpha, and I am so glad you are here to bring happiness to him."

"Thank you." Some of her urge to get up and stomp out left.

"Neither would I." Kyra smiled. "And I think in a few minutes it'll be time to get his quite intoxicated sister home to bed." Kyra stroked Lake's hair. "She's not usually this type of drinker." Lake stared off into space as though she'd missed the whole conversation. "Something has plagued her lately."

"Jensen knows you're here, and he lets you come anyway?" Betsy took another sip of her drink and winced. It was really too sweet for her. Maybe she wasn't meant to drink anything but water, milk, and coffee.

"He's outside in the car."

"What?" Ruth—whose name was obviously not Raquel—slammed down her drink. "He's outside? That spoils the whole point of not having a guard dog roaming around in here killing all the good times."

"Oh really?" Kyra's tone said she'd had enough of Ruth's crap. "Did his sitting out there every other time we've gone out spoil your fun? You went home with how many random humans? Did Jensen say a word? And if you call him a guard dog again, I'll rip out your eyes." Maybe female company was going to be really out of the question. Leaving the two of them to fight it out, she stared back at Liana. "How does it work if you're not true mates?"

"What do you mean?" Liana smiled.

"Well, you commit to each other, like a marriage, right? You have kids, form a family?" Liana nodded happily. "Exactly. We're hoping to start one the next time I go into heat."

"That's really wonderful. But I guess I'm confused because what will happen if you are in a committed relationship and then one of you finds your true mate? How will you handle that? Is there a system?"

The other woman's face fell. "Most of us will never find a true mate. If such a person exists for us, they are somewhere we'll never find them. With the exception of the Alphas, most of us will never leave our territory. Ever. It's not safe. And, as for me, if it happened, I would never leave my family under any circumstances. Besides, this is all so hypothetical. I can't believe the moon would ever be so cruel."

"In other words…" Lake slurred her words, apparently tuning back into the world around her. "They all hope really hard that it's not going to take place."

Something was going to have to be done about Lake. Betsy didn't know her mate's sister at all, except that she'd been really kind to her when Betsy had almost vomited in the basement. Afterward, Betsy had felt heaps better and had thanked her. Lake had seemed sweet, now just despondent. Of course, the woman had also turned Betsy from latent to full shifter without asking permission. Maybe she had a volatile personality.

She'd no sooner had that thought than her attention shifted. There was a change in the room. Something smelled wrong. Her nose twitched, and she tried to make sense of it. A group of men and women had entered. It smelled as though they'd bathed in perfume or cologne. Betsy gagged and, seconds later, so did several of the women at the table. Lake and Ruth didn't seem to notice. Maybe alcohol dulled their ability to scent things.

Betsy turned around to stare at the stinky people. Who walked around draped in so much fake scent that it was practically a noxious gas? The group of eight stared back at her table, which seemed kind of odd. To an outsider, her group was a pack of women talking loudly. She didn't know that much about bars, but surely their like could be found in about any drinking establishment any day or night of the week.

TV was filled with shows of women talking about inappropriate things while they sipped way-too-expensive cocktails. It was fashionable, and this was Manhattan, where fashion was king.

A feeling of dread filled her stomach. Something was wrong. "We need to get out of here." As a human, she'd ignored her instincts, but if she'd learned nothing in the last forty-eight hours it was that her instincts were far more accurate than she could have imagined. Her hands shook, and her heart raced. She wasn't a fighter, not really. It seemed pivotal to flee.

"I agree." Kyra jumped to her feet, tugging at Ruth, who was sluggish.

"What are you two fussing about?"

A woman with long white hair got up from the table, making Betsy nervous, and moved to the door. She closed it and stood in front with her hands on her hips. Now that really couldn't have been misinterpreted as anything but weird—if not downright threatening.

Kyra walked to the side of the table and took her hand. "Listen to me. I think we're in trouble here."

Lake stumbled to her feet. "What's going on?"

Kyra pushed on Lake's shoulder, pushing her back down in her chair. "Quiet."

Betsy spoke to Kyra, a bead of sweat traveling down from her neck to her back. "I agree.

These people—"

"Are here to do us harm. Yes." Kyra nodded. Betsy was glad Kyra was so calm because it kept her cooler than she'd otherwise be.

"What should we do?" Her hands shook, and she shoved them in her pockets.

"Well, we don't know how dangerous they are. They might be here to spit evil nonsense at us, or they might mean to attack us. In the meantime, I've sent Jensen a text. He'll get in here. I know he will. And I'm sure he's let the Alpha know we feel threatened." "Great. Cyrus can ban bars." Lake rolled her eyes.

"Would you shut up? We're here, we're in some kind of trouble, and we are responsible for the Alpha's mate. She's new to this. Nothing can happen to her. It will kill your brother.

Despite whatever is up your ass tonight, you would never want to harm him in any way."

"All right," the woman by the door called out loudly. "If you are a human, get out the front door. Now. This is your last chance to leave."

"If we're human?" a man screamed out from the back of the bar. "Funny joke, lady. Have another one."

She opened her jacket and pulled out a large silver

knife. Any doubt Betsy had about their intentions disappeared. Yep, these people were here to cause violent trouble.

The other seven people at the table rose, pulling out their own versions of the knife from their articles of clothing.

"Do we look like we're kidding? We're actually here to protect you from the scum that is here to destroy our lives. So, if you're human, get out now." She gestured her knife in their direction. "And don't try to fool me. We know who all of you are. You're not sneaking out, creatures."

"Where is Jensen?" She turned to Kyra. "Shouldn't he busting through the door?"

The hordes of humans in the bar rushed forward, and the knife-wielding woman let them out, the whole time glaring at the group of werewolves.

"I don't know. But we're not got going to sit here and let these knife-wielding psychos hurt us. Stay behind me."

As Kyra spoke, a strange sensation took over Betsy's brain. Her vision tunneled. All she could see was the woman with the knife. How dare she threaten them? How dare she put any members of her pack in danger?

No, she wasn't going to tolerate this anymore. She pulled out her shaking hands and stared at them. What she really needed was a weapon, and she had one. Or two, to be exact.

Betsy knew exactly what she had to do, and it was so damn simple. Even though she had never done it before, she had no doubt about how she could accomplish her task. All she had to do was will it.

Her hands shifted into hairy claws, which might have

disturbed her if they hadn't been so completely what she needed at that moment.

Kyra gasped, staring down at her. "How did you do that?"

"Can't you?" She shook her head. "We'll work it out later. I'm getting rid of her."

"No." Kyra held onto her. "Please don't do that. I can't let you get hurt.'

But she wanted to take care of this situation. She craved retribution for the threat.

Growls sounded around her. She didn't know which werewolves had made the noise, but she joined in on the sound. These humans should be cowering. They should be on their knees hoping they didn't get torn to bits.

Whether she wanted to fight or not, the option had been taken the moment the woman had issued her challenge. The knife-wielding humans rushed at them, and all Betsy saw was red.

"BETSY." Liana shook her, and she stared down at the other woman. There were screams deafening her, and blood dripped from her hands. What had happened? She sucked in her breath. She'd seen red, and then she had no idea what happened.

"Liana." She said the other woman's name as though it were a lifeline because, in that moment, it was.

"That's right. You've been in battle haze. It's normal." Liana shook her again gently. "Happens to all the new werewolves. But, listen to me, we have to get out of here."

"What happened? What did I do? Where is Kyra?"

Liana's face fell. "Let's not worry about that now. You were remarkable. I can't keep you safe here any longer."

Just then the door flew open, and a large group of werewolves pushed through the door howling. She briefly saw Jensen, Mitchell, and some of the others she had met briefly, but she had eyes only for the man who led the charge.

Her Alpha. Cyrus.

He rushed through the door, slamming into one of the humans holding a weapon. The man went down to the floor and was immediately picked by up by Mitchell, who twisted his neck into an unnatural position.

Cyrus was here. He was coming to her. She stared down at her claws. There was blood on them. *Whose blood is that? What has happened?*

Her gaze flew to the door where the gray-haired woman lay with her throat slit. Had she done that? Where was Kyra? Something was in the back of her mind, something she should know.

Cyrus' arms came around her, pulling her against him. "Are you okay? Betsy, are you okay? Look at me."

She forced her eyes upward. "My hands."

Betsy held up her hands to show him the claws. Cyrus took them in for a second. "Okay. It's rare. Not all of us can do that. I can't. I don't partially shift. I'm really glad, in this case, that you can. Are you okay? Shit, I've never been so afraid. When I heard—"

Behind her came a sound she'd never heard before and hoped she never would again. A howl of pure and total pain filled the air, and everyone in the room went silent.

Betsy twisted in Cyrus' arms. She had to see, had to know what could have caused such pain. It was a werewolf crying out. It had to be. But why?

Cyrus let go of her and moved toward the sound of the pain. She stared toward where he walked. Jensen was on his knees on the floor, his face a contorted version of his strong, tense features. Tears streamed down his face.

Only one thing could have done that to him. *Kyra. No.* The woman had been with her when it had all gone red. Was this her fault? She had no memory, no idea of what happened. *No. No. No.* This couldn't be happening.

She rushed to Cyrus' side. Kyra lay in Jensen's lap, her eyes open and staring lifeless at the ceiling. Jensen rocked her back and forth, howling at the ceiling, and next to him, Lake wept openly.

"I'm so sorry. I couldn't help." Lake covered her face with her hands. "I'm so sorry. It's not working."

It was the alcohol. Lake hadn't been able to smell the perfume. She'd been out of it. None of them should have been drinking like they had, and Betsy couldn't consider herself blameless. She'd known something was wrong. How could this be happening? Kyra had been talking about true mating, and now she was dead. Betsy couldn't even remember how it had happened.

They were supposed to be going to the movies. She was supposed to be making friends.

"I'm so sorry, baby." Jensen put his head down on his dead mate's body. "I couldn't get through the door. There were too many of them outside. I'm so sorry. Take me with you. Don't leave me here to do this alone. Don't go, Kyra. Please, Lake, I'll do anything you ask for. Bring her back. Anything you want."

Cyrus squatted down next to Jensen. Her mate had yet to utter a word. Jensen was covered in blood and not all of it was Kyra's. How long had the werewolf fought on the street? *Oh no.* They'd been on the street.

"Cyrus." She could barely think, barely speak. "We have to go. The humans. I hear sirens."

"They're being kept back." He didn't look at her, his

eyes on Jensen. "We have procedures, but they won't work forever."

Jensen's voice hitched. "Cyrus, we can't do this. We can't let Kyra die here, my Alpha.

Not like this. Not by the hands of the true believers. Not when it's my fault for not getting in."

"It's not your fault." The voice behind her startled her, and she whirled around. When had Alexei gotten here? Had he been with them the whole time? Like the other males in the room, he was covered in blood that wasn't his. "The question is, what are you going to do about it, Cyrus?"

"War." Finally, Cyrus raised his head finally and stared straight at Alexei. "I'm going to war, and God help anyone who gets in my way."

Her mate threw his arms around Jensen. The strong warrior sobbed, large heaving gasps into his Alpha's arms. A howl started somewhere, and it wasn't from Jensen. She had no idea who had begun it, but before she could question it, they were all howling, even her. They'd lost someone tonight, a woman she hadn't known long but had connected to, had belonged with even for the short time they'd been together.

This was goodbye. It was only fitting.

Someone had to tell her what she'd done.

Chapter 13

There were five true believers still alive. They'd all been part of the group that attacked Jensen, and then the rest, on the street. None of them inside the bar had taken a breath again. Cyrus stared at them in the darkness. He wasn't certain all of them would make it to morning. Some of them would bleed out before the new day. There wasn't a thing Cyrus was willing to do for them. They had done what no one should have been able to do, what had never happened since he'd taken over as Alpha. The humans he held captive had hurt his pack in such a way that it might never recover.

Jensen would never be the same. Cyrus couldn't imagine how the other man would even get through the night. Cyrus had known Betsy for only two days, but if anything happened to her, he'd stop breathing. Life would be over. Jensen had lived ten years with Kyra. How could he face even a day without her?

Cyrus shook his head. Jensen had children. He'd find a way. The warrior werewolf would never leave them to suffer without both parents. Cyrus would see the kids at the

160

goodbye ceremony. He would forever be in their memory as the werewolf who sent their mother back to the moon. Shepherd would forever live in his own memory that way.

"Two of them are goners for sure." Alexei leaned against the wall next to him. "I know Lake is out of commission for the night. Do you want me to get my Healer here? I could put her on the plane and have her here in no time."

"No. Thank you." Cyrus didn't care if they all dropped dead.

Nathan, who rocked back and forth in his cage, mumbling to himself, was all the collateral he needed at this point. "You're going to have to keep feeding Nathan for me a few more days. Restrain yourself from killing him for a bit longer."

The trip to Montana would have to be delayed until after they laid Kyra to rest. Then they would go.

"I will, of course." Alexei nodded. "Because he is involved in whatever is going on with Betsy's parents that you won't be more detailed about."

"Exactly."

His negotiations with Alexei had gone well and had ended with a blood oath of nonaggression minutes before the call had come in about the problem with the women. He hadn't asked the other man to come help them, but the other Alpha had fought beside him as if it were the most natural thing to do so.

"Are you okay?" He turned to Alexei. "Hurt?"

"I'm fine."

"Good. Then I'm going to go home."

"These moments… when there's nothing more to do for anyone, but it feels like there should be something… they're the most frustrating because of how ineffectual it makes us." Alexei yawned. "If anyone really knew what it was to be an Alpha before they took on the challenge, no one would do it."

Cyrus didn't want to talk to about his feelings, not with Alexei. He wouldn't attack the other man's territory, and his people would be safe from Alexei's pack. That was enough. Nathan had been given as part of the deal. That was enough.

With a nod, he left the room. All the problems in his basement would still be there in the morning. Or they'd be dead. Either way, he needed to go home to his mate. His human legs wouldn't move fast enough.

HE PASSED several of his wolves on the way in. Cyrus hadn't asked them to guard his mate, but it was nice to see they'd all done it anyway. He nodded to each of them, letting them know that they could leave. There was nothing more to say, no comforting words, nothing he could ever say to make tonight okay.

Shepherd would have given them platitudes. He'd been full of them when he and Lake had been orphaned. *Greater good. War. The life of a werewolf.* Screw all those meaningless nothings spoken to make the speaker feel better, not the person enduring the pain. Cyrus wouldn't do that to any of them.

This was awful. They'd know he felt it too.

Finally, at his door, he saw Mitchell. He stared at the other wolf for a second before speaking. He never saw Mitchell without Jensen. They'd been the closest of friends before Jensen's mating, and nothing had changed afterward.

"What are you doing here?" Mitchell should be with

Jensen, not standing at his doorway. There were others to fulfill that duty tonight.

"I failed Kyra." Mitchell's voice sounded hoarse. "I won't have your mate hurt. Not while I can be here to guard her."

"We all failed Kyra." Cyrus had to look away for a second, lest he give in to the urge to start howling in the hallway. "I'd never seen such a lineup of armed humans waiting for a fight. They knew we would come. They waited for us."

"Maybe if Jensen hadn't been alone when it started…" Mitchell fisted his hands.

"Maybe if I had stopped the bar outings when he first told me about them." It had seemed relatively harmless. Jensen had always watched them. Cyrus had believed that as long as he kept the pregnant females out of view, then the rest of them would be safe. Kyra was dead because of his arrogance.

"You couldn't have known."

"I appreciate the words, Mitchell." But they didn't absolve him. Ultimately, the responsibility fell to him. They all belonged to him, and it was his gift to be able to lead them, protect them. "This was the world I grew up in. So did you, although you were a baby. Maybe you don't remember it."

Outside a car honked, reminding him of the real world that would too soon make this day nothing more than a memory.

"I remember the drills. I remember my parents were afraid. They're not anymore. Not since you." Mitchell's words struck Cyrus hard. The fact that he stayed upright was a miracle unto itself. All this time and it turned out that all he had been was lucky. None of the things he'd arranged had made the slightest difference. When the humans wanted to attack them, they'd been perfectly able to accomplish their task.

"I would keep you all safe if I could. If working at it day and night could accomplish true safety, that is what I would do."

Mitchell nodded. "The blame for tonight does not fall to you."

"It does. As it should." Cyrus shook his head. "We'll bury Kyra tomorrow, and then I have to leave for Montana."

"What time should we be ready to leave?" Mitchell's jaw was tight, and Cyrus could feel the aggression radiating from the other man's body. He couldn't blame him. Cyrus also craved a fight.

"You're not coming with me."

Mitchell's eyes widened. "Sir? Have I done something to make you lose trust in me?"

"Just the opposite, actually. I have to leave New York and go to Montana. We're not at war with Philadelphia or Boston. I've made arrangements that should secure that peace. . But I need someone to hold Manhattan in my stead. I've never chosen a second-in-command. It never seemed necessary. Now it's clear to me that too much time has passed and that I've been remiss in not selecting one of you. Mitchell, would you be second? Would you hold Manhattan until I return and, if I don't come back, will you lead the pack? Keep it strong and safe?"

Mitchell fell to his knees, his head facing the floor. "Sir, I don't deserve such an honor."

"You do." Cyrus shifted his weight. A "yes, sir, I'll take the job" would have sufficed. These traditions were old and long-standing. Maybe he shouldn't have been surprised by the reaction. "Stand up and take it if it's what you want."

Mitchell stood up. "It would be an honor. I won't fail you. We'll find this threat, and we'll destroy it."

"We will." Because Cyrus would die before he ever let this happen again. His mate would be safe in Manhattan for the rest of her days. His people would know peace again. He'd work to make that happen until he drew his very last breath.

———

BETSY WAS asleep on the couch. She'd left the shades open in the living room, and the lights from the street illuminated her resting figure in colored shadows that made her look, for a moment, unreal, as though she might disappear into the darkness of the colorful display from outside if he blinked.

He took a deep breath, drawing in her scent, which confirmed to him that she was real. Cyrus walked closer, and she didn't stir. Her mouth was slightly open, her tongue pressed against her teeth. He wished he could have been here to hold her while she cried, the scent of her distress still evident in the room. Her hair was knotted and wet. She must have showered before she changed her clothes. He'd have the bloody ones burned so she never had to look at them and remember.

Cyrus' gaze fell to her hands. They were still shifted into semi-wolf form. It was so amazing she could do that. He couldn't. Cyrus either shifted or he didn't, and as an Alpha, he could manage to shift when it wasn't a full moon, but most of the pack would never even be able to manage that. The ability to change at will showed the strength to be an Alpha. It was a rather big sign of a pup's future.

Betsy had managed to half-shift her hands, but she was obviously not able to get shift them back. He placed his fingers on top of hers and stared at them for a second.

Turn back.

Betsy's hands glimmered before they shifted back to their human form. He smiled at the sight. Cyrus would never be able to do all the things he needed to do, but that, at least, he could manage.

She stirred, her lids fluttering open. "Hi."

"Hello there." He smoothed his hand over her forehead. She felt warm from sleep. In a kind world, he'd get to pick her up, carry her to the bed, and snuggle in for the rest of the night. But they had things to talk about before then, and he wasn't sure he could sleep anyway. Truth was he might never rest easy again.

"I wanted to wait up for you, but I guess I crashed."

"Perfectly normal after the adrenaline surge."

She sat up, and he moved until he could position himself right next to her. Sleep might be out of the question, but he needed her presence. She wasn't the only one who needed to come down from the stress of the night. His blood still boiled too hot.

"Cyrus, that's the problem." She rubbed her forehead. "I can't remember any of it. Something happened. Kyra is dead. Did I do that?"

"What? No, you didn't." How could she even think that?

"One second she was telling me I couldn't fight, that she would protect me, and the next thing I remember, Liana was shaking me. There was blood all over me, and Kyra was dead." "Not from your hand." Cyrus wished he had known she been worried about this earlier. He could have reassured her before he sent her home. "Kyra died from a gut wound delivered to her by a sharp knife. From what you're telling me, she was probably protecting you if she made you stay behind her."

He'd always admired Kyra, but now she would forever hold a place of honor in his memory. The woman had gone down protecting his mate. That kind of sacrifice could never be paid back.

"But I don't know what I did. I must have done something. My hands—claws—were covered in blood." She sounded so forlorn that he pulled her onto his lap.

"Betsy, princess, you killed the woman who stabbed her. That's what you did. That's what Liana told me. And then you were lost to the haze, and, thank goodness, she brought you back from it. Most of the time, we don't suffer the haze when we're wearing our human skin. That's a new werewolf problem. Teenagers suffer for years. But you're rapidly catching up, and maybe because of your ability to shift part of your body, it triggered the response."

"I killed the woman who killed Kyra." She said the words into his shirt, and he stroked her back.

"How do you feel about that?" He knew how he felt—tremendous relief and pride. But Betsy still needed to adjust to all of this. Humans took the repercussions of killing very seriously. They didn't see the necessity of it the way werewolves did. The woman had killed Kyra. Of course, she'd had to die.

"Good." She sniffed, pulling back. "Right. Justified. Glad I did it even if I can't remember it. Cyrus, does that make me a sociopath?"

"No." He put his hands on the sides of her head. "It makes you one of us. You protected my people tonight. Thank you, Betsy, thank you. I'm sorry this happened to you. It never should have."

"They're mine too. Or at least they feel that way. Like I know them, even though I don't."

"That's pack. They are yours. We all belong to each other." He kissed the end of her nose. "But when I got the call, all I could think about was you. Getting to you. We were trapped outside. Humans everywhere. I've never seen them so organized in their attacks on us."

"I knew you would come, and then when I saw you, Cyrus, all I could feel was relief. You were there. You were okay. We were all going to be okay. But it wasn't." The catch in her voice tore at his heart. "Kyra was dead. Lake couldn't save her, I guess. I don't remember."

"My sister's abilities were not on track. Alcohol does that to us. I should have forbidden it, I knew what was going on, but I didn't think it was a problem. We were safe. I really believed that. I'm such a fool."

"No." She placed her hands on his chest. "You're not. Something is happening, escalating. I don't know what it is. But me, Lilliana, my parents, these crazy psychos coming after us, it's all related. You couldn't have known this would happen. You can't predict the future any more than I can."

If only he could believe her words. But she forgave him for too much. He'd wanted the young females happier. Lake was so dissatisfied with her life. Ruth always seemed pissed. He could go through the list. Letting them go blow off some steam had seemed a good option. So he'd pretended not to know, hadn't interfered more than making sure Jensen went every time, and now a worst-case scenario, the kind that haunted his dreams, had happened He'd gotten weak. It couldn't happen again. "Cyrus, look at me." He raised his eyes.

"This isn't on you. You're in charge, but as with any person in a position of power, sometimes bad things happen, and sometimes things we can't possibly control take place. Cars crash. Boats sink. People disappear. Crazy, knife-wielding werewolf haters come into bars…"

He nuzzled into her neck and closed his eyes. Being pressed up against her had lowered his heart rate. "I have to perform Kyra's goodbye ceremony tomorrow. We try to not let more than one night pass between death and the speaking of the words. We'll go to Montana afterward."

"What happens at the funeral?" She closed her eyes, and he could feel the exhaustion pouring out of her scent. The vanilla odor he loved so much had ebbed to a dull scent.

"I give her back to the moon." And he felt like a complete fraud doing it, considering he thought the whole thing bullshit.

"That's nice. I like the idea of you doing that. There's no one better suited for it than you."

In that way, Betsy had completely misunderstood him. But, then again, he'd let her, having told her the whole Lily and the three werewolves fairy tale as if it were something he bought into. There was no reason to change undo her belief. Like the rest of the pack, she could think he believed if it kept them all feeling better. Travis believed. Alexei probably did too. Lucian had.

There was something wrong with him that he couldn't believe himself.

"Come on." He picked her up in his arms. His mate needed to rest, and he had to figure out how to burn off the energy that wouldn't leave him before the moon ceremony.

Cyrus placed her gently on the bed, and she opened her lids to stare up at him. She extended her arms. "Come on."

"I don't think I can lie down yet. I promise to try not to conk out on my desk, but I can't lie down and rest."

She shook her head. "Who said anything about resting?"

Her words sank in, and his cock took note, jerking in his pants. "You can't possibly have the energy."

"Not for what we did last night, no. But a quick, sweet coupling with you? That I can do. Anytime. And I want you now. I need you. Please. Make me feel alive. Make this day go away. Let me do the same for you."

He walked to the bed and then pushed her down beneath him as he kissed her lips. She tasted sweet, tempting, and completely alive. Betsy kissed him back with total abandon, a soft moan releasing from her throat.

Cyrus stroked down her body, starting with her neck and moving downward. She squirmed beneath him. She'd said she wanted quick, but he didn't want to be ridiculous about it. Every time he looked at her, he got hard. It would be no problem to push inside of her and drive away the day in her willing arms. But, first, Betsy had to come.

They fumbled and tugged at each other's clothes. Eventually they were all discarded. He stared down at her. She was so small beneath him, so delicate, and yet he knew now that she was also made of steel. Betsy possessed a shifting power not one in a million wolves could do. Untrained, and still not having gone through her first full moon, she had killed a woman who threatened them. His mate was…breathtaking. And beautiful.

"You're looking at me like you've never seen me before."

"Every time I see you, it's like the first time, like I have new eyes. Does that sound corny?" He shook his head. "I'm sorry. I don't mean to be so…whatever this is."

Her eyes were serious when she spoke. "Cyrus, when you came into the bar, and I was coming out of the haze, all I could think was, oh, there he is. My heart melted. I've known you two days, but I am in love with you. How can that be? How can I feel like I know you when I don't know basic things like your favorite color or what you like to eat on Sunday mornings?"

He took her nipple into his mouth, sucking on it. She gasped, and he smiled, loving the sound of her responses. "I like black. I know it's a shade not a color, but it is what I like. And I don't know what I like to eat on Sunday mornings. I'm usually sitting in the office. Coffee?"

She dug her fingers into his back, drawing him closer. "That changes, okay? No work on Sundays."

"Okay." He kissed her on the mouth again, letting his hand travel down to her pussy. He stroked her sex, pushing one finger and then two inside of her.

"I mean it." She bit down on his shoulder, and his cock hardened to the point of pain. *Yes.* She could do that anytime she wanted. Maybe that's what it was like for her when he bit down. If he'd been less in control, he would have come right there.

"Yes. I'll stay home on Sundays." He kissed her again, positioning his penis by her entry. Since her little bite, there was no time to waste. If he didn't get inside of her, he wasn't going to make it there.

Cyrus pushed inside of her, feeling the welcoming heat and pulses from her muscles. She fit him like a glove, and he groaned out his appreciation. Betsy raised her hips, and he pushed deeper.

"Yes, more like that, darling, please." He loved the darling.

Picking up the pace, he pushed and withdrew until they were both in a frenzy. His mouth hurt, and it took him a second to realize his canines had descended again. What the hell? He shouldn't have to mark her again so soon. She wrapped her legs tighter around his waist and knew he was lost.

All sense fled him, and as he pushed both of them over the edge with a grind against her clit, he bit down on her shoulder, marking her in the same spot again. Betsy writhed beneath him, calling out his name again and again as his cock filled her with his seed. Finally, when he could breathe, he let go of her shoulder, licking the spot again. At this rate, her skin would never heal, and he felt fine with that idea. Always his, always marked.

"Betsy," he whispered in her ear. Her eyes were closed, but she smiled.

"Yes?"

"I love you."

He lay down and rolled her against his side. She yawned, snuggling deeper. "It's red." "What?" He hadn't followed what she said. Was she talking in her sleep?

"My favorite color. Just so you know. And I like pancakes with maple syrup." He was going to be sure to get some in the house.

Chapter 14

Betsy sat in her seat listening to Cyrus talk about the moon, about the earth, about being part of things. Several of her pack mates wept, and one woman had actually gotten up and left. Betsy could feel their misery as if were own, and it pressed down on her shoulders like a mountain had formed on top of them.

But she knew her burden to be nothing compared to her mate's. Cyrus had stayed home from work, and although she hadn't known him long, she knew enough to understand how odd that happened to be. He'd slept well into the morning, and, although he'd answered questions if she spoke to him, he'd all but shut her out otherwise, their closeness from the night before long gone.

They were all gathered on the roof of the office building. A hush had descended on the place when Travis, Lilliana, and Alexei had arrived for the ceremony. Travis and Alexei had left guards at the entrance of the building so all of Cyrus' people could attend. Betsy took in the gathering. She hadn't even known there were so many wolves in Cyrus' pack. Somewhere around five hundred, she would guess. Some women clutched babies, and old couples held each other's hands.

All of them had stared at her when she'd entered in on Cyrus' arm. Betsy didn't want to imagine what they were thinking about her. Who was the woman who had stolen away their Alpha? Why hadn't she been able to help Kyra? What use was a woman mated to an Alpha if she was so clueless in what to do for all of them?

Betsy sighed and forced her attention back to Cyrus. He stood silently in front of them. It must have been unusual because whispers started behind her. The wolf pack didn't know why their Alpha had failed to finish the ceremony.

"Can everybody hear me?" Cyrus raised his voice, and the whispering hushed. His eyes met hers, and she nearly jolted off the seat. Her mate was in pain, and it dug into her soul. This went beyond the sadness of the rest of the group.

"Good." He stared out the group, and after a moment, the pain she'd glimpsed vanished as if it had never been there. Her love was certainly proficient at hiding his feelings. "If, at any point, you can't hear me, please raise your hand."

He took a beat before he spoke again, and she wondered if he considered his words. This couldn't be standard to the ceremony, which, up until this point, had felt pretty rote.

"I realize it isn't traditional to do this during a moon ceremony. Please know it is only out of respect for Kyra that I speak this way. She was not only an amazing pack member, mate, and mother, but I have recently learned that she gave her life to save my mate."

Betsy stared down at the ground. That was right. Kyra would never draw breath again because she had saved

Betsy. How was she going to live with this for the rest of her days? Was there even a way to make it right?

"I can't seem to stop my eyes from going to Jensen and his children." Kyra and Jensen had two children, both girls with their mother's light brown hair. They sat on either side of their father, the older one looking stoic and the younger periodically breaking down into tears. "And I remember when Lake and I were children and how we sat through a ceremony like this one for our parents."

Lake was missing. It hadn't dawned on her that the Healer wasn't there, but now that she looked, it was very clear the other woman wasn't present. Betsy leaned back in her seat. Something was going to have to be done about that girl. If only she knew her better.

"I remember watching the Alpha, Shepherd, talk about my parents and feeling like didn't really know them. No one could have understood them like we did, and even now I'm not sure I really did grasp who they were. I was a child or, rather, a teenager, which may have been worse, and there is a certain kind of blindness in that."

Some murmurs of agreement crossed the pack. Betsy still wasn't sure what Cyrus was doing. She concentrated on trying to keep a calm look on her face. Everyone would be able to smell her nerves, but maybe she'd get credit for trying.

"Anyway, what I wanted from Shepherd was something he never delivered. Something I'm going to make sure your children get, Jensen." Cyrus nodded, and she wondered if he was there in the moment with them or if he'd travelled with his memory back to the time he'd sat at his own parents' moon ceremony. "I'm going to get you retribution. It won't bring back Kyra. But I can promise you that we will taste their blood. They will know pain."

A roar sounded, and she turned around to look at who

had made the noise. Was this standard for a funeral? Shouldn't they all be crying and patting each other on the back? Why was everyone applauding? Her mouth watered at his words. She'd like to see retribution, and Cyrus' words filled her with a warmth that had been missing for most the day.

"I can promise you their deaths. Or the end of my life trying."

Her heart may have stopped beating for a second before it picked up in a rapid one-two punch that left her feeling as though he'd taken his foot and kicked her hard. *His own life.* Cyrus seemed so casual with his disregard for his own existence. She squirmed in her seat, wishing to be anywhere else. Somewhere she could catch her breath. Why was this throwing her so completely off balance?

Cyrus had killed the Alpha to become the Alpha. That was the way things worked. He'd been in wars. Someday some young werewolf was going to come and want to replace him as Alpha. They'd challenge him, and there would be a fight. Maybe Cyrus would die. Betsy shoved her head between her knees. If she wasn't careful, she was going to hyperventilate.

"Are you okay?" Liana whispered in her ear.

"No." She sat back up. "I think I'm having a hard time with some of the truths of our lives."

"The dying part." Liana nodded. "I know. Sometimes hearing them speak about it makes me really hot, and sometimes it makes me really scared." She shook her head. "I think it's one of those ways male werewolves are different. They're almost eager to run off and die in a battle to prove something. It makes them fierce protectors and fine men. But it makes them reckless as hell. Maybe this isn't a really good time to ask, but are there real differences between men and women who are human? I think there must be. I watch this television show called *Sex and the City*…"

Liana continued, but Betsy ceased listening. Was Cyrus really okay with running off and dying? Leaving her alone while he had his name inscribed in some kind of book for the glorious dead? *No.* That couldn't be. None of this would work without him. Being a werewolf could be okay because it also meant being his mate, but she didn't want to be a werewolf if Cyrus didn't live in the world.

She smiled at Liana stood up and left, even though Cyrus still spoke. She couldn't take any more. Hopefully, the other woman would forgive her and think she was spacey, but she needed to get some perspective, and that wasn't going to happen on the roof while everyone applauded the idea of Cyrus potentially getting himself killed.

Of course, wishing she wasn't a werewolf was probably akin to wishing she'd been born with brown hair instead of blonde. There wasn't anything she could do about her genetics, and no one sold beauty products to make her less moon-dependent or non-furry. She walked down the staircase back into the office building. The cool air of the air conditioning hit her skin, cooling her, and she suddenly realized she'd been sweating.

How had she not noticed? Betsy slowed down and pushed her head up against the wall. The hallway spun, and if she kept moving, all she was going to do was collapse. How had the reality of Cyrus' existence not dawned on her before now?

She'd gone and fallen head over heels in love with a man—her mate—who had a job, no, a *role* in life, where the very nature of his position meant that people would want to kill him. If someone else wanted to be Alpha of

Manhattan, all they had to do was challenge Cyrus to a fight and win.

Her mate had gotten the job at twenty years of age by killing Shepherd. If some young kid got a good swipe in, her whole life would shatter.

"Betsy." Cyrus' voice moved over her, and she lifted her head from the wall as he placed his hand on her back. She hadn't scented him, which showed how floored her revelation had left her.

"What's the matter, princess?" His voice soothed her nerves like a cold balm on a heat rash. He was alive right now. That had to count for something.

"Sorry. I guess I'm having a breakdown. Finally. I hope I didn't spoil the ceremony. I suddenly had to get out of there."

He pulled her against him. "It finished. All is well."

She fit her head on his shoulder and breathed in his scent. "Good. I would have hated to have spoiled it."

"What caused this response?" He kissed the side of her chin. She loved the warm feel of his breath as it brushed against her skin. They were totally exposed in a hallway, but she felt as though they were alone in the universe. "I know I haven't been communicating a lot today. I had to consider things."

"Right." She pulled back, his words shattering the illusion of the quiet moment. "The decision to announce you would taste her killer's blood or you would die trying. That decision."

"Which part bothers you?" He crossed his arms on his chest. When he continued, it was not with gentle tones. "The eating, the blood, or the dying?"

"The dying, my Alpha." If he was going to yell at her, then she'd speak to him as the others did and see how he liked it. "The sacrificing your life. And also—because I'm truly an idiot for not realizing it earlier—the fact that you could die any full moon if someone decided they wanted your job. One good lunge and you're dead on the ground. It freaked me out."

He shook his head. "I'm going to assume you said that because you are ignorant of my strength and fighting skills and not because you are doubting my ability to hold this pack, protect you, and defend myself from usurpers?"

"Assume whatever the hell you want." She turned on her heel and stormed towards the stairs and then down them. He could get pissy by himself. She'd heard too many proclamations of death and destruction from him to fill a lifetime, and she couldn't listen to any more. She had to deal with him on the airplane. Until then, she needed to think. Just a little distance to...

She heard Cyrus a bare second before he yanked her against him. "You don't get to say that to me and walk away, mate." He must have charged down the stairs to get to her so fast.

"You know if you run, I chase."

"Okay." She shoved at his chest. "Then I won't run, my Alpha. I'll tell you exactly what I'm thinking since you seem disinclined to give me any space."

"Stop calling me that. I don't want that from you. There's no such thing as space between us, Betsy."

"Oh really? Seemed there was lots of it today while you worked things out in your head when you didn't share your plan with me what you decided to proclaim to the pack. So, is it only me who never gets any alone-time, but you can take it whenever you want to?"

"I am the Alpha of this pack. I don't discuss my decisions with anyone."

"So then I'm your mate, Cyrus, when it's convenient, but the other times I can go screw myself. Is that it?"

"That kind of language is beneath you, princess. I don't like it."

She threw her hands up. Why was he focused on small details when he should be listening to what she said? "Are you paying attention to me? I'm angry with you." She clearly had to spell this out for him as though he was a child. "You decided to risk your own life—to announce your intention to do so to the whole pack—without even informing me that you meant to do so first. And it has made me angry with you."

"Your temper shows how human you still remain." He shook his head. "I'm the Alpha of this pack. I don't discuss pack business with anyone if I don't want to. Things that relate to us, I'll be happy to bring to your attention, but this is me as the Alpha. I don't talk to you about it. Ever."

She felt as though he had smacked her over the head. "I see."

"No, I don't think you do. I have to live many lives, and one of them now is being your mate. I don't think it'll come as a surprise to you to hear me say that it's my favorite part, the best moments of every day, and some- times being with you is going to mix with the rest of my life, my role as Alpha of this pack." He took a deep breath, fatigue radiating from his pores. His scent smelled acidic. Why had she brought this up now?

Her temper had always been an unpredictable entity in her life. One second she'd be angry, the next she wasn't. His scent had defused her. Not that she wasn't correct, but they clearly couldn't have this discussion while he was so exhausted.

"Fine. I understand. I won't push this, for now. But

you're too smart to believe that a mate can be sidelined like that. You need me, and you know it."

He sucked in his breath, and she turned around but then thought better of it. If she ran, he would chase, and she wasn't in the mood for where that would end. They'd be right back in this situation. She closed her eyes. Her father had sometimes gotten really unreasonable with her mother. What had the woman who raised her done? She'd cooked him something, calmed him down, and then tried again. Sure enough, he'd ended up giving her what she'd wanted.

Betsy opened her eyes to regard Cyrus. "Sweetheart, I don't really want to have to start managing you to make you be reasonable. Why are you acting so obstinate? Are you feeling guilty about something?"

He opened and closed his mouth, still not saying anything. Wow. Her simple question had silenced him. Finally, he spoke. "I guess. I'm feeling guilty, as you put it, that Kyra is dead, that I let the bar outings happen."

"Right." She nodded. "Those are all huge factors, I'm sure, but I'm asking you if you are feeling guilty in relation to me, outside of Kyra. Is something else making you feel that way, which is why you are acting like such a goat? What is it? Let's talk about that instead of going around in circles and you saying things I don't believe you actually mean."

Cyrus growled, and she sighed. He was going to exasperate her before they ever got to the airplane. "You can growl and fuss if it helps. I don't mind."

"You were screaming at me a minute ago."

She nodded. "And now I have my temper under control." "Just like that?"

And now he was going to focus on how and when she got angry? "This time. I can't promise to always be able to do so, but tonight I can. Count yourself lucky. You've had a hard day. I don't want to be the crazy mate who screams at you when you're down." "Shit."

"Now who's using inappropriate language?" She wasn't going to yell, but it didn't mean she would forget everything he'd spewed at her.

"All right, I apologize. Yes, I'm feeling guilty."

She shook her head. Weren't women supposed to be complicated to deal with emotionally? Betsy needed a roadmap to navigate Cyrus. "About what?"

"Because you're right, and I don't like it."

She stopped for a beat and bit her tongue. Her first instinct had been to snap at him. What did he mean he didn't like it? Why would it bother him that she should be right? But she tried to breathe through that response. He'd told her she was right. Rather than make things worse, maybe she could try to figure out how to make them better.

"I'm right?"

"Yes. You are. I'm wrong, and you're right. Happy?"

This was the strangest apology she'd ever heard. Forget a roadmap, she needed a GPS to find her mate in this strange, raving lunatic who had taken over his body.

"No, not particularly."

"Why not? I've told you that I did the wrong thing by not telling you what I meant to say to the pack. I contemplated it, but I knew what you'd say—that I shouldn't make them that promise—because I know what I would have told you if our situations were reversed. I'd tell you no way in hell should you be promising your life to anyone but me. That being said, this is my role. I can't be Alpha if I'm unwilling to throw myself in one hundred percent. They deserve nothing less from their leader."

A bead of sweat had broken out on his forehead, and

she wiped it away. "And that's why you consciously decided not to speak to me most of the day and not tell me you were doing this."

He swallowed, his Adam's apple bobbing up and down. "Correct."

"That's pretty much akin to lying to me." She wasn't going to automatically let him off the hook, even if he seemed kind of sad standing in front of her confessing his sins.

"I suppose if you want to look at it that way." He stalked over to the side of the stairwell and stared outside.

"How else should I look at it?"

"That I'm the Alpha of Manhattan and I'm not used to explaining myself. I don't know how to do things differently, and I handled it badly. I apologize."

She walked over and put her arms around his waist, leaning into his back. "I grew up on a ranch in the middle of nowhere, just me and my folks. You had all this family around you all the time. How do you not know how to communicate better?"

He snorted. "Betsy, everyone has done what I wanted since I was twenty years old."

"Then you're overdue to have a mate who doesn't always feel inclined to obey your every order." She really wanted him to understand what she said to him. "Particularly when it comes down to your safety. You belong to me, and I know you belong to all of them too. But you belong to me differently, and I'm going to cherish you whether you want me to or not." "I want you to." He kissed her forehead.

"And you will eventually figure out you actually want to share with me." Maybe if she put that out there to the universe it would happen. Maybe the moon would listen. "I'm not used to it."

She nodded. "I know. And you realize this puts to an end your whole speech about not lying, about always telling the truth."

"Betsy, it's not exactly the same thing."

She shook her head. "How am I going to know when you're holding back? When you're not telling me things you should?"

He let out a long breath. "Okay, I promise to not keep things to myself that you should hear. I promise it. I swear my oath by it."

"Okay." She nodded. "That's good enough for me." She smiled at him, but when he didn't return one, she had to ask him again. "What's wrong, Cyrus?"

"No one is going to kill me, Betsy. No one is going to beat me in a fight or take

Manhattan from me. I've never been bested, and I never will."

"Oh no?" She raised an eyebrow. Male egos were clearly all the same regardless of whether they belonged to humans or werewolves. "When you're one hundred and ten years old, you don't believe that it's possible someone could come and beat you in a fight? It must be possible, Cyrus. Look what happened to Lucian."

He sucked in his breath, and she knew bringing up Lucian had been a low blow. But it was a fair point, nonetheless. He worshiped the man, whether he should or not. How could he forget that someone had murdered the Alpha Prime? If that were possible, it would certainly be possible for a strong, would-be Alpha wolf to show up and take Manhattan from him. "I'll step down at one hundred." He nodded, as though he appreciated his own idea. "That'll work. At one hundred, I won't do this anymore."

"Is that possible? Have you ever heard of an Alpha stepping down before?"

He shrugged. "New precedent. It's not like we all belong to some organization that can tell us what to do. There's no Alpha Prime to oversee us. If I want to step down, I'll step down." His words should have warmed her, but they didn't. Nothing in her life had ever been simple. Even her parents had lied to her every day of her existence. It wouldn't be as simple as Cyrus stepping down at one hundred years of age. Someone would want his head before then. One of her jobs, it seemed, would be to see that no one got it.

"Will we retire to Florida at that point?" She squeezed his fingers. "Become snow wolves?"

If he noted that she covered up her distress in humor, he didn't remark. Instead, his mouth came down on hers, and she forgot to think. Cyrus had a way of doing that to her.

Chapter 15

With Betsy conked out on his lap, Cyrus stared at his sister across the aisle of his plane.

This trip to Montana was going to make his accountant nuts. They would bill it to the company. The fact that his accountant was a thirty-year-old member of his pack helped things. He shook his head. This was technically pack business, thus also company business. Even if it was sometimes complicated to make the federal government see it that way.

His sister wasn't really sleeping, but she was certainly pretending she was. Her scent, always citrusy, told him she remained wide-awake. But she'd closed her eyes during takeoff and hadn't opened them since. He sighed and ran his hands through Betsy's hair. His mate, by contrast, slept solidly. Cyrus would do anything to scoop her up and take her somewhere they could have privacy. Their romp in his office earlier after their fight hadn't satisfied him. Maybe nothing ever would.

Cyrus drummed his fingers on the armrest and studied the plane. He'd take eighteen werewolves with him.

Twenty, total, including he and Betsy. Almost everyone slept, although a few lights shone, indicating a few others were as awake as he.

Something had to be done about Lake. She'd been off before Kyra's death, she'd not shown up at the moon ceremony, and now she pretended to sleep instead of talking to him.

He kicked her seat, and she jumped, her eyes widening as she looked him. "Yes, my Alpha?"

He heard the proper amount of respect in the term. If she'd said it sarcastically, as she sometimes did, he might have woken the whole plane with the way he would have hollered at her. Instead, he regarded her silently for a second before answering.

Lake had been a very happy child, even remaining that way after the death of their parents. When had she lost her *joie de vivre*? Had he not been paying attention? Empire building had taken up his time for a long while.

"Tell me what's going on with you."

She shifted in her seat. "I'm not having a very good day. I lost a pack member, and it's entirely my fault. What did you think was going on with me?"

"Well…" He took a deep breath and sought the kind of patience Betsy had shown when dealing with him earlier. "For one, I think you're lying to me, or, at the very least, you're avoiding the question. That's okay, little sister. I tried something like that earlier today. My mate wouldn't let me get away with it, and I'm going to do you the same courtesy. I'll try again. What is happening with you?"

His sister dug her fingers into her palm. He watched the brief act before she spoke again.

"Listen, we have more important things to be doing now."

"I don't. I have hours ahead of me before I can act. So

talk to me. We'll never have a better opportunity than this."

She looked all around, her dark hair flinging over her shoulder. Once, when she'd been twelve, she'd chopped it all off and spent the whole summer acting like she loved the boy cut she'd given herself. He'd known she hated it. He had smelled her desperation whenever she glanced in the mirror. Cyrus couldn't scent an emotion coming off her now. His baby sister had figured out how to mask her scent from discovery, a trick his mate didn't know even existed. Cyrus was both proud and horrified of Lake's success. How much effort had she put in minute-by-minute to smell like nothing was out of the ordinary?

It must have been exhausting. But if she lied to him again, he wasn't going to continue being pleasant. Family or not, Lake was his Healer. She constituted a very important member of his pack, and if she was having a nervous breakdown or had a major problem with something, he needed to know what it was before someone else died.

"Look, none of this is new. Why do we have to talk about it at all?"

He'd expected fabrication, but her hostility grated at his nerves. Flippancy from any member of his pack, save Betsy, was not going to be tolerated.

"Why do we have to talk about it?" He forced himself to stay seated, to remain calm. They hurled through the air at thirty thousand feet, trapped in only a steel rod with wings to protect them. His mate slept peacefully in his embrace. Both facts meant he had to stay calm— even if he wanted to throw something across the room.

"Well," he continued, "we have to talk about it because your behavior, as of late, is unacceptable. You're rude, diffi-cult, and sarcastic. You're drinking too much. You don't show up to pack-mandated events, and, yesterday, a member of the pack died from an injury you should easily have been able to handle. That's why we have to talk about it."

Tears flowed from her eyes as he spoke, a steady stream falling down her face. "I wondered how long it would be until you got to the point, until you blamed me for Kyra's death."

"I don't blame you for Kyra. I blame *myself* for Kyra. If you had been to the moon ceremony, you would know that. I should never have let you all continue going to that bar, not after I knew about it. I should have had my female pack members better protected. I blame myself. What I want to know is why my Healer was so unhappy that she drank herself into a stupor and couldn't manage to call on the genetically driven, magical talents that allow her to save our lives when need be? For the love of all that's holy, what is going on? What are you so afraid of? Tell me, for fuck's sake."

She wiped at her eyes. "What's the point of any of it?"

Well, he certainly hadn't expected that. Cyrus adjusted Betsy until she lay across the seat and he could stand up. The plane had hit a spot of turbulence, and he was certain that, had the flight attendant not been a member of his pack who wouldn't dare contradict him, he would have been ordered back. But his sister had made a statement that was better addressed face to face.

He placed his hand on her arm and squatted in front of her. "Lake, I'd like you to explain what you mean." He should have gotten his degree in psychiatry instead of a master's in business.

"Are you out of your mind? You're going to get killed, hitting the ceiling or something."

"Oh, imagine that, you'd have to save my life." He waited a beat, wondering if he should finish his thought. "Or maybe you'd let me die because there's no point to any of it?"

She gasped, covering her mouth. "Cyrus, that is not what I meant."

"Then I guess you'd better explain, sister, before I decide you're unfit for your position." Truth was, he'd been considering that all day. But what would they do without Lake? He'd have to actually advertise for a new Healer from another pack. Alexei would torment him about it for years. Lake had always been one hell of an asset for his pack, the Healer to rule all Healers. But whether or not she could work for him anymore was moot. His sister had said something really dark, and as much as the Alpha of the pack had to consider logistics, as her brother, he'd freaked out inside.

"I mean we go about every month doing the same things. We get up, come work in the concrete hell you think of as heaven, and go home. And then we do it all again except for two days out of every month where we go to upstate New York and change into our animals." She sniffed. "Oh, I'm sorry. There are also the times I go into heat and then I get to pick out someone

I don't care about to have sex with, which is like scratching an itch or putting on a Band-Aid." Cyrus let her words sit for moment. "Are you saying you're bored?"

"Not bored, brother. Miserable. What am I doing with my life? Sitting at a desk acting as your assistant? You don't need me. Ten different pack members could take over that job and do it better. I'm offering nothing, doing nothing. And the one time I had to step up and do something crucial, I screwed up. And now Kyra is dead. Whatever you say about it being on you, it's on me. End of story."

"Sweetheart." He shook his head. "I'm not sure what you want me to say about all of this. I built that business for all of us. Don't you remember what it was like before? Or were you too young? Everyone running for their lives. Losing jobs. Changing into werewolves in the middle of the street in the rush to get home?"

"There has to be a middle ground, Cyrus."

"No," he shouted and then lowered his voice. Everyone remained completely still. "Not on this. Not after Kyra. I'm sorry you are so disappointed with life. I'll work on figuring out something to make you happy." Because that was his role, he saw to the needs of his people. "But I'm not compromising on the work issue. You may not go into the human hospitals where anything could happen and we could be exposed. I will not allow it."

"I know." She turned away from him. "I'm not drinking anymore. You don't have to worry about that."

"Good." He stood up and pinched her cheek. "I know I can count on you."

He didn't believe that, but she needed to hear it. Maybe saying it would make it true. He moved back to his seat and adjusted Betsy again. Lake blinked rapidly and then nodded to him. There were things he would compromise about and things he would not. After Kyra's death, there could be no relenting. If they did things his way, everyone went home to their families at night. He shook his head. They had to get in and out of Montana before the full moon. Seven days until it hit. His pack couldn't be forced to change so far from home.

That was another thing he wouldn't allow. Betsy's first full moon would not be in a situation he couldn't control.

"ARE YOU OKAY?"

He was becoming concerned. Betsy hadn't spoken since they'd gotten off the plane.

The pack had settled into the house he'd rented. It had seemed smarter to have a home base to come and go from rather than a bunch of hotel rooms. It turned out that they'd been able to rent one large house that had three guest homes associated with it. Between the three structures, they all had rooms, and no one had complained about sharing.

"I guess I didn't realize how much I do not want to be back here."

He knew what she meant. He'd have to be dense not to. Still, teasing her might get her out of her funk. He pointed to the floor. "Here? In this house? Have you used Vacation Home Rentals before? Stayed here?"

She pursed her lips. "Ha ha ha."

"Oh, come on, it was amusing."

He could see her trying not to grin. She looked away from him, and eventually her cheeks turned pink. Finally, she must have given in because a smile crossed her face. "You know I meant I didn't want to be back in Montana."

"Doesn't seem so bad to me. I mean it's been pitch-black and cold, but the air smells nice, and it seems like a person could hear himself think out here. Isn't it considered to have a big sky or something?"

A knock on the door cut off what she would have said. "Come in," he called out.

"My Alpha." One his pack mates, John, stood at the door. "We went ahead and secured the perimeter. No unusual smells catching our attention. I think it'll be safe for the pack to rest."

Cyrus nodded. "Thank you."

He'd had to leave Mitchell and Jensen behind. They

were his two most trusted pack members. Mitchell was now his second-in-command—he had to hold New York in Cyrus' absence—and Jensen needed to be with the kids. It was incredibly gratifying to see the others step up in their places. That was how a functioning pack was supposed to work. If one part fell, the others filled the void.

"You're welcome. I'll guard the door tonight. You and your mate can sleep peacefully."

"No," Betsy called from behind him. "You go to bed too, John. Get some rest."

"Ma'am, I have to insist. It is our duty and privilege to keep you safe." John planted his feet shoulder-width apart. Cyrus could read the insistence in his eyes. He'd once been the same when he'd been young. At seventeen years old, he'd wanted to die for Shepherd. Then he'd gotten a better sense of the man. How old was John? Eighteen? Nineteen?

Thanks to Betsy's earlier conversation, all he could do was imagine the young man challenging him for Alpha. Cyrus growled, and John took a step back.

"Sir? Have I displeased you?"

"No." *Damn it.* "Are you happy in this pack?"

"Happy, my Alpha?"

Cyrus tapped his foot. "Do you need a definition of happy, John?"

"Is that a trick question, sir?"

Betsy stepped forward. "Go to bed, John. The Alpha didn't sleep on the plane. He's tired. You're doing a good job. But give us some privacy. Ten feet from the door, won't you?" John nodded, looking between them. "Yes, ma'am. As you say."

When the other male had left, Betsy rounded on him. "Have you lost your mind? You were terrifying that kid."

"I kept wondering if he was gunning for me. Thinking about becoming Alpha himself."

His mate groaned and put her arms around him. "Sweetheart, when I brought it up earlier, it wasn't to make you think all the members of your pack were gunning for you."

"I know that." He shook his head. "Maybe I am exhausted."

"Don't you think you'd be able to smell it?"

"We can't smell people's thoughts. Emotions some-times. But I don't know what you're thinking based on scent alone." He sometimes wished he could. That would certainly give him an edge in business meetings.

"The hostility would be obvious. And, besides, the only thing I got from John right now was how much he wanted to look out for us. Forget I said anything. If anyone came after you, I'm sure you'd be able to handle them. If you couldn't, I would, so there's nothing to worry about."

His mate was so darn cute. He pulled her against him. "You would, would you? Take on an Alpha challenger for me? Going to act like some kind of enforcer werewolf? My personal bodyguard?"

"Don't laugh like I couldn't do it." She pushed at his chest. "Don't forget, in stressful situations, I can shift my hands into claws."

"That's good. I'll count on you to claw my opponent to death."

Betsy sniffed at his neck, and it sent shivers down his spine. He loved the thought that she was taking his scent into her blood, the same way he did hers. "John isn't so close that he can hear us, is he?"

"Oh." He laughed, finally understanding why she wanted him not to guard their door. "If he can hear us, I'll count on him to use the good sense to never, ever say anything."

He cupped her breast through her shirt and tweaked her nipple until it budded in his hand.

She sucked in her breath. "How can you be awake? You haven't slept in forever."

"I'm an Alpha werewolf. Despite the fact that I find myself able to rest better with you than I ever have before, I actually don't require very much sleep."

"Oh. I get it. You're such a tough guy. Big strong Alpha doesn't need to get his *z's* like the rest of us."

He picked her up in his arms, carried her over to bed, and then he laid her down on it. "Well, if you would prefer me to go to sleep instead of ravishing you, I'm sure I can manage to do that."

Although the truth was he'd not be able to conk out if she denied him. His balls had tightened to the point of pain, and his cock tented his pants. Betsy smiled, her eyes slitting into what he thought of as her sultry gaze. He got even harder and had to adjust his pants. Wow, the woman unmanned him, made him feel like a teenager.

She reached between him and cupped his balls through his pants. "I think someone down there is excited to see me."

"He's always ecstatic to be in your presence. Trust me on this. I may spend the rest of my life two seconds from totally hard at all times."

She kissed him, her soft lips drawing him in to her like a moth to a flame. If she burned him to death, he'd die happy.

They pulled at each other's clothes until there were no barriers between them. Betsy reached up to stroke his face. "From behind this time?"

His heart rate kicked up a notch. "Really?"

"Yes. I want to try it every which way with you. This

time I want you deep inside of me, pushing in as far as you can go."

She didn't have to tell him twice. He flipped her over, running his hand down her smooth ass. Betsy was rounded in all the right places. The curve of her ass filled out her pants, and now, bare to his gaze, it made his mouth water. Because he had to, he pinched her rear.

She yelped and then laughed at him. "Are you goosing me while I'm naked and totally exposed to you?""

"Yep." Just for good measure, he did it again.

She hissed. "Watch out. Payback will be a bitch. I might just decide to grab your behind while we're in public."

The idea amused him more than it should. What would his pack do if his mate went around goosing him? There would certainly be a scandal to manage. The gossiping tongues would wag. That was all right. He'd take the talk if it meant he could continue to mark up her hot ass.

Cyrus pushed one finger inside of her, relieved to find her warm and ready. She moaned at his slight touch, and he smiled. It took so little to get Betsy excited. She was always so perfectly responsive.

"Like that, princess?" He found her clit and stroked it with two fingers until she vibrated against him.

"You're cruel." Her voice had lowered. "Getting me all excited and then leaving me to wait like this."

Her hips pushed back against him, indicating her readiness for his entrance. He kissed her back, running his tongue on her skin. "You're not the only one suffering, my love. But the longer we wait, the sweeter the reward. On your knees."

She complied. "Yeah. Yeah. Yeah. You like to torment me."

"Not true. Your every need is my privilege to fulfill." He pushed deeply inside of her.

She'd wanted him as far as he could get, so he swept in balls deep. She cried out. "Better?"

"Cyrus." She gripped the headboard so tightly her knuckles appeared white. "Oh my god, you're so deep inside of me."

"That was the idea." And if he could somehow manage to not embarrass himself by ending all of this too quickly, he'd consider himself a lucky man.

Nothing could be more perfect, and he wished he could spend eternity right where he was. But his body quivered, begging for release, for him to give both of them what they needed, and he'd be able to deny the need to move only for so long.

Still, if he could take a second, one moment to live within her, then he could bring the memory to surface whenever he was alone or unsure or bored.

"Cyrus." She said his name again, and he knew he couldn't wait any longer. His woman never needed to beg for her release.

He pumped in and out of her, pressing against her clit with every movement. Their bodies slapped together, the sounds of wet, hot sex mixing with his groans and the sound of her voice calling out his name.

Betsy threw her head back onto his shoulder and came, covering him with her juices. He held on for dear life as she milked him with her muscles until it was too much, until he had to release deep inside of her or he'd never breathe again.

Cyrus had never come so long or so hard—over and over again. He saw stars before his eyes, and his ears rang.

It took every ounce of strength he possessed not to collapse on top of her when he bit down on her shoulder.

Would he ever stop doing that? He didn't know, and for the first time, he didn't care. Betsy liked it. Biting her every time worked for them, and he intended to stick with it.

"Love you." She panted.

"Me too, princess, me too." More than she would ever know.

Chapter 16

Betsy groaned and grabbed her head. Light pushed its way through her sore lids and forced her to open them. The cold ground dug into the small of her back where her shirt had ridden up. She shivered and felt her head again while she tried to sit up. Her hand was covered in dried blood and so, from the residue on her fingers, was her head.

What the hell had happened? She stared left and then right, realizing for the first time that she had no idea where she was. Not one clue. Or why she was alone.

Her heart rate kicked up into a rapid gallop, which made her throbbing head only hurt worse. Okay. Okay. She had to get control of herself and figure out where she was and how she'd gotten there.

A big blank nothingness filled her brain. Had she blacked out somewhere? Had something happened? Why didn't she know where she was or why she'd been bleeding?

Betsy sniffed the air. There were some things she did know. Her name. Cyrus' name, he was her mate, and they were both, strangely enough, werewolves. She'd come to

Montana to figure out what happened to her parents, what the truth was once and for all…

She caught her breath. Montana. That's where she was, back in her home state. They'd gotten on an airplane and come here. Then what?

Betsy staggered a bit as she tried to get her feet to work. She felt drained, as though her body didn't want to function. She rubbed her head again. Something obviously *had* occurred. And if she really dwelled on her current situation, it terrified her even more.

There was no way she should be alone on a country road somewhere in Montana. There was no way Cyrus would have allowed that to happen if he could have done anything to prevent it. She'd been alone, unconscious, on the side of the road with a gash in her head. Something terrible had happened. Tears poured out of her eyes, and she sniffed before pushing them away. She wasn't going to be able to help anyone if she didn't get herself under control and fast.

If he lived, Cyrus would do everything in his power to get to her, and if he didn't, then the world was too horrible to contemplate and she couldn't let her mind go there.

The first problem was that the last thing she could remember was going to bed in their rented house. Had something happened there? Had John attacked Cyrus and tried to take over the pack? She dismissed that thought and tried to ignore the constant throb of her head.

If John had attacked them in their bed, she wouldn't be lost on the side of the road. That didn't make sense. She growled and stuck her shaking hands in her pockets. Pockets! She had them. In fact, she was completely dressed. Black slacks, white turtleneck, and winter jacket. Gloves in her pockets She had not gone to bed dressed like this, so she must have gotten up and dressed at some point. But when? How? She was on the road. When had they left the hotel?

The plan had been to hit the road after breakfast and drive the hour to Destiny, Montana, the closest town to where she'd grown up. They'd go to her childhood home and assess the situation there before heading over to Nathan's family's compound. Cyrus' plan had been less clear at that point. Or maybe he hadn't told her everything, which was what she suspected from the way he went silent whenever she asked him about it.

He wouldn't have wanted her to worry. Her mouth felt dry, and she felt around inside her coat until she pulled out a peppermint. She didn't always carry them but she felt lucky they were still in there. Popping it in her mouth, she tried to figure out what to do next. There had to be a street sign at some point somewhere. Didn't there? Could she be lost forever on this road?

"Oh, don't be ridiculous, Betsy. You are a strong woman. You survived your childhood. You survived Nathan in New York. You became a werewolf and mated an Alpha. Extremists have attacked you. Certainly, you can handle walking down the road Just suck it up and stop being such a chicken."

The sound of her own voice jarred her into action, and, even though the dizziness hadn't gone anywhere, she walked faster. The sun's position in the sky told her it was mid-day, but it wouldn't stay that way long. If she didn't make headway to somewhere habitable before nightfall, she'd really be screwed. Cold would only be part of the problem. Predators would be in the woods on the side of the road, and at night, she'd seem like a tasty morsel.

If only she could shift into her werewolf form on demand like her mate could. That sort of ability would be very useful.

But that was one of the reasons he was Alpha.

Okay. So something had happened since leaving the house and getting to Destiny. She either walked in the direction of Destiny or away from it. The latter might be preferable since she wasn't exactly sure if she was ready to deal with Destiny on her own yet. What would she say to people? How would she keep her parents from being killed?

A car sped by her and slammed on its brakes. She darted backward, wondering if she should make a break for it into the woods. Not knowing what had happened left her feeling tremendously vulnerable.

Panic made her sloppy, and as she turned to flee, she slipped, hitting the pavement with a thud that jarred her bones and cut up her skin through her clothes. Damn it, what was wrong with her?

She pushed herself up. Somehow she had to run from whoever was in that vehicle....

The door to the car flew open, and a scent she recognized wafted out. Citrus. She took a deep breath and whirled around. Lake, her mate's sister was the first to exit. Three werewolves— John, who shouted orders, Kirk, and Taylor followed. She didn't know the other two very well, other than they had come on the trip, but she'd never been so happy to see four pack members in her life.

Lake reached her first and drew her into her arms. The Healer trembled against her. "Oh, Betsy, thank the moon."

"Lake." Her voice sounded hoarse, and suddenly her idea of keeping it together seemed pretty far-fetched. Tears swam in her eyes, and her vision blurred. "What happened? What is going on?"

The other woman pulled back to look at her. "Are you serious? You don't know?"

"No. I woke up about half a mile back. Or maybe less.

I don't really know how far I walked." Everything was so confused, jumbled, as though she'd never make sense of it again. How much time had gone by? She really didn't know.

Lake shuddered. "I can feel your pain. You need to let me heal you, and then we'll talk." Despite herself, Betsy laughed. "You mean you need my permission to do that?" She hadn't when she'd taken her from latency to full-fledged were.

"I could see how you might think I don't, but I'm turning over a new leaf, so to speak. I'm asking before I interfere. Can I make your head stop hurting?"

"Yes please."

"Everything okay, Lake?" John's voice interrupted the moment. "Where is the Alpha?"

"I don't think she knows. Give us a minute." Lake placed her hands on her head and a slow warmth spread inside of Betsy.

"You don't know where Cyrus is?" Some of the warmth in her body dissipated. Where was he? What had happened? Why couldn't she remember?

"Shh. It's okay. We have a general idea of what happened. And we're all going to work this out together."

The heat picked back up again, and for a moment, she couldn't keep her eyes opened. She knew it was ridiculous. She couldn't be falling asleep standing on the side of the road, but it had to be something Lake was doing. Would the other woman let her fall? Right at that second, she really didn't care. There was such peace in the warmth flowing through her.

Her eyes flew open, and Lake smiled. "Better?"

"Yes. Thanks, wow." Even her muscles felt looser. Her body felt something akin to having gotten out of a hot bath.

"You're welcome. Any memory return?"

Betsy bit her lip. "No, damn it. Shouldn't that have helped?" What was wrong with her? Could someone have reached inside her brain and pulled out her memories for a whole chunk of time?

"Only if the loss was from the head trauma. I strongly suspect it was not, but I'm reaching in the dark here. I can only fix what ails you on the outside."

"And this is not that?" She scratched her head. Did Lake think she'd become emotionally damaged in the hours since they'd arrived in Montana?

"I think it's possible you had another blackout from fighting. Like the one you had in the bar."

Betsy shook her head. "Cyrus said that would only happen once."

"Some people take longer to adjust. Don't forget, most of us have our first encounters with werewolf aggression as children. How do we really remember how many times we blanked out? Maybe we did it as babies. You're a bit of a unique case. Even your sister hasn't faced the same kind of endless battering since her shift that you have."

Betsy let Lake's words sink in. "Then I was in another fight."

"It would seem that way. A few hours ago. We got left behind. Cyrus didn't want to bring everyone with him in case something like this happened." Lake nodded.

"The true believers, they somehow knew we were here and got to us?" She was going to string Nathan up by his toenails, assuming he was still alive after being left in Alexei's gentle care for over twenty-four hours.

"We don't think it was the true believers." John stepped forward, holding out his phone. He handed it to her, and it took her a minute to realize what she was looking at. She and Cyrus were not yet communicating using cell phones. But it seemed that her mate had sent him a message.

It read: *under attack by wolf pack* with a set of directions. "We darted out to the car."

"And all you found was me." It wasn't a question. If Cyrus had been around, he would have popped up by then.

"Betsy." Lake leveled her eyes to hers. "Mated couples can sometimes tell. Not always. Jensen didn't know Kyra was dead until he saw, but sometimes a mated couple can tell if one half of the pair is dead. Are you feeling anything?"

"What?" She didn't mean to shout, but that was what she did. "No, nothing like that. Cyrus isn't dead." She would know deep inside of her where her heart beat if he was. Wouldn't she?

"Okay. So then I'm going to suggest that we return to the house, hole up there, and wait for Cyrus to contact us. I trust my brother to get himself out of this situation."

"No." She spoke the word almost the second she thought it, instead of considering what she wanted to say, a usual occurrence for her, especially in this kind of uncertainty. "I have a different idea. I know exactly how we're going to help him. Cyrus is in trouble. And I'm not going to leave him that way. Tell me, can you get Alexei on the phone?" She hoped she wasn't about to make a terrible mistake.

―――

NOTHING MUCH HAD CHANGED in Destiny, Montana, since she had left. She hadn't expected it to be different. But it hadn't been until they had driven through what amounted to the downtown with its one stop sign and white aluminum siding everywhere she looked that she realized how addicted she had become to New York City.

Some people might crave the solitude that living in Destiny provided. Betsy never would again. Her mind worked better with the constant noise of Manhattan instead of the oppressive buzzing silence of her small hometown.

They pulled up to the compound in silence. It really didn't look like much of a compound but Betsy knew looks could be deceiving. The red brick building had one gate in front of it with a doorbell she was going to have to ring before she gained access to the people inside.

Behind the red house would be other buildings. She'd heard her father discuss this place. Although she couldn't see the rest of it, she knew it was there.

"You sure you want to do this?" Lake chewed on her bottom lip. Cyrus' sister was worried. Betsy could smell it in the way the other woman's scent kept twisting in strength. One second it was light, the next almost over-whelming.

"Yes." No. She hoped her own aroma didn't betray how unsure she actually felt about this endeavor. She knew what Cyrus would want. He'd be ordering her back to the house and out of sight. But if her mate and the thirteen others had been taken by a wolf pack, then there was only one group she knew to ask for information.

The true believers.

And she had the one thing they wanted. Nathan.

"All right." Betsy tried to open the door, and John stopped her, reaching around her to put his hand over hers.

"You can't do this, Betsy. Not alone. The Alpha will kill me."

She had finally gotten John to stop calling her ma'am. If the five of them were going to survive this, it was going to have to be on equal footing or not at all. When Cyrus returned, they could all scamper to be polite. For now, they could treat her like a woman about to step off a cliff with only them to keep her from plunging to her death. .

"Okay." John made a good point. Cyrus would freak out if he found out the others had let her go into the compound alone. But she wouldn't be responsible for getting any of them killed. "Then you come along. The rest of you, stay here with the car running."

"Like bank robbers." This from Kirk, who had an acerbic wit she'd come to like in the last few hours. He really knew how to lighten the mood.

"Hopefully we'll be more successful than most bank robbers." Otherwise, they'd be carting her out of there in a body bag and even Lake's considerable skills wouldn't be enough to bring her back.

Cyrus would have to conduct another moon ceremony. She shuddered at the thought of her poor mate having to give her back to the moon as he wondered why she had been such a complete idiot and not gone back to the house.

She walked toward the entrance to the compound, and John grabbed her arm. "You can change your mind. We'll go back. No one will think the less of you."

Betsy looked down to where he held her arm. "I would think the less of me." John let go of her, and she kept walking. "I'm not a coward, and even though you can smell my fear, I don't want you to think I can't do this. I can. That's bravery, right? Doing things that frighten you."

"Maybe for humans. We're not often afraid. Why don't you let me do this for you? I can handle it on my own."

"John." She let out her breath as she raised her hand to knock on the door. "Remember the part about not being a coward?"

"I can't help wanting to spare you this. For my Alpha's sake as well as your own." "Thanks for that."

She thought about what he said. Werewolves were not often scared. That was probably true, at least not in physical situations. They were bigger, stronger, and faster than humans. Inside the other buildings she could hear someone walking toward the door. Someone, other than Nathan's father, was going to answer the door, but maybe she should start off the way she intended to continue.

The skeptic in her, the part of her that had been born the day Nathan had dragged her off to save her from her sexuality and force her into marriage to save her parents, knew they were likely already on camera. Nathan's father, Joe Jones, would already be aware she stood at the door. Alexei was on alert in Boston. He had Nathan's cell phone. Nothing would happen on that end until he got the go from her.

She regarded her hand. The kind of focus she'd had at the bar flew back at her. All she could see were her fingers. They appeared human, and that wasn't what she wanted. No, right at that second, she needed claws and fur. The true believers inside the compound would know fear.

It hurt, but it worked. As she watched, her smooth skin grew fur, and her fingers reshaped into the long, sharp weapons that would kill in a fight. To call the pain agonizing would be too small a word, but she didn't have time to care.

Betsy had never met the middle-aged man who opened the door. He had brown hair, graying on the sides, and brown eyes to match.

She smiled, and he opened his mouth to say something, only he never got the chance. With her shaking, shifted hand, she grabbed the human by the throat.

"I want Joe, and if you want to see another day of life, you're going to get him here.

Immediately."

"Betsy?" She hadn't cleared this part of the plan with John. It didn't surprise her one bit that she'd startled him, but he was going to have to get with the new circumstances fast.

"Do I smell scared, John?" She hissed out her words.

"No actually." He shook his head.

"Then don't worry." She turned her attention back to the man whose throat she held.

"Did you hear me? Call for Joe."

"There's no need for that, Betsy." Joe Jones came slinking out from farther down the hall. She caught a whiff of his aftershave. It was lemony and fresher than she would have liked. The man should wear a scent that matched the degradation in his soul. Something coarse and disgusting. Something that would make her gag.

"Joe." She nodded to him not letting go of the throat she held

"I see you've found your claws. I'm very disappointed. You were our example of how the damned could be saved. All of those years you never turned, not even when provoked. Now look at you."

There were a number of things she could say to that, including questioning him about what exactly they had done to try to provoke her, but she needed to keep her head in the game. Her objective was to find Cyrus and free her parents. Playing a game of words with a man who she knew hated her kind wouldn't amount to anything useful other than satisfying her growing need for blood.

The claws must be bringing out her wolf side.

She smiled, and Joe took a step back. Good, he should

feel fearful in her presence. Maybe she could be the monster he'd named her.

"Joe, you aren't going to ask after Nathan? In all of this, he isn't your first concern?"

His eyes widened. "I don't believe you'd hurt him or that you'd even be capable of it. My son is a trained were-wolf hunter."

"Your son is sitting in a cage at the mercy of the Alpha from Boston."

Joe sucked in his breath. "I don't believe you."

"John, if you would."

Her companion dialed the phone, and Alexei picked up on the first ring. John handed it to Joe without being told to. She was glad he'd gotten into the moment. Directing him was going to destroy some of the mystique she was going for.

From where she stood, she could hear Nathan whimpering into the phone. Her werewolf abilities were proving to be useful. Joe turned redder and redder as he spoke to his son. She wasn't sure what bothered him more, the fact that his son was crying like a baby or that it was the Alpha of Boston who held him captive.

Without saying a word, Joe hung up the phone.

"I'm going to imagine that you've heard of Alexei before since your people had his females killed." She didn't give him the chance to answer. "He's vicious and mean on a good day. Lately, he's not been feeling particularly pleasant."

Well, she assumed those things to be true based on the way the rest of the pack reacted to Alexei. She'd known him four days and didn't have much to judge him by.

From the way Joe's red face turned pale instantly, she knew she had hit a nerve. "Alexei has agreed to keep your son alive." Not indefinitely, but she would lie, cheat, and steal to get what she wanted right then. Bending the truth would have to be something she lived with. Somehow she didn't think it was going to be a problem.

"Your parents aren't here. They never were, you stupid girl. They've always been with us. Go by your house. They're living there like they always have."

Betsy swallowed. His words really shouldn't have thrown her off. She should have been prepared to find out her parents had been part of the betrayal the whole time, that there had been no coercion, that she'd always been a pawn. It burned in her stomach. Some day she would cry about it. When she had Cyrus back and he could put his arms around her. That day wasn't today.

"Who said anything about my parents? You think we didn't know?" Her throat felt scratchy, and she ignored it. "I want to know where the local werewolf pack is, Joe. You tell me that, and Alexei won't slit Nathan's throat and don't act like you don't know. There's a werewolf pack here and for some reason you haven't been able to kill them yet. But I bet you know where they are even if you haven't been able to kill them." She tried to steady her breath. Bluffing wasn't easy for her.

For tonight anyway. She raised an eyebrow, begging him to challenge her. If it hadn't been Cyrus' head on the line, she might even want him to dare to call her bluff. Because she wasn't bluffing—the whole lot of them could rot in hell.

Chapter 17

"I'm going to kill you, Beaux. Just so you understand that. I'm going to eat your insides." Cyrus hadn't seen Beaux Nelson since the third year on Lucian's farm. Beaux hadn't been back the next year, having not been invited to join them again. The fact had surprised Cyrus because Beaux had been a top werewolf, and Lucian had seemed to favor him in year three. And then nothing, not even a blip of anyone's radar until the man's pack had jumped their cars and dragged Cyrus and his people into a fight in the middle of the road. It had been bloody. He studied his pack members. Thirteen of them were in various states of capture and distress. Some of them needed a Healer, and Beaux had certainly not offered one.

Betsy. By the moon, he wished he knew what had happened to her. He'd ordered her to run. Had she? *She isn't dead.* He couldn't allow himself to think about that. Sending her off had saved her life. Lake *would* find her, assuming his sister was functioning properly and not lost in her own needs. He'd been so distracted with trying to keep Betsy safe that he'd not seen the attack by Beaux coming.

The other man had struck him with something on the side of the head. He'd awakened tied up to the wall.

Beaux shrugged. "I imagine if I untied any of you that you'd certainly try to kill me. That's why you're all confined."

Cyrus growled, disliking Beaux's nonchalance more than anything "Why did you do this in the first place? We were not here to bother you."

Beaux clenched his teeth. He'd always seemed a man on the edge, but it seemed he had gained some measure of control.

Beaux liked the "old ways", as if they should all be romping through the woods communing with the trees and hiding from human ways. When no one else had seen things the way he did, he'd grown bitter and angry.

He'd been the best fighter among them. And now here he was. In Montana.

"Is it customary in New York to allow a group of were-wolves passage into your territory without them asking permission of the Alpha first?" Beaux growled his words.

"I had been told there was no Alpha in Montana. Lone wolves, no pack. It isn't necessary to request anyone's permission when dealing with a bunch of rabid dogs."

Beaux launched himself forward, getting in Cyrus' face. "You won't talk to me like that. Not now. Not ever. You are on my land. You will respect me."

Cyrus lowered his voice to keep from shouting. He needed to treat Beaux like a child, a misunderstood youth who needed to be taught. "It's easy to demand respect while you have my people injured, have not offered them care of a Healer, and have me tied to the wall. It's easy to demand respect when you hit me over the head so I can't take you on properly. I'll respect you when you've done something to earn it. There is no Alpha in

Montana. You're a pretender to the role. Pathetic actually."

"How dare you?"

"My Alpha." One of the wolves who'd fought beside Beaux entered the room. The wolf had to be over six feet seven inches tall. Cyrus didn't know if he'd ever actually seen anyone that large before. His mouth fell open before he realized it, and he closed his lips together. "May I see you for a moment?"

Beaux snarled through his nose when he spoke. "Right now?"

"Yes, sir. It's imperative."

It didn't bode well for his you're-not-an-Alpha argument if the others were referring to him as Alpha. If Cyrus were wrong about Beaux's status, he'd apologize later. What he needed was to get off the wall, free his people, find out what had happened to Betsy, and then beat Beaux into the ground before he handled Betsy's family situation.

He tugged at his restraints. Beaux had been thorough; that was for sure.

"My Alpha, don't worry about this," Lachlan called from the back of the room. "We don't require his assistance."

"You let me judge what you do and do not need." What Cyrus needed was a jackhammer. Or a stick of dynamite he could stick up Beaux's ass. Lit.

Beaux reentered the room. "Who is Betsy Webber?"

The entirety of Cyrus' pack trapped in the room erupted in growls. No one liked hearing her name on Beaux's mouth. Cyrus would have smiled if he hadn't wanted to rip the other man's face off. Cyrus' pack had accepted and protected his mate.

"Where did you learn that name?" He was going to shift and get out his chains. He'd been holding off doing so, trying to figure out what Beaux wanted, what his objective had been.

But the time for talking had ended. The cuffs on his wrist wouldn't hold him in animal form. And then he was going to tear Beaux's heart from his body.

"She's at my door. Or so my people tell me. Four other werewolves accompany her, and she's offering to trade some kind of information we need for your release. Who is this woman? Is she the one you helped to flee from my men?"

When he got a hold of John, Lake, and the other wolves who should have been protecting her, he was going to string them up by their toenails. What were they thinking letting her come here? How did she even find this place?

He forced himself to take a deep breath. "She isn't going to trade you anything. She doesn't know anything. Get her gone."

Cyrus would protect her whether she wanted to be or not. Betsy needed to be far, far away. India might be far enough.

"Who is she to you?"

"That's not your concern." He wouldn't let Beaux make her a bartering chip. Not in this lifetime or any other.

"Let's say I make it my business. She's an attractive female, and she smells like heaven. We don't have an abundance of females here. Perhaps one of my wolves would like to woo her." The pack growled again, and Cyrus narrowed his gaze. He was going to have to be cleverer with this man. Beaux had always lived by the old rules, the ones that had worked before they embraced their human side. There had to be ways to get them to favor Cyrus for a while. Much as he wanted to kill him right off the bat, he was going to have to let his human side rule for a few minutes. As hard as that proved to be.

"Your pack doesn't want me putting men in front of her. Why is that? Have I been misinformed? Is she not attractive?"

Cyrus took a deep breath. If his idea didn't pan out, he was royally screwed. He'd have no choice but to shift and end all of Beaux's guys where they stood. For the sake of peace, it was worth a try.

"She's my mate. My pack objects to their Alpha's woman being discussed at all."

Beaux crossed his hands over his chest. . "She didn't identify herself as such."

"Betsy wouldn't know to do so. She's new to this. It's a very long story and one I would be happy to share with you if you would let me go"

Beaux shook his head. "I never would have imagined it. What happened? Did you need a new political alliance now that someone finally took out Lucian? Is her family well connected? Isn't that what you guys do? Take over packs for political reasons; marry to assert your power? Act more human than the humans themselves?"

The dig at Lucian's death had clearly been meant to raise his ire. But Betsy stood outside at risk. He couldn't afford to give into temper. Not yet anyway.

"Actually, we're true mates. I found her in a coffee shop."

Beaux opened and closed his mouth. So he'd finally managed to stun the man. Good, then they were moving in the right direction.

Beaux hissed out his breath. "Are you telling me that the moon gifted you with a true mate? How could that be? You're so undeserving."

"And you've always managed to be holier than thou,

haven't you?" Cyrus shook his head. "Regardless of whether or not I've earned a true mate, I got one, and I'm going to call on you to give me mate protection. She is not to be touched, molested, or in any way harmed in whatever is going on between us."

Beaux groaned. "You played me like a fiddle."

"Do I have your word, Nelson? You won't harm one hair on her head and neither will any member of your pack?"

The other man nodded. "You have it. The true mate of an Alpha is always exempt from any Alpha challenges."

"I don't want your damned pack, man. I don't want anything to do with it. That isn't why I'm here, and had I known you were now Alpha of Montana—something I couldn't possibly have foreseen considering: a, you never announced it and b, are from Ohio—I would have made a proper request for travel over your lands."

"Then what are you doing here? I know your games. I watched Lucian play them, and I saw through them even then. I won't be used as a ploy, and neither will my pack. We will not submit to another Alpha Prime and certainly not to you."

Cyrus shook his head. "Listen to the words coming out of my mouth. I am not looking to be Alpha Prime. I never wanted it, and I never will. I do not desire that kind of power. I am Alpha of Manhattan. I have enough on my plate, and I would not abandon my pack to go running around taking care of hunting rights in Iowa. I don't want Montana. I want to do what we came here to do, and then I want to get out of here, never to return or to look at your ugly face again."

"I might almost believe you if I didn't know what a manipulative bastard you are."

Cyrus had enough. He'd tolerated more than he ever would have in the past for Betsy's protection, but if he took any more of the werewolf's puny excuses for abuse, he would look weak in front of his pack and feel pathetic as a man. Neither of those things could be tolerated.

"Let me out of here, and we'll talk like men. Or you could continue to act the coward. I suppose it's up to you."

Beaux growled, and Cyrus suppressed a grin. Sometimes it was too damn easy.

"I have never been a coward, and I took you in a fight. You're my prisoner."

Cyrus shifted into his wolf form. Really, enough was enough. His pack responded in kind, filling the room with the sounds of their tempers and excitement. He had one moment to see Beaux's eyes widen with what amounted to respect before he himself shifted into his werewolf form.

Well, maybe the son-of-a-bitch really is an Alpha. Only an Alpha could shift like that outside of the full moon.

He snarled, letting his wolf take over. He didn't need reason and logic, not when he meant to tear the asshole's face to shreds. Cyrus leaped forward, knocking Beaux backward onto the ground.

No one fucked with him or threatened what was his. No one lived who harmed his pack. Cyrus sniffed the air. He'd bloodied Beaux. There would be more where that had come from.

Beaux lunged toward him, and Cyrus ducked right but not before Beaux got a swipe at him. It burned, but who cared for small pain when there was death to doll out?

"Stop it." Betsy's soft smell drifted over him as her words filled the room. "Don't hurt each other. We need to work together on this."

Cyrus wanted to look up and see his mate, but he

didn't dare. If he looked away from Beaux, the other wolf would wreck him.

"Oh my gosh." Lake choked on her words as she saw his injured pack. "You all need some help. Here, let me. John, help me."

He was glad she'd see to them. Perhaps Lake could be counted on again.

Beaux yelped and jumped back as though Cyrus had struck him. Only he hadn't. For at least thirty seconds, neither of them had moved. What the hell had happened?

In the blink of an eye, Beaux had transformed back into his human form. He now sat, open-mouthed, staring at Lake.

Cyrus couldn't attack another werewolf in wolf form if the other wolf wasn't covered in fur too. It didn't seem a fair fight, and his animal instincts didn't like it. With a real threat, he couldn't justify the assault.

He concentrated on shifting back until he, too, had regained his human physique. "What's the matter, Beaux? Never seen a Healer before? Can't your so-called pack manage to bring one in?"

His sister stood facing away from him, her back stiff as she checked on several members of his pack. She jolted when he spoke but didn't turn around while she got to work on someone's torn leg. What was wrong with her?

"This is your Healer?" Beaux's voice sounded strained, edgier than it had earlier. Cyrus hadn't swiped at him that hard. *What the hell is going on?*

"Yes." Cyrus stood up. "And my sister, as it happens. Beaux, this is Lake. Lake, this is Beaux. Apparently he's Alpha here, but that's still up for debate."

Cyrus had no intention of letting that chestnut go. Not for a while at least.

"Hi." Lake didn't turn around, which was horribly

rude. But maybe she was really involved in who she was helping? How badly injured were his pack mates? Cyrus stared at Betsy, and she shook her head. Either she didn't know, or she wasn't going to talk about it right then.

Betsy took in the room. "Listen, I think this is something we should be working with the

Montana wolves on. Don't you, my Alpha? This is their territory. They may want to help."

Now he was *my Alpha*? He groaned. Now she chose to act respectful and obedient? After she'd not stayed protected and stormed into the room in the middle of an Alpha fight?

"Are you okay?" He tugged her against him. They'd deal with the particulars of the whole thing after he'd assured himself of her welfare. "You hit the ground hard before you finally ran. What were you thinking?"

Betsy shrugged and bit down on her lip. "I hate to tell you this, but I had another blackout. I have no memory of any of it. I came to on the side of the road with absolutely no idea of how I got there or what had happened."

She must have been terrified. He inhaled the scent from her hair. Lake had fixed her. He smelled the familiar warm scent of pack magic on her. If his sister was back in her game, there wouldn't be permanent damage to his mate, and for that he could be grateful.

"What information did you think you could share with this pack?" It burned him to even use the word. There were legitimate ways to form a pack, and if Beaux, the rule follower, had done any of them, they wouldn't be in this situation now. Of course, maybe that was the problem. The other werewolf had never believed the rules Lucian put in place to be true werewolf law.

The whole thing made Cyrus' head hurt.

"How should I address, uh, Beaux? Is there protocol?"

Cyrus shook his head. "Not for him, no."

Beaux growled, and Lake made a strangled sound in her throat. What the hell was going on with his sister?

"Well, okay." Betsy scratched her head. "My parents and some others have been involved for some time in stealing werewolf babies. They did so with me."

The wounded pack remained quiet and turned around to look at her. She continued speaking. "I'm not entirely certain what they're doing with the babies, as a rule. But they kept me and raised me as if I were human. I'm not sure why they did that. I have a lot of questions. But I think we need to take down the whole lot of them, and, having come from their compound, you're going to have to trust me. We need as many hands on deck to do that as possible."

Cyrus listened to her words, trying not to howl at the moon from the pain he heard percolating beneath them.

Beaux spoke before he could. "Did you say you came from somewhere where they are stealing werewolf babies?"

Betsy nodded, taking Cyrus' hand. Her fingers felt small trapped within his. She was so tiny everywhere. How on earth would he ever keep her safe in this world where all the precautions he'd taken over the years had been blown to shit?

"That's right." She nodded. "I went to them. I knew they'd know where you were. I had to find Cyrus. And since you'd apparently attacked," she stared back at Cyrus. "And I couldn't remember any of it, which is a real problem, I had no other choice."

"They told you we were here?" Beaux yelled roared his response, and Cyrus held up his hand. He agreed with the other man on sentiment, but he wouldn't have Betsy spoken to in any kind of disrespectful way.

"Obviously, they did. Actually, I think it's brilliant. Go

to the true believers since they know where we are, even if we don't know they know."

"How can that be?" Beaux paced from the window to the center of the room several times. "We have taken precautions."

Cyrus rolled his eyes. "We've all been doing that for generations. They always find out. Why do you think Lucian wanted things run the way he did? There would be accountability for being a traitor."

"Lucian himself was a traitor, and it's what got him killed," Beaux snarled.

"How dare you?" Cyrus stepped away from Betsy. He wouldn't have her harmed in the crossfire of the explosion Beaux had triggered. "Lucian was a great man. He didn't think you were worthy, but that doesn't make him a traitor."

Beaux moved until they stood face to face. "He was a traitor to what it is to be a werewolf. In trying to make us more like them, he killed the best part of us. Why try to fit into their society? Why have to figure out how to co-exist in their midst without detection? We aren't like humans. We don't belong with them. It's no wonder he got himself killed. It was inevitable the second he meddled in pack politics, sticking himself at the pinnacle, in a role that should never have existed."

His words slammed into Cyrus with the force of a freight train. How had Lucian done what he did? How had he become Alpha Prime? These were questions Cyrus had never had the answers to, and Cyrus had been too busy trying to hold together Manhattan to worry about the logistics of it.

"He dropped me," Beaux continued, "because he knew I'd never cow-tow to bullshit. He had all of you too wrapped around his fingers to notice. Maybe you would have always been Alpha of New York. Or maybe you wouldn't have been. But that would have been your choice, your fate to decide."

Cyrus shook his head. "In that, you're wrong. It was my choice. No one stood over me and made me challenge Shepherd."

"The weight of expectations watched over you while you did that. Twenty years old kids don't overthrow their Alphas, not unless someone puts that idea in their heads. You might have taken over New York. Eventually. Now perhaps. When you're fully in your power and you know what it is to be a man, a leader." Beaux shrugged. "You really had no choice in that matter. None of Lucian's prized Alphas did. And, for that, I pity you."

He would have spoken. He would have told the man he could take his opinions and shove them where the sun didn't shine. Cyrus never got the chance. Betsy lunged forward, throwing her small weight against Beaux's body. She wouldn't normally be strong enough to do any kind of damage to a werewolf Beaux's size, but the other man hadn't anticipated her attack.

Beaux stumbled backward. His eyes widened as he stared at Cyrus' mate.

"I don't know who you are," Betsy snarled, "but you aren't going to speak to him like that. You don't know the first thing about him or what he is capable of. Maybe you weren't able to take over a pack in your twenties because you're mentally deficient, but Cyrus can do anything he sets his mind to. Anything."

Cyrus stepped forward. If Beaux said or did anything to Betsy in response that was anything less than respectful, he'd show him the meaning of pain.

"My Alpha," said one of Beaux's pack members, a

small man for werewolf standards, with brown hair graying on the side. "There are humans coming in cars."

"Is this a problem?" Cyrus walked to the one window in the room that had been covered by a dark sheet. He pushed it away to look outside. What was the problem with humans? They had humans around them all the time in New York.

"This isn't Manhattan, and this is private property. If humans are coming, then it's because your mate stirred them up."

"I..." Betsy started to speak, and Cyrus placed his hand on her arm to stop her. There wasn't time for her response. Not if this really was an attack. The humans were coming on pretty strong. They must think this was going to be a walk in the park. Or they'd come on a suicide mission.

"Are you prepared for an attack?" Cyrus regarded Beaux. "You're not yet, are you? There aren't enough of you to do much beyond whacking people over the head when you ambush their cars, are there?"

Beaux growled. "We can defend ourselves. Can you, city boy?"

It had been a long time since Cyrus had gone to war. But he was fairly certain he remembered how. His blood heated, and his wolf senses went on high alert. "Bring it on."

Chapter 18

Beaux pounded his fist on the wall. "Boys, it's time for Plan B." Cyrus responded to him, and they must have been debating a battle plan, but Betsy couldn't focus on any of it over the ringing in her ears. Had she done this? Had she brought the true believers to Beaux's pack's doorstep? The idea made her stomach turn, and she gagged, trying desperately not to lose the contents of her stomach onto the floor of Beaux's lair.

Lake moved up behind her. "Come on, we need to get out of the way."

"What?" Betsy shook her head. "I'm not going anywhere." Cyrus needed her, and if she had caused this, then she had to be right by his side to see it through. Or maybe she'd go outside and see if she could talk to the men getting out of the Jeeps. They'd never killed her all the years she lived here. Maybe they'd listen to reason now.

"I know you want to help. I would too, and I can see it in your expression. But this isn't the time for us, okay? I'm a Healer, and you're still untrained. You still black out in fights. We need to let Beaux, Cyrus, and the others do what they do. They can't do that if they're worried about us."

Lake made a good point, even if Betsy didn't want to hear it. She really didn't know anything about fighting. What good would she be in the middle of this mess? She took a step back toward Lake.

"Where should we go?" She turned to Lake. Would heading out the back door help?

"Stay inside." Beaux turned around but had eyes only for Lake, not for her. Betsy glanced between them. It wasn't the time for this, not by a long shot, but clearly there was something happening with Lake and Beaux. It wasn't that she could smell it. They were both carefully guarding their scents but she could see it in the way they kept trying not to look at each other and failing. If they lived through the rest of the day, she was going to ask Lake exactly what was going on.

Cyrus nodded toward the door. "We're going out."

Betsy took a deep breath. "Look, I agree with Lake. I'm out of my element here, but I have to ask you something before I get out of your way."

"What is it, princess?" Already she could hear a growl in his voice. He was going to go wolf soon, and then reasoning with him on any kind of human level would be impossible. His fight with Beaux earlier? It had been nothing but show. Now she'd lose him to the animal until it was over. How did she know that? She chewed on her lip. Maybe from the fights she couldn't remember? Oh hell, all of this was terribly confusing.

"They aren't werewolves. Do you have guns? I can guarantee they have them. They're all hunters and experts at it to boot. You guys go out there charging like this is some kind of war from old times and they are going to pick you off one by one until you're all drowning in your own blood."

"Oh, I have something else in mind." Cyrus smiled, and she shivered. How could she be both so intimidated and ecstatic over his aggression? "We are going to take them entirely by surprise."

She hoped he knew what he was talking about because if anything happened to him she'd never be okay again. Those men had weapons. What did Cyrus and Beaux have besides shifting? Animals could be shot easily. This was too horrible to vocalize and she tried to swallow her fear.

━━

BETSY PACED THE ROOM, unable to stop.

"It's been quiet for a long time." Lake chewed on her fingernail, pacing around the basement with Betsy. But for every lap Betsy took, Lake made two. Where did the other woman get her energy? All she wanted to do was collapse onto the floor with worry. How long had it been since they'd been sent downstairs, and why was it so damn quiet?

"Do you want to be distracted?" Lake tapped her foot on the floor.

"No." Betsy shook her head. She stared down at her hands. Maybe thirty seconds passed, but it felt like an hour. "Yes, okay, distract me."

Take my mind off the fact that Cyrus might be dead. Or dying on the floor. Bleeding to death. Shot. Maimed. Stabbed. Decapitated… Make it so I can't hear the noise outside and scent the humans. Do that for me.

"I think… that is to say… I'm wondering if Beaux is my true mate."

"What?" She stared at Lake. Could that be? She'd

known something was happening but she hadn't seen that coming.

"Can you tell me how you knew that you were mated to my brother?"

"Well…" A loud boom sounded upstairs, and they both stared up at the ceiling. What had caused that?

The door to the basement swung open. John charged down the steps two at a time. A grin exploded across his face when he saw them, and Betsy let out the breath she held. He wouldn't be smiling if her Cyrus lay dying somewhere.

She rushed toward John and then up the stairs behind him. Lake followed in her wake, but Betsy had only one thought, and it was all about finding her love. She sniffed the air when she reached the upstairs and didn't scent Cyrus inside the house.

"This way." John opened the front door, and for the first time since he'd come into the basement, she felt a moment of trepidation. Her hands were unsteady, and she shoved them in her pockets.

"Is everything okay?"

"Yes." John laughed. "Look."

A wolf paced around a group of humans. It wasn't Cyrus. She'd know his brown and gray coat anywhere. It was the darker black fur of Beaux. Cyrus stood behind the group. Eight men knelt on the ground, their heads bowed. One of them was Nathan's father.

"Hello, princess. Sorry that took so long, but these humans had to be dealt with using very little fuss. That took some arranging."

She cleared her throat. "It's not like I had any appointments I had to miss today. My schedule is rather open."

"Well then," Cyrus grinned. "That's good."

"Monsters." Nathan's father bled from a wound on the

top of his head. Blood covered the side of his face as it flowed downward.

Beaux laughed. "Now now, Joe no one hurt you until you took a shot at us. Then you left us no choice."

John snickered. "We may have made ourselves easy targets to encourage that stupidity."

"I see." And suddenly she did. The wolves had given the humans enough rope to hang themselves with. Now there would be no question in how they should be dealt with.

"Joe, I think we talked about what you're going to do now, remember? If you don't want to see us go after your family and friends with the vengeance of a pissed-off animal, you're going to do what we said."

"Betsy, I'd like to apologize for any wrongs we ever did to you."

She blinked, not sure if she'd heard him correctly. "What?"

"Say it again." Cyrus tugged on the back of the other man's head, yanking his hair.

Joe yelped, and several of the pack let out joyful howls. "I'm sorry for anything we ever did to you. All of it. From moment one when we decided to keep you."

This was her chance to get some answers. Her heart rate kicked up, and it took a half a minute before she could speak again. "Why did you decide to keep me and send my sister off?"

It might seem a simple question considering the large problems they had to deal with. But it had pressed on her mind since she'd met Lilliana. What had happened?

"We meant to keep both of you. Twin werewolf girls who didn't show any signs of shifting? It was a real coup. But one of our group got chicken-shit and decided to take off with the two of you, rescue you. He nearly got out of town with both of you. Big battle. Shots. We got you out of the car, but the asshole still managed to hightail it with the other baby. I can assure you that we searched. Never found the baby demon."

She kicked him, hard, in the ribs. He gasped, and Cyrus laughed. It took Betsy a moment to realize what she'd done. In all her life, she'd never resorted to violence so casually. This time, though, she'd not even given a second thought before she'd kicked.

She met Cyrus' gaze, and she saw amusement radiating in his blue depths. "I guess I really am a wolf now."

"Oh, you are." Cyrus smiled. "Do you have any other questions for this little man or shall we haul him off now and let Beaux's people do what they will?"

"Why take us at all? What did you do with the other babies?"

Joe shook his head. "We waited to see that you all really were werewolves. Babies start to show their shifting around age one. They howl. Growl. Start to act more like animals than human babies. You never did that, so we didn't do to you what we did to the others. Some of us foolishly thought you could be saved."

Cyrus spoke before she could. "What did you do with the ones who weren't latents? How many of them did you have hold of over the years? Where did you get them?"

Beaux shifted into his human form. "That last point is pivotal. Where did you find them?"

"You really are evil creatures, aren't you? I mean the way you did that. The way your body shifted from one form to another. How can that be anything but evil?"

Beaux shook his head. "Give me your knife, Cyrus. I want to slit his throat."

"After he answers our questions. Of course, I could contort his body in lots of way if he really wants to know how to shift. His muscles won't accept the alteration, but he can get to know the pain."

"I...I...I...that is to say, we had the abominations put down. Slit their throats. They didn't suffer long. That was less cruel than sending the creatures off to be experimented on, which was what we originally wanted."

The silence that fell over the moment was so thick Betsy wasn't sure she could draw in a breath. She forced her body take in air. The information Joe had dumped on them was like a physical blow.

Betsy turned to the other werewolves. None of them seemed as floored as she felt. There wasn't a scent of shock in the air. For his part, Cyrus remained as calm as after the delivery of the news as before when he'd asked the question.

Was she the only one who hadn't expected all of those werewolves to be...dead? Tears swam into her eyes. Why was she so dumb about these things? What else could have happened to them? If the werewolves had been somewhere, at least some of them would have escaped by now. Someone would have known about this.

She turned her back on the scene and walked toward the tree line.

"Where did you get them?"

Maybe she should listen to the answer. It would tell her where she'd come from, but all she could think about were all the other babies that hadn't been as lucky as she had. For some reason, she'd been latent. Perhaps one of her parents had been human, but who knew? Why had she been born without the ability to shift? Her latency had saved her life.

Betsy doubled over. Her hands ached, and she stared down at them before standing back up straight. Without meaning to, she'd shifted her hands again. Betsy sighed.

Every time this happened, she ended up going into a haze and losing periods of time. Damn it, she wasn't going to allow that to happen again.

Why had her hands shifted? She wasn't in any danger, not that she could tell.

Cyrus' hand felt warm on her back, and she turned around to look at him. "Didn't see the dead wolf babies coming."

"I was afraid that was the case." He ran his hand over her cheek. "I'll forever be grateful that you couldn't shift. You and Lilliana. It saved you."

"What will you do to him now?"

Cyrus pulled her against him. "I won't do anything. This is Beaux's land. And, as it turns out, the werewolf babies came from all over. So none of us have jurisdiction over this. I'm hoping to build some good will with Beaux in case we need him again." Cyrus smiled, showing a lot of teeth. "He can play hunt the true believer next week during the fool moon."

"Actually sounds like fun."

"Betsy." Cyrus tilted her chin up so she'd look at him. "This isn't your fault. You didn't determine who would live and who would die. There's no need for survival guilt."

"How did you catch them? I would know, if you hadn't made me stay in the basement." It was better to focus on the injustice of being sidelined than to think about all those dead babies...

"I lured them out. They took a shot at me in my human form, and then Beaux's men and our pack took them out from behind. It was all pretty fast actually."

"You let them take a shot at you?" She whacked him in the arm. How many times was he going to risk his life without a second thought?

Cyrus rubbed his arm where she'd hit him. "Ouch,

woman. You're a strong werewolf lady. Watch where you put those claws."

"Like I could ever hurt you." She laughed. He always seemed to be able to do that. Disarm her temper with a word or a look. How could he make such an awful situation feel better just by being with her?

"It's your claws. Put them away before you take out your eye by mistake."

"Oh." She took in her hands again. . He'd made her laugh, and she'd forgotten that she'd partially shifted. "I don't know exactly what's going on with this. Can you help?"

"Sure. Don't worry. New werewolves have to figure out this stuff one day at a time."

She knew he was pacifying her. How could it be anything else? It wasn't like anyone had all that much experience with changing latent werewolves into full-fledged versions as adults. They'd done it with Lilliana, but she had no idea if her sister could partially shift or not. It was sweet Cyrus made the effort, but he might as well have told her the truth—that it was really odd she kept doing that. Even if it had proved a useful tool when dealing with the true believer earlier.

"Relax." His voice moved over her when he placed his hand on her claw. Warmth travelled up her spine, and her hand shifted back to human. "See? No big deal."

"Right." She tried to smile but must have failed because he furrowed his brows.

"Cyrus," Beaux called out. "Come say goodbye to these fools. They have to go meet their maker."

Her mate smiled at her. "Give me a second. Then we'll talk about what to do with your parents."

That was a subject she really didn't want to broach. It obviously had to be dealt with, and apparently Cyrus wasn't a fan of hide–under-the-covers-and-hope-it-goes-away behavior.

"Sure."

He turned and walked toward Beaux. What was she going to do? Just hang out by the tree line and wait for him? Surely there had to be something she could do. Was there a place to order dinner somewhere within fifty miles? Her hand throbbed, and a second later, it shifted into its wolf form again.

"Oh. Damn it." What the hell was going on? Maybe she should have Lake take a look. Was something wrong with her?

A scent caught her attention, and she turned around. What was it? Foul, like rotten meat, the aroma wafted over her nose. She turned back at the group of werewolves. No one else seemed to notice or else they weren't concerned. Maybe the scent hadn't reached them yet.

Betsy covered her nose with her hand and started walking in the direction of the smell. Something had to be dead. That could be the only explanation. An animal that needed to be disposed of before it stunk up the entire surrounding area.

This was something she knew how to do. Growing where and how she had, she knew how to take care of maintenance issues, including the removal of dead carcasses. Probably not something she'd have to do in New York City anytime in the future.

First, however, she needed to find the thing. Her nose would go a long way to helping, and at least it gave her something to do while Cyrus and Beaux did whatever Alpha thing they were going to do.

The dead deer had been there a long time. She bent over to look at it. Why had Beaux and the others left this to rot so close to their home? Maybe they had some weird thing about not moving things they had killed? Had they been the reason the deer had died?

She sighed. Why did she care? Was she looking for ways to distract herself from the fact that things kept getting worse and worse?

Betsy bit her lip. Was she going to start killing deer and other animals when she shifted? Was that what happened?

"I didn't expect to catch you alone so quickly."

Betsy jolted. It had been months since she'd heard her mother's voice, and rather than the pleasant tones she was used to, even if the words the woman spoke were distant recently, the menace in the other woman's tone made goose bumps appear on Betsy's skin.

She could now smell her mother, although her approach had been completely masked by the scent of the rotting animal. Her mother's scent came across as spicy, and it burned Betsy's eyes.

"Mom."

Her mother had always looked as though she stepped out of a sitcom. Now gray-haired and wrinkled, she raised a gun and pointed it at Betsy. "Why did you have to succumb to the darkness? Why couldn't you have remained pure?"

Betsy raised her hands in the air in what she hoped was a gesture of surrender. Her mother's eyes widened when she did, and Betsy silently cursed the impulse to have brought her hands up since they were, in fact, claws.

"Look at you." A tear slipped from her mom's eyes. "You're a monster."

"I'm not a monster. I promise you. I'm still the same as I ever was. I'm as I was meant to be. But I'm still the same girl I was before. The one who lived with you—who *loved* you."

"No." Her mother shook her head. "You're not."

"Betsy."

Cyrus called her name, and Betsy tried to swallow through the fearful lump that had formed in her throat. He would find her. The second she didn't answer, he'd sniff the air, and even though she stood near what she now suspected was a purposefully placed dead carcass, he'd find her.

He'd stop this.

"Mama, if we can talk about this, then I'm sure we can—"

The loud noise stopped her breathing, and she blinked rapidly as she tried to identify where the explosion had come from. It was then she noticed the smoke coming out of her mother's gun. They'd had that thing forever. It was antique, belonged to her great-grandfather.

Strange thoughts but all she could focus on...

"Mom?" Something was wrong, but she couldn't seem to make any sense of it. What had happened?

"Goodbye, Betsy. I won't let them take me." With that, her mother turned the gun on herself. A second blast later, her mother fell to the ground. Dead.

"Mom?"

She tried to move forward, but her body wouldn't comply. Betsy knew she needed to look down. She had to. But she couldn't make her neck work. It felt like it took a year but with no other choice, she glanced down and saw a large red spot seeping through her shirt. What had happened?

"Betsy." Cyrus rushed toward her.

"I've been shot, honey." Her voice sounded hoarse. "How could my mother have done this?"

The world went black. In the distance, she thought she heard wolves howling. And then she heard nothing at all.

WHEN BETSY WOKE UP, she was alone. Raising her head, she looked left and right. The world felt ten degrees colder than it had been when she'd…. *when I'd what?* She couldn't seem to remember.

She pulled herself to her feet, hearing the sounds of wolves howling. Where was she?

A sound caught her attention, and she sucked in her breath. Although there was no light except from the full moon, she could see three figures approaching her. They were male, and each one was naked. She gasped, covering her mouth with her hands.

This had to be a dream. It was too…bizarre.

"Relax, fair princess, the moon has returned you from where you came. You are back with us, where all the sons and daughters of the moon come when their time on earth has passed.

In a few more minutes, you will be fully with us. And then you will no longer know any pain." Betsy reached out in front of her as though she could stop their words with her hand alone. "Are you telling me that I'm dead?"

The figure in the middle spoke. "Almost. My name is Lucian, little sister. I don't think we knew each other on earth."

"No." She backed up a step. "No. No. No." Betsy shouted to the moon as though it might listen to her. "I'm not dead. It's not time yet. I refuse. Do you hear me? Put me back. I'm not done."

Because Cyrus would destroy the world if she didn't wake up, and she'd never want him to know that kind of pain.

Chapter 19

"Fix her." Cyrus' hands shook as he stared at his sister. The last few minutes were a blur but they'd moved her back into Beaux's house. They were in a back bedroom that had become Lake's makeshift healing room. Betsy was sprawled out on a bed, her red blood soaking into the sheets beneath her.

Lake leaned down over his unconscious mate. Blood flowed way too quickly from her open wound, and he worried that she soon might not have enough in her to live. What did humans do when this happened? *Transfusions*. He would gladly give Betsy his blood. "What do you need, Lake? I'll give you anything. Do you understand? Anything in the universe, it's yours."

Lake had her eyes closed, and she sat unmoving with her hands positioned over Betsy's body. Why didn't she say something?

Cyrus was hauled backward. He snarled, whirling around to attack whoever had dared touch him. To no surprise, it was Beaux who yanked him toward the door.

"Your Healer can't do what she has to do with you

badgering her. You want your mate healed? Give the woman some room to do that. She has your mate's soul in her hands at the moment. Do you want her to lose focus and let the moon take her?"

"It's all bullshit." He shoved Beaux through the open doorway. "She's got the ability to help werewolves. That I can understand. All of this moon-taking shit has always been crap, and the fact that you buy into it makes you pathetic."

On a normal day, he would never speak to anyone like that. Even as he said the words, he almost couldn't believe they'd come out of his mouth. But his mate lay dying, and he didn't want to hear shit about the moon and souls. He wanted her fixed. End of story.

Beaux shook his head as he closed the door to where Lake worked. "That's tremendously sad. The moon has gifted you with so much. Health, strength, power, money, a pack of your own to run, the intellect and instinct to do that relatively well, safety most of the time, and a true mating that most werewolves will never know. The fact that you cannot believe, even now as your sister performs magic that might save your mate from a fatal gunshot wound, makes me enormously sorry for you."

Cyrus didn't have it in him to have this kind of discussion with Beaux without ripping his fucking head from his shoulders.

"It's always a choice," Beaux called after him when he stormed from the house out onto the lawn. His pack was giving him space, which was a smart move. If Betsy died, he'd start tearing things, and he knew he wouldn't be able to stop himself.

Her damned mother had shot herself before he'd had the chance to end her. Or keep her tied up until the pack could eat her alive.

Betsy might already be dead. Betsy might *already be dead*. He fell to his knees on the grass. If she perished, he'd go wolf and never turn back. He was Alpha. He didn't have to be human. Mitchell would run the pack. There could be no life without Betsy. No way to exist in a world without her presence.

"She's not dead yet." He spoke aloud so he could hear his own words. Why hadn't he told her everything that needed to be said? Why hadn't he simply explained to her that he needed her to hide in the basement because if this happened, if this very scenario took place, his life ended? Why hadn't he shared with her his intent to come to Montana and why he needed to risk his life for her, for the pack? Why the fuck had he left so many things unsaid?

The light of the moon shone down on him. It wasn't full, but it made him shiver. Cyrus stared up at it where it sat in the center of the sky. He never looked up at it anymore. Not since he was a child. His knees gave out and he hit the ground.

"Hello," he called upward. "Can you hear me?" If anyone else could, they'd think he was nuts. This wasn't how werewolves communed with the moon. Silent prayer was fine, but no one shouted at the big blob in the sky.

Except he didn't give a shit. Wasn't this how his forefathers had done it? Hadn't they howled for the dying Lily and begged to be human to save her?

"I'm here. I'm right where I've always been, one step from lost and making all of this up as I go along. I can't seem to figure out the damn plan. I don't really even understand why we are werewolves. What good does it do in modern life? It gets harder and harder to hide us. And we've all fallen from whatever purpose we were apparently supposed to have."

He cleared his throat, knowing he needed to shut up.

Instead, he kept speaking because, really, what did he have to lose anymore?

"I killed Shepherd. I won where so many had failed, and I've worked every damn day since to take care of everyone. You took my parents. You took Lucian. I fight, I struggle, and I work. I don't sleep. I never complain. And then you give me Betsy, the first thing that I ever really wanted for myself, for only me. And now you take her back like this?" He growled. His whole body ached, feeling as though it were being torn from the inside out.

"She's not dead yet." Beaux knelt down next to him. Cyrus hadn't noted his arrival outside. The whole world could come marching in, and he'd probably not note it.

"What are you doing out here?" Cyrus didn't want company. Of course, Beaux might be the perfect person to begin his rampage of destruction on. Why hadn't he made this whole lair more secure? Why had he dragged them to his place to begin with?

Betsy would not be in this situation if it weren't for Beaux…If the other Alpha hadn't attacked their car, they wouldn't be now faced with Betsy being critically injured. .

Cyrus growled. Maybe Beaux did need to die.

"You think I'm not blaming myself?" Beaux correctly interpreted Cyrus' growl, which really pissed Cyrus off. Why did he have to be so correct all the time? "I've found myself here more than once. On my knees. Particularly when my mate died."

"What?" He hadn't known Beaux had mated. Not that he'd kept up with him. He hadn't even known Beaux still lived in the world. But the news of the mating still took him by surprise. It seemed something the proclaimer of all things wolf would have mentioned.

"She wasn't my true mate, but we loved each other." A muscle in Beaux's jaw ticked. "She was killed, struck down by a car on the street when she'd gone to the grocery store. Ten years ago. We'd been living like you live—pretending to be human most of the time—when she died. After that, I hit my knees and swore I'd find a way to return to the way things should be."

"I'm sorry about your wife." Cyrus sighed. "But I don't pretend to be human." He gritted his teeth. "And I actually owe you some thanks." "What for?" Beaux shifted on his knees.

"For reminding me I'm on my knees." Cyrus stood up. "I'm never on my knees. I'm the fucking Alpha of Manhattan, and someone still needs to be punished for this. That I can take care of."

His mouth watered. He could still spill blood to avenge his mate's pain.

BETSY'S CHILDHOOD home smelled cold. It made his nose tingle and his hands itch. Had it always been so completely soulless? He doubted it. Anywhere Betsy lived would have been lively and joyful, but her scent no long permeated the walls.

He took a deep breath, searching for her scent somewhere, anywhere.

"Have you come to kill me?" The man, Betsy's father, or kidnapper depending on how he wanted to look at it, leaned against the wall sipping a cup of coffee. He had a gruff voice like he'd smoked too many cigarettes. Cyrus took another breath and then cursed the urge that had made him do so. Betsy's father was riddled with disease.

"Looks like I needn't bother. You're a dead man walking."

The other man laughed and then exploded into gut-wrenching coughs that doubled him over for a few seconds. Cyrus waited, not moving. He ached for the man's death, but a fast destruction of the husband of the woman who had shot his mate might be too kind an end. Maybe it would be better to leave him like this, to cough himself to death alone in a stale home with no one to love him in the end.

"I told her not to go there and do that. I told her to leave the girl alone. It all seemed downright nonsensical to me. Can't change the nature of a werewolf, any more than you can change the nature of a person. Killing her was only going to drag you monsters out to commit more destruction. Better to put you all down like the abominations you are." He shook his head. "But Joe told us to raise her, to try to save her soul, and we did the best job we could considering the girl couldn't keep her legs closed."

Cyrus struck him across the face before he could think about it. No one insulted his mate, and even though Cyrus would never use the word slut to describe a woman's sexuality, he knew that Betsy's father had meant it as such.

Blood seeped out of the other man's mouth, and he spit it on the floor. "Damn it. If you're going to kill me, do it already."

"I'm not going to. I'm going to let you suffer. Your wife is dead. She took her own life. Your compatriots are all dead too. Beaux had them all shot. I would have preferred to let them suffer in terror but I guess he's kinder than me." The house creaked as gust of wind hit it. "It's going to be a long, cold winter. Maybe if you're lucky, you'll die from pneumonia. You humans are so weak, your bodies failing with every little ailment. And Betsy didn't die. So your wife failed. You won't have any satisfaction from her having succeeded in her mission."

Cyrus turned on his heel and left the cabin. It didn't

surprise him to see Beaux leaning against a car, watching him when he walked out.

"Are you stalking me?"

"I'm feeling rather determined to keep you alive." Beaux shrugged, but his usually benign scent surged for a second. The man was hiding something. Cyrus didn't know if he had the energy to delve into exactly what that entailed.

"Anything from Lake?" He headed toward his car. If Beaux wanted to follow him around, he could chase him back to Betsy. Screw Lake's concentration. His mate needed him, and if there was no one to kill, he wasn't leaving her side until she opened her beautiful eyes. And, when this was over, he was going to see to it that she never knew pain like this again. When he drove away, it burned his guts that he'd left the man inside the cabin alive. Even if he was only a temporary problem.

━━

CYRUS SLAMMED through the door in time to see his sister stumble from the room where he had left Betsy in her care.

"Lake?" His voice shook. His sister's eyes were red, her hair wild, and her skin two shades paler than usual. "Is she gone?" Wouldn't he know? Didn't true mates always feel a death, or was it more bullshit about their werewolf lives that would prove to be nothing but nonsense?

The world suddenly lost all its color. Everything dulled.

Lake placed her hand on his arm. "Cyrus. She should be dead, but she's not. Do you hear what I'm saying? She's not."

He took a deep breath, feeling the sunlight coming

back into his soul and the colors of the universe returning. "She's not dead?"

"Listen to me. I don't know why she's alive, but she is. I did everything I could, and I don't know why it was enough. It shouldn't have been. But it is, she's healing. She's going to be okay."

He grabbed his sister and tugged her closer against him. "Lake, I don't know what to say. You saved my mate. You did it. Anything you want, Lake. When we get home, work wherever you want. Do you hear what I'm saying? Anything."

"Okay." Lake laughed. "Why don't we see if you feel that way after you've come down from shock?"

Cyrus ran into the room where Betsy lay. Her eyes were closed, but her color was good. She didn't look gray, and although her clothes were still covered in blood, it didn't bring on a sense of panic. Her body functioned normally. He could smell it, and he could see it with his eyes. It was okay for him to believe it.

"Betsy, princess." He sat down next to her and took her hand. "Can you hear me?"

Her eyes fluttered open. Her gaze appeared glazed, but she smiled at him. "We could hear you. Loud and clear."

"We?" She was really out of it. Did she even know what she said? "Who's we?" He didn't care what she said. Just the fact that she could say anything at all meant the world to him.

"Lucian, me, the entire group of wolves standing at the gate." She closed her eyes and then opened them again. "You sounded so sad to me. Some of the others heard anger, but Lucian and I could hear the sadness. He says you won't always feel this way, that they'll be a time you'll know the moon again in your soul and that the moon still knows you. You're an Alpha wolf, chosen by the moon, given to me. She loves you."

He took her small hands in his. "Sounds like you had quite the dream."

"You would say that." She squeezed his fingers. "I still don't like what Lucian did, taking your choices away at such a young age, but he did love you. Told me you scarred him once during a training exercise. Left him a permanent mark across his chest from his shoulder to his belly button. On a full moon, before you could totally control yourself. He stood as a human, and you launched at him."

"How the hell could you know that, princess?" He never talked about it. It was one of the humiliations of his training. Alpha werewolves didn't go around attacking without thinking. The ability to remain human in his mind while looking like a wolf helped determine the power of the Alpha.

"Guess I must have had a hell of a dream."

He kissed her knuckles, his heart in his throat. It was hard for him to believe, hard for him to choose a life where someone other than him had set everything in motion. The implications of all of the wolf myths being true were hard to take. .

It didn't make sense. How could the moon have turned three wolves into werewolves? How could it all have started there? A wish and a moon and now they all had a destiny.

"Betsy." He needed to say what was in his heart. "I would have chosen you, so you know that. If it hadn't been anything to do with a true mating, with scenting you in a Starbucks, I would have still picked you. If we were two humans on the street, I would have crossed it to talk to you."

"That's sweet, Cyrus. I would have picked you too, but

I would have been part of a crowd, I think. Rich businessman in New York City? I don't know that I would have gotten close enough to you for us to make a decision like that. Thank goodness for true mating."

"No. I think you don't understand how observant and determined I would have been as a human." It mattered that she understood this. "I would have found you. I would have picked you because you're smart, funny, loyal, and beautiful. Because you have freckles over your nose. Because—"

"Cyrus, you must have been scared to death I was going to die. I'm so sorry you went through that." She paused. "I love you. I don't care what brought us together, okay? Fate or the moon or good luck." She yawned. "I think I need a nap. But you have to do something for me." "Anything." He'd move the mountains away if she wanted it.

"I want you to give this," she tugged at the necklace he'd given her with female werewolf on it, "to your sister. She's going to need it now."

"I tried to give it to her once. She wouldn't take it. The necklace was meant for you."

"It was." Her voice sounded husky. "But now she'll take it. She needs it now."

He took it from her hand. "I'll give it to her if that's what you want."

"I'm going to sleep now. I'm sorry. I really want to talk more."

"That's okay, baby." He had tears in his eyes. Shit, was he actually crying? He wiped them away. "You sleep. I'm going to watch over you. Always."

"I DON'T CONTROL the full moon any more than you do." Beaux shook his head. "I'm sorry you're still stuck here, but you're going to have to shift with us. If Lake says she can't be moved yet, then she can't be moved."

"What is going on with you and my sister?" It might have taken him longer than it should have to notice, but he had finally clued in. Every time his sister was in the same room with Beaux, one of the two ran away. That kind of uncomfortable didn't happen out of nowhere. "I think that is between me and your sister."

Cyrus growled. Beaux better watch his damn mouth. Hours from the full moon, even he got twitchy. "In addition to her being my sister, she's my Healer and a member of my pack." "Do you monitor the personal life of every member of your pack? Paid a lot of attention to Lake's life in the past? Or is it bothering you because, this time, it might be me that she has something going on with?"

"Forget that I asked. I need to figure out the full-moon politics with you. If we're all going to shift here together, there have to be rules."

Beaux laughed. "You keep your rules back in Manhattan where they belong. Tonight we all get to be wolves. Understand what that means anymore? Even Betsy will shift, and when she does, she'll heal completely. We'll be the part of ourselves that we only get to be once a month."

"Oh for the love of the moon." Sometimes he really wanted to break Beaux's stupid neck. "We're not pack, Beaux. When rival packs get together on full moons, there is violence unless the Alphas speak up ahead of time. The time Travis' pack came to New York, I told my people not to touch them. We need to do that for each other."

"I don't think that's going to be necessary. You and me, we're connected. Our pack isn't going to hurt each other."

"Bullshit. We're not connected." What the fuck was he talking about? "If you want to risk it, go ahead. We can kill each other and see who is still left in the morning."

"We're all children of the moon. We'll all be fine in the morning." Beaux sauntered away like a man who thought he knew what he was talking about.

They were leaving Montana in a few days. Cyrus had to put up with this for a few more days, and then he'd be back among the concrete jungle he'd missed more than he thought he would. Give him noise, 3 a.m. takeout, and honking horns.

Betsy walked behind him, placing her arms around his waist. "I'm sorry we can't leave tonight."

"It would be a big disaster. We'd all shift on the airplane. Or if we did make, we'd land in New York, and it would be too late to get to safety. One more night here and then we're out."

She nodded, and he leaned over to kiss the spot on her neck that met her shoulder blade. Alone time would be a great thing about returning home as well.

"When are you going to tell the pack?"

He turned his gaze to the sky. . Maybe another hour until her first shift. "Tell them what, princess?"

"That you're going to let them all choose their own careers. That they don't have to work for you anymore if they don't want to."

"When we get back." He paused. "How did you know that?"

She smiled. "Still think I had a hell of a dream?"

Cyrus shook his head. He didn't know what he thought anymore, but if the moon or Lucian or a bunch of giant two-headed rats had something to do with her returning to him, then he was grateful.

"I need to keep you safe tonight, and when we get back

home, forever. And I'm not sure I can do that and be Alpha in this time of war. The longer we go without an Alpha Prime, the more I think it will come to that." He kissed her forehead. "How would you feel about me stepping down?"

"I think that would be the stupidest thing you could ever do."

Well, he hadn't expected that reaction. "What?"

"You're Alpha. Stop questioning it. I can keep myself safe. If I'd paid better attention to the fact that my hands kept shifting as an instinctual warning instead of a weird phenomena, then I wouldn't have gotten shot. I'll learn as time goes on. And you'll keep the pack safe until someone worthy, someone you think you can follow, steps into the role. Until then, don't waste time worrying about things you can't change."

He grinned. No one but Betsy would ever speak to him like that. "Yes, my mate. Whatever you say."

"That's right, my Alpha. It's whatever I say. Don't forget that."

He kissed her soft lips. Cyrus was Betsy's. And thank the moon for that.

Epilogue

His sister fiddled with the totem around her neck. She stared out the window and bit her nails. Had she suddenly gotten horribly afraid of flying? They were still on the tarmac. What was the problem? He sniffed the air. Sure enough, the pungent aroma of fear crept through his nostrils. Lake was terrified.

Cyrus stroked Betsy's leg, not caring if anyone noticed. Another day of being so completely desperate to make love to her and he might decide to take her in public. Screw anyone who wanted to watch. He'd make sure they got a good show.

"Is something wrong with my sister?" He asked Betsy, who stared back at him with hooded eyes. Between her injuries, the lack of privacy, and her first full-moon shift, she was as needy as he to fuck. Maybe even more so. Hours left. That was all they both had to endure.

"Um…" She turned to regard Lake. "I imagine her anxiety has to do with Beaux."

"With Beaux?" He raised his voice and then lowered it. They were leaving Montana. He didn't have to be so worked up about the asshole anymore. "Why would she be scared of

Beaux?"

The plane jerked forward as it started to travel down the runway. Movement outside caught his eye, and he glanced to see what occurred. Three cars pulled up next to the plane, and as though he'd appeared because Betsy spoke his name, Beaux dashed out of one of the cars. He waved his hands as if he wanted them to stop.

"Brother, my Alpha, don't let them stop this plane. Please."

He had no intention of doing so. If Beaux wanted something, he could call or email. Hell, he could text. Cyrus would ignore him the way he did the rest of the world.

"What did he do to you?" He shifted in his seat and leaned forward. "You guys were weird the entire time."

The plane lifted off, and Lake exhaled loudly. "He didn't do anything to me. I mean, really, Cyrus, he's not that bad. Nice even. He told his wolves not to engage with yours. What more do you want from the man?"

"He told me he wasn't going to do that, that it wasn't necessary." *What has changed?*

"I asked him to. He did it for me." She turned away.

Cyrus didn't like this conversation, not one damn bit. "Why would he do that for you, Lake? Why would the Alpha of Montana change his decision because you asked him to?"

His sister pursed her lips. He knew that look, had seen it far too often in childhood.

Unless he ordered her to tell him, she wouldn't.

"Cyrus, don't be dense." Betsy kissed his cheek. "They're true mates. I think everyone has caught on to that but you. I get that relationships aren't really your thing, but this one is pretty transparent."

"Oh. Hell no." Cyrus moved to unbuckle his seatbelt. He didn't care if they were taking off. News like this made him want to move before he exploded. "Lake, are you telling me that you, my sister and this pack's Healer, mated the Alpha of another pack—true mated—and didn't think you should tell me about it?"

"Did you stop to discuss your mating with me? Besides, I don't accept it. I'm not giving up my life to live in Montana with him. I like New York. End of story."

He moved to take off his seatbelt and Betsy placed her hand on his to stop him "Stay seated. Nothing is going to get solved while we're airborne."

"He let you leave?" Cyrus took some deep breaths. It didn't seem to help. "What kind of a mate does that?"

"No." She bit her lip. "He told me not to leave. Ordered it, in fact. And I drugged him. I guess I didn't give him enough."

Cyrus cracked up. His sister had drugged her true mate to get away from him. "You do realize he will chase you."

She nodded. "That's what he told me."

Cyrus squeezed Betsy's hand. He could keep Beaux out of Manhattan for a while. There were protocols, and as Beaux himself had pointed out, one Alpha couldn't go traipsing around in another's territory without permission.

Still, eventually, he'd have to let him in. Or there would be war.

Betsy smiled. It's okay. There's a plan for this. It'll all work out. The moon will see to it. What has fallen will be set right"

Maybe Betsy was right, maybe it would. Or maybe they really were in the midst of chaos that would have to explode into war because there was no other choice. He kissed Betsy's hair, loving the feeling of closeness that came from being so sure of her. Whatever happened, he had his mate. Everything else would have to work itself out without him. He planned to spend the next few days in his apartment with his mate. With the doors locked and the phones off. Their destinies would have to wait patiently for a while. He had his own plans to take care of."

Afterword

Thank you so much for reading Alpha's Strength, the next book Alpha's Truth is available now. If you enjoyed the book I'd very much appreciate a review. Reviews help authors reach more readers. If you are not already, I'd love it if you would join my reader group on Facebook here: https://www.facebook.com/groups/458490741256283/ Its called Rebecca's Randomness and we have a lot of fun in there. Also, please turn the page for a complete list of my over 80 books.

About the Author

As a teenager, I would hide in my room to read my favorite romance novels when I was supposed to be doing my homework.

I am the mother of three adorable boys and I am fortunate to be married to my best friend. I live in Austin Texas where I am determined to eat all the barbecue in town.

I am in love with science fiction, fantasy, and the paranormal and try to use all of these elements in my writing. I've been told I'm a little bloodthirsty so I hope that when you read my work you'll enjoy the action packed ride that always ends in romance. I love to write series because I love to see characters develop over time and it always makes me happy to see my favorite characters make guest appearances in other books.

In my world anything is possible, anything can happen, and you should suspect that it will.

I'd love to hear from you! Please visit my website at www.rebeccaroyce.com to sign up for my newsletter and learn about my books!

Here's where you can find me online:

www.rebeccaroyce.com

Rebecca's Randomness Reading Group
https://www.facebook.com/groups/458490741256283/

https://www.facebook.com/authorrebeccaroyce/

www.twitter.com/rebeccaroyce
Instagram: rebeccaroyce79
Cheers!!
Rebecca

Other books by Rebecca Royce...

Wings of Artemis

Kidnapped By Her Husbands

Rescued by Their Wife

Crashing Into Destiny

Meeting Them

Reclaiming Their Love

Loving Them

Ship Called Malice

Saving Them

Dark Demise

Light Unfolding

Still Waters (coming soon)

Last Hope (completed series)

Tradition Be Damned

Past Be Damned

Destiny Be Damned

Compassion Be Damned

Future Be Damned

Dragon Wars (completed series)

Forever

Eternal

Always

Evermore

Endless

Wards and Wands

Hexed and Vexed

Curse Reversed

Meow, Baby (novella, Coming Soon in <u>Petting Them</u> antho
written with Ripley Proserpina)

Tragic Magic (Coming Soon)

Safe Haven

Everywhere and Nowhere

Dimension X (coming soon)

More coming soon….

Soul Bound

Prisoner of the Dragons

More coming soon….

Shadow Promised

Strange Days

Weird Nights

Bizarre Years

More coming soon…

The Warrior (completed series)

Initiation

Driven

Subversive

Redemption

Justice

Warrior World (spin off of The Warrior, completed series)

Deacon

Micah

Jason

The Westervelt Wolves (completed series)

Her Wolf

Summer's Wolf

Wolf Reborn

Wolf's Valentine

Wolf's Magic

Alpha Wolf

Angel's Wolf

Darkest Wolf

Lone Wolf

Fallen Alpha

Alpha Rising

Alpha's Strength

Alpha's Sacrifice

Alpha's Truth

Alpha Enticing

Hidden Alpha (coming soon)

The Capes (completed series)

Seductive Powers

Adrenaline Rush

Last Ascension

The Conditioned

Eye Contact

Embraced

Unlawful (coming soon…)

The Outsiders

Love Beyond Time

Love Beyond Sanity

Love Beyond Loyalty

Love Beyond Sight

Love Beyond Expectations

Love Beyond Oceans

Love Beyond Flames

Love Beyond Lies (coming soon)

Cascade (completed series)

Haunted Redemption

Phoenix Everlasting

Fragility Unearthed

Persuasion Enraptured

Reverse Harem Story (completed series)

Unconventional

Unexpected

Undeniable

Kiss Her Goodbye

Sacrificial Lamb (coming soon)

Martyrs

Saints

Stand Alone Titles

Planet Bear

Under The Lights

No Quitting Allowed

Mr. Wrong

Bite Marks

Bitten Surrender

The Vampire and The Virgin

Demon Within

Crimson Lust

Call Me Crazy (coming soon)

Writing with Ripley Proserpina

The Storm

Lightning Strikes (coming soon)

Thunder Rolling

www.ingramcontent.com/pod-product-compliance
Lightning Source LLC
Chambersburg PA
CBHW011027260626
47153CB00020B/2965